The Summer of '39

by the same author

NOVELS
Carrying On
Madonna of the Island
The Reluctant Devil

NON-FICTION
A Ring of Conspirators: Henry James and his Literary Circle
Life on the Grand Scale: Ottoline Morrell
Life on the Edge: Robert Graves

The
SUMMER
of '39

A Novel

MIRANDA SEYMOUR

W. W. Norton & Company
New York • London

c.1

To Toby

Copyright © 1998 by Miranda Seymour
First American edition 1999

Originally published in England under the title *The Telling*

Manufacturing by The Haddon Craftsmen, Inc.

Library of Congress Cataloging-in-Publication Data
Seymour, Miranda.
[Telling]
The summer of '39 / Miranda Seymour. — 1st American ed.
p.   cm.
ISBN 0-393-04806-3
I. Title.
PR6069.E737 T45 1999
832'.914—dc21
99-30005
CIP

W. W. Norton & Company, Inc., 500 Fifth Avenue, New York, N.Y. 10110
www.wwnorton.com

W. W. Norton & Company Ltd., 10 Coptic Street, London WC1A 1PU

1 2 3 4 5 6 7 8 9 0

The castaways thought they were home and dry,
running aground on the hunched back of a sleeping whale,
so they pitched camp and raised a fire, burning
the ship's oars and the main mast. The whale turned tail

and dived, and they were each man drowned. There are those
taken in by the whale's breath, and those
who think of the whale as a symbol of birth.
But the whale is a grave, and its meaning is death.

Simon Armitage, 'Cetus'

PART ONE

1

November, 1979

My DESTRUCTION OCCURRED forty years ago, in the space of a single month. Recovery took somewhat longer. But I triumphed. I am still at Point House, looking out over the cliff at my familiar bay. I have lived here, unguarded, for twenty-five years. That counts for something in the survival stakes, wouldn't you say?

Sane? As much as any woman can be who's learned to keep herself to herself. Regarding the past, it is not a subject on which I am ever likely to achieve a settled view. It doesn't do to depend on love. Let me leave it at that for the moment.

I keep pretty quiet. The garden's my passion. I'm up by seven and out there for as long as I've light to see by. I had Silas Cooper at the hardware shop out from Falmouth last year. Fixed me up a couple of tree-lamps so that I could work on after sundown. I told him how I almost pitched off the cliff path hunting for my trowel one night and he slapped a coat of luminous paint on all my tool handles then and there. Free of charge. On account of my being a good customer, he said, though I never spend more than two dollars a year in his shop. Too fancy and tricksy for my taste, the stuff he gets in. I told him so, but he just laughed.

When I'm done with working in the garden for the night, I settle down with a sandwich and hot soup at my desk by the window, try to gather my thoughts and make a tidy shape out of them. Everything has to be set down now, but writing isn't

3

my trade. I always seem able to find an excuse, drawers to be tidied, photographs that need sorting out, anything that keeps my hands busy. If they're busy, they can't fluster me.

Prattling on paper like this may be the way to get going. It's becoming quite pleasantly conversational, like talking to a friend in another room. Not that I'm lonely. Why should I be?

And why should I not? Be honest with yourself, Nancy. If I am occasionally a little downhearted, I've no one to blame but myself. Living to an old age has become a kind of victory over circumstances, but I haven't yet learned to behave as the old should. I'm not grateful, and I'm not tolerant, and I don't like small talk. That should be enough to keep away those well-meaning souls, newcomers all, who make a vocation out of doing good to those who never did enough harm to deserve it.

It doesn't stop them at all. I had a whole rash of them over the place this summer, worse than measles.

– Oh, Mrs Brewster, we wondered if we could help care for your beautiful garden.

– if we could persuade you to join the Golden Age Voyagers' Club.

– if we could take you on a visit to the church . . . the whaling museum . . . the old harbour.

I do my best to be polite. But why should I be, when all they've come for is a peek at the hermit, a spoonful of gossip to be carried off and shared out at the next club convention. I see the gleam in their eyes as they shout their charitable invitations. I used to see such faces in my nightmares, pressed up against the bars of my room, waiting for the freakshow to begin.

There have been occasions when I've felt sufficiently angered by these intruders to show them the door with a donation to their chosen cause, as if they were no better than hawkers. On the whole, I'm gracious. Point House always had a reputation for hospitality and I'm proud enough to cherish family traditions. I thank them for their thoughtfulness and explain that gardening and housecare don't leave me much time for outings.

4

Then I call in Joe Finnis to give them a tour of the place. That's
what they've come for, apart from a personal sighting of the
freak. Joe's job is to see that they don't start taking cuttings from
the shrubs. They ask him questions, of course. But he's a good
boy, Joe. He doesn't give any secrets away. He came here too late
to have any worth the telling. Isabel had gone south by the time
I returned in the summer of 1954. For which, while sceptical of
any power above nature, I am prepared to thank God.

I love this place. I always have. Every summer, when my parents
and brother left the house in Louisburg Square to visit my
mother's family in Vermont, I came here, to spend three months
with my father's childless older brother, Caleb Parker, and Aunt
Louise. They treated me as if I was their own daughter and, for
all the old-fashioned ritual of their ways, they offered me an
ease I never knew in my parents' house.

They called this the Gold Coast in those days, on account of
the millionaires who were building themselves Tudor palaces
and baronial castles above the shore. But the Parkers were the
first to settle the place and my aunt and uncle kept themselves
as distant from the newcomers as I, for other reasons, do now.
They lived in a different world, in a different time. The newcomers' big yachts swam out of Falmouth harbour each day
like a flock of haughty white swans; their long shiny cars went
tooting and swerving along the narrow roads with never a stop
for the beauty of the overhanging woods or a glimpse of dark
water between the trees. No more sense in them than in a flock
of sandpipers hopping this way, then that way, over the glisten-
ing sand washed down by the waves.

I had just turned seven when my mother brought me here for
the first time in the summer of 1914.

'Will you stay too?' I asked her in the car.

She shook her head. 'I've told you so many times now, Nancy
– don't you ever listen? Daddy and I will be taking Michael to

5

Aunt Sarah for the summer. The doctor says the sea air will do you good. You need to get your appetite back. You haven't been well.' She shot a look at me as I slipped my hands between my legs and the hot sticky leather of the passenger seat. 'Uncle Caleb and Aunt Louise aren't as young as they were,' she said. 'It's kind of them to offer to have you, but they've no knowledge of children. Just try not to cause any trouble.'

I shut my eyes and closed her out, letting the roar of the engine fill my ears.

My first visit. I saw tall green woods and the house floating above them, lying at the highest level of a terraced lawn. The car crunched gravel. I jumped out before my mother could stop me and ran in through the open door.

I saw long cool rooms, hushed by canvas blinds and smelling of roses and lavender. A wind from beyond blew against the blinds and spattered them with shadows. If I closed my eyes, I was on a ship under sail for the tropics.

'Nancy? Nancy! Come back here at once before I –'

I ducked under a blind and came out onto a broad, stone-flagged terrace. Below me, bright as a tray of silver, I saw the bay, curving forward from a wide arc of sand. Out in the water, straight ahead of me, a little island of yellow rock and rough grasses jutted up from the sea. The wind caught hold of white feathered birds and whirled them up at the sun; all about me, the air vibrated with shrieks and cries and the low lion's roar of the ocean. I stood still as if my feet had grown roots.

A hand lay on my shoulder. I looked up to see my uncle Caleb peering down at me and smiling in the shy way I came to love.

'Well now, Nancy, and would you like to go down there?'

I nodded. 'Take this along,' he said, handing me a rusty tin pail. 'Follow the path down to the right and see what you can find for us.' He glanced at my fancy little city shoes. 'I'd take those off first. Barefoot's best, but don't tell your dear mother I said so or we'll both be in trouble.'

I stayed down on the shore for the best part of two hours and

6

came back triumphant with a harvest of pale oyster-turret shells and the plump hollow body of a cushion star.

'Quite a treasure trove, Nancy,' Uncle Caleb said. 'But we'll see if you and I can't find something even better before you go home.'

'Not on the rug, ma chérie,' Aunt Louise said in her light whispering voice as I started arranging my trophies on the floor. I pretended not to hear.

'Don't make me ashamed of you.' My mother spoke against my ear as she bent to kiss me. 'We've had trouble enough already.'

I clung to her hand. 'Will I have a nightlight in my room?'

'A light! At your age!' My aunt's sandy lashes fluttered open. Her eyes were blue and soft. 'She's surely a little old to be afraid of the dark, Evelyn dear? Or is it something that the doctor . . .' Her voice trailed away uncertainly.

'Nothing to do with doctors.' My mother's narrow fingers nipped at the flesh of my shoulder. 'We don't want any more nonsense, Nancy. Stop it now. This minute.'

I knew better than to say any more. But I cried so hard when Aunt Louise put me to sleep in a black room with not even the glint of a passage light under the door for comfort, that she took pity on me and pulled open the curtains on a sky bright as a box of diamonds. Then she bent down and put the starfish I had picked up on the beach under my bed. 'There you are,' she said. 'Stars in the heavens and a pretty pink star of your own under the bed. There's nothing to harm you here, ma petite –' Sobbing, uncomforted, I shook my head until she sat down on the edge of the quilt and took my hands in hers, gently rubbing them. 'What frightens you so much, little Nancy? Won't you tell me?'

I couldn't say. I would have let her throw me into the cold salt waves before I told her the cause of my distress. But she was right. There was no threat in the murmuring, sea-filled darkness of Point House. And, when I held my five-pointed trophy in my hand and looked out at the peaceful bay and the glitter of starlight on the water, wonder swallowed up my fear. Soon, I could hear the creaking of floorboards without feeling a responsive flutter of terror, of wings beating against my ribs. I began to loiter near the kitchen door in the hope of treats between meals from the slow old cook. My cheeks grew plump. Aunt Louise made cuts in the side of my dresses to give me room to breathe.

'I'd hardly know her for the same child,' she remarked to Caleb after one of these operations.

'Rosy as a peach,' said Caleb. 'You'll have to make us another visit, Nancy. Would you like that?'

'Most of anything,' I said. And, for once, went uncorrected.

Because I was a child, I saw nothing as eccentric. It seemed to me tedious but unremarkable that we should drink hot water out of yellow Worcester cups every afternoon because Aunt Louise didn't care to waste the contents of her tea caddy on family occasions.

There was no quarrelling at Point House, although my aunt and uncle divided in their passions as neatly as astrological signs. Louise, brought up in Normandy, had given her heart to the earth and everything that grew in it, while my uncle cared only for the sea and the sky. A feather or the broken rim of a shell were all he needed to identify the owner; every singular fish he had caught was mounted on the staircase wall in its own iridescent skin. It was from Caleb that I learned about the wreck of the *Hesperus* not far from our shore and of how the skipper's dead daughter was found floating on the water, bound to the mast by her own father to save her from drowning. My uncle sat by my bedside one summer when I was ill, telling me tales of the sea and reciting – he had it all by heart – the poem I loved to hear.

> *Her rattling shrouds, all sheathed in ice,*
> *With the masts went by the board;*
> *Like a vessel of glass, she strove and sank,*
> *Ho! Ho! the breakers roared.*

Caleb was a natural storyteller, although I wonder now at the kind of tales he chose for a child. Of a privateer that took two English prizes and vanished the next day with a hundred and thirty men aboard, never to be seen again. And of a cruelly cold winter when a cart bringing blocks of granite overland for one of the new houses along the shore went through the ice and down into the long salt marsh inland from Point House, drowning the driver and the oxen. He showed me where the granite blocks could still be seen, buried in the reedy water. But Caleb told his stories with a smile and I never trembled as I did at the cautionings against wilfulness that came with my mother's reading of fairy tales.

My uncle was a tender-hearted man. I remember when Aunt Louise told him to shoot the heron which had been taking carp out of the ornamental pond. I offered to go along with him, seeing how sad his eyes were as he strapped an old cartridge bag over his shoulders and peered down the dusty barrel of his rifle. He did it with his first shot, brought that lovely sharp-beaked predator down to lie like a ghost in the grass, and then he burst out crying, caught hold of my hand and gripped it as though he meant never to let go again. He stayed in his room for the next two days, refusing to answer my aunt when she hammered on the door. I never heard the heron mentioned again.

Sailing was my uncle's passion; Louise used to say that his schooner, the *Dryad*, was as troublesome as having another woman about the place. But the *Dryad* was more of a refuge than a threat, an escape from my aunt's gentle insistence on the fulfilment of local obligations in which Caleb took no interest. I was sixteen and spending my tenth summer at Point House when my uncle gave me a pretty little racing sloop and taught me how to master her giddy ways. I sailed her into Falmouth harbour the next year. I was so proud. I wouldn't have exchanged her for any of the yachts and schooners belonging to our neighbours, although she looked no bigger than a cockleshell bobbing in the shadows cast down by their gleaming hulls. That year still has a kind of glow on it when I look back. Nineteen twenty-three. The last summer before Louise died and those gentle interludes at Point House came to an end.

My uncle named his boat in teasing acknowledgement of my aunt's nature-loving activities. The well-ordered garden was her province, but she seemed happiest when she let me follow her into the rustling woods beyond it, separating us from the outside world. If I grew up knowing where to look for a saw-whet owl in the thick foliage of a hickory tree, or the ruby eyes of a whippoorwill glinting up from a drift of leaves, I have my aunt to thank for it. Even now, I only have to sniff the shavings from a new pencil to remember the red cedar she showed me when she was still trying to cure my fear of the dark. And I still smile.

Louise was convinced that my fear could be helped by the trees in which she placed an almost mystic trust. I was eight when she first bandaged my eyes with a strip of cotton and led me, her light papery hand clasping mine, into the green depths where willows and cottonwoods and creaking elms shut out the sky. Each time I snivelled and fumbled with the knotted material behind my ears, she pressed my hand to a trunk or leaf, telling me to remember how it felt before I heard the name. From her, I learned how to tell the silk-smooth bark of an alder from the light, breaking skin of a birch. Gently rubbing my hot arms with velvety mullein leaves, she taught me how to ease the salty pain of sunburned flesh; giving me a sappy stem of cow parsnip to munch as we went along, she told me how to distinguish the flower head from those of its poisonous hemlock cousins.

Further on, deep in the tawny, tangled labyrinth of the forest, was Astarte's Grove, a circle of white oaks, osiers and birches enclosing a dark pond. Light flecked the surface of the water with yellow motes, but the air was always rank. Sinewy branches of undergrowth trapped my ankles, holding me fast; the darkness of the water, so still, so unimaginably deep, suggested hidden things, slow-moving, blind. The place filled me with terror, but here, unluckily, my aunt had captured some of her finest butterfly specimens and here I was compelled to stand and watch with unbandaged eyes while she darted and stumbled after an elusive skipper or peacock, soon to be pinned and added to her collection.

Years later, I discovered that witches used to meet in Astarte's Grove and make all kinds of ghoulish sacrifices for their spells. I knew nothing about that when I was a child but the place filled me with dread. Even now, I cannot bring myself to go there. But that is for a different reason.

I respected and feared my parents. I was torn between love and resentment for Michael, my older brother. My uncle and aunt were the only relations for whom I felt unqualified tenderness. I never felt so sad as when the southbound swallows began to swirl and eddy over the chimneys of Point House and I knew that the time had come for me to travel back to Boston.

Thinking about those days has made me sentimental. There is danger in that. There is dishonesty in sentiment and I have committed myself to being entirely truthful.

I have only one audience in mind for this story and I am not such a fool as to suppose that my memories of childhood summers here will be of any great interest to them. My two granddaughters, Judith and Catherine. It's five years now since I last saw them. Judith turned eighteen last month. I wonder whom she looks like now. As a little girl, she reminded me of my husband. The same light brown hair and big hazel eyes. There were times when it actually hurt to look at her.

I wrote their mother a couple of years ago, reminding her that the house is big and that it could easily be divided up between us with no discomfort to anyone. She never answered. I don't intend to humiliate myself by repeating the invitation.

My daughter Eleanor is a shrewd woman. She has not had an easy time, not altogether, but she has made the most of herself.

11

I'm told that she has quite a reputation now as an attorney. I doubt if such a successful career leaves much time for the girls. I could have given them all of mine. However. However.

I can't blame her for wanting to keep the girls away from me. Eleanor has her reasons for being uneasy, even afraid. I took notice of her feelings the last time they were up here in the summer of seventy-four. I wanted to take Judith and Cathy out in my old dory to the Point, to show them where to pick up the shells of Angel Wings and fiddler crabs, washed in on the spring tides and stranded high on mossy ledges of rock. This was my own secret spot when I was young and I wanted them to share it, to feel the thrill I had known when I first discovered the place. But just as the children were wading out at the side of the boat and shrieking at the coldness of the water, Eleanor came hammering down the cliff path. The girls were laughing until they saw her; I think they shared my relief at being away from her guard-dog eyes. Eleanor's face was red as a beet as she came running across the sand, arms waving like semaphore flags, hair flapping down her back. I laid down the oars.

'You'll give yourself a heart attack tearing about like that,' I said. 'Now don't tell me you came all the way down here to say they can't go.'

I'm sure she meant to be diplomatic, but the excuses poured out of her mouth with such crazy fluency that even the girls must have guessed she was terrified. The tides were unpredictable, the coastguard had informed her. Judith and Cathy already had more shells than they knew what to do with in the apartment. I hadn't checked the life-jackets. And on. And on. I didn't utter a word. I knew what she didn't have the courage to say. I just kept looking at her.

We climbed the path back to the house in silence.

2

Boston, 1914–1925

FAR BACK, ON the other side of a closed door, is fear. The memories are so confused and indistinct that I can never be certain I have separated the false from the true. I am six years old. I see myself curled up in bed, knees nudging at my chest as I squint up the side of a high white pillow to make a mountain of it and myself an intrepid skier flying down the slope. Beside the bed, a pink-shaded lamp creates an island of light, floating on the darkness. The curtains are unusually thick in order to keep out the gas lamps of the square over which the mossy heads of Christopher Columbus and Aristides the Just, a tax assessor, keep unpaid guard. I have allowed the curtains to be closed. Later, I will slide out of bed and pull them an inch apart, searching the shadows for any sign of the devil, fiery eyed and cloven footed, stepping lightly through the square in the high-collared black coat of a Boston gentleman.

The faint, sooty smell of the central heating gusts up through the floor vent, making me cough and bury my face in the sheet.

I can hear the sharp click of the front door as my mother sets out for one of her evening meetings. Not for the first time, she has forgotten to kiss me goodnight. I have often prayed that I might become a little beggar girl, since it is clear that my mother would find me more interesting if I was poor and helpless. My mother nearly died of diphtheria as a girl. When she recovered,

13

she decided to become a missionary. Instead, she married my father and made causes her vocation. School boards, Chinese missions and temperance societies occupy her time. I have never seen her show affection towards my father; I sense that she feels little for me. My brother Michael, a sulky red-lipped boy of fourteen, is the exception. I do not think Michael has ever known what it is like to feel unloved.

The house is quiet, but it hums with expectation. Something is going to happen. Imperiously, nervously, I knock on the wall to make sure that my brother is awake. No answer. Either he is already asleep – unlikely – or he has locked himself in the bathroom to read something unsuitable. I know what he reads because I opened the box in which he keeps his sports clothes. Hidden at the bottom are some bottles and a book of photographs, heavily tinted pictures of pink and yellow flesh, legs in black stockings, bosoms that look ready to burst. I have studied them with care and can see that my brother has been driven mad by years of proximity to Mrs Higgins, my nurse. Mrs Higgins has jowls that quiver like jelly when she nods her head. Cushions wheeze where she drops her weight. The ironed front of her white blouse swells before her with the pride of a filled sail. At six, I, too, am in love with the thought of vast female bodies. Comfort is not far from the warm, sour odour which rises from under Mrs Higgins' broad lap as she dozes by the fire.

This is Mrs Higgins' night off and she will be shut behind her door, chanting appropriate passages of the psalms to ward off the Beast who, in her mind, and therefore mine, is always prowling under the gas lamps of the square, ready to cleave the earth with his tail and send us flying down to a lake of eternal darkness. By listening at the keyhole, I have learned to watch out for the Beast's accomplice, a lady dressed in purple and scarlet. Her name is Mystery and she is the mother of harlots and abominations of the earth. Miss Craven, whose house I have just begun visiting for Wednesday afternoon dancing classes, is the most likely candidate. She wears a long purple dress and scarves of red chiffon swirl about her and brush our arms when she glides among us, urging us to droop like snowdrops or prance like little ponies. Mrs Higgins says that all forms of imitation are temptations sent by the devil, so I hold myself straight and refuse to droop or prance.

Now the pictures grow confused. I hear no footsteps. It is not I whose hand puts out the light. The room is thick with darkness. I call out for my brother, frantic: 'Michael! Michael!' Now the pillow is under my face, stifling me until I think my head will burst. My thrashing legs are pushed apart and fingers move up and between them, stroking and probing until I quiver and my body jumps. There is sighing, a groan and then a sudden sharp smell, strong as disinfectant. Sobbing, I twist and kick, trying to push the pillow away. I am sure I am going to die. I can't breathe. My body is all twitching and raw and strange to me.

The pillow is lifted. A voice speaks close to my ear. It whispers hoarsely. The words are kind, but the voice is angry. It growls. It says: 'Dear Nancy, good Nancy, all better now, all safe again. The dream's gone. Time to go to sleep.'

The voice is so rough and I don't understand what he means or what is happening. I wait for my goodnight kiss, but he goes out of the room and closes the door behind him. I wait for the creaks to tell me he has reached the staircase before I dare move. I am squashing my body up against the wall to stop the shaking, and the darkness which never scared me before has the smell of a wild animal.

It was imagination, they said. It was only in my head that the darkness rose from the floor and stretched itself until there was no breathing space left in the room, no breath for a word, no space for a thought, no feeling beyond the heat burning up my body like a flame from hell as the velvet arms of darkness slid up to hold me still. I suffered from bad dreams, my mother said as she shook herself free of my desperate, clutching fingers.

Imagination deprived me of the wish to eat. Imagination required that a light should be kept burning in the room all night and that the curtains should be pulled wide apart. Imagination drove me to ask if I could have a bolt put on my door and, when this was denied, to bar the way in by dragging my bed across it as a barrier. Alone, I rubbed at the dry slit between my legs, as if rubbing would make my mind a blank. I was sent home from school one morning for behaving dirtily. 'Miss Lennox says you were touching yourself,' my mother said, and she wiped her mouth with a corner of her handkerchief as if to take the words away. 'Touching yourself in class. In public. Do you understand how horrible it is for a mother to hear that said of her own child?'

'She made it up,' I said, weeping. 'I didn't do anything.'

'I'm fixing an appointment for you to see Dr Rowntree,' she said. 'And we'll see if he thinks Miss Lennox is lying.'

The doctor was a thin, worried young man with gold-rimmed spectacles and a watch on a long chain which he allowed me to play with while he questioned me. I couldn't say the things I wanted to, not with my mother watching us from her chair in the corner of the room. The doctor made light of my behaviour at school. Little girls don't always know what they're doing, he said to my mother and he gave me a hard yellow sweet out of a jar on his desk. He seemed more concerned by the fact that I was underweight for my age.

He must have said something else to her when he sent me to sit in the waiting room. My mother took me to a shop on the way home and bought me a little musical box with a picture on the lid of mountains and a lake made out of fragments of mother-of-pearl.

'But my birthday isn't for two months,' I said, holding it tight in case she took it away again.

'It isn't', she said, 'a birthday present.'

When the holidays began, I went on my first visit to Point House, away from my father.

The fear of dark rooms has never left me.

*

I was a gangling eleven year old, no better at dancing than I was at making friends or getting a school star for my class work, when the cable arrived. The maid came into the drawing-room, where I was being measured by my mother for a new winter coat while my father sat reading his paper.

'It's from France, Mr Parker,' she said and, dropping the envelope on the centre table, she scuttled back through the door like a crab under siege. Slowly, my parents went towards the table, facing each other across it.

'Aren't you going to open it?' I was puzzled by their stiffness, the silence. 'Is it about Michael? Have they made him a captain?' This was the only military rank I had off pat and I thought it sounded awfully fine and swaggering.

'Quiet,' my father said, and I saw his hand shake as it crept over the cloth towards the envelope. My mother's hand was quicker. She pulled the envelope free of his limp grasp, slit it briskly open with the little ivory knife which was always in her pocket. She held the piece of paper up to her eyes for a moment before placing it on the table and smoothing two creases out of it with the careful tips of her fingers. When I looked up at her face, she seemed to be smiling.

'I knew,' she said. 'I knew.'

'He's coming back!' I crowed, pleased to have discovered the answer. She made a movement with her hands, pushing space away from her.

'Go upstairs, Nancy,' my father said. 'Go now.'

I went to the door. Turning, I saw my father take out his handkerchief and start to polish his spectacles with small, fierce movements. My mother stood by the table, staring straight ahead. I understood then that Michael was dead and that I was not to share in their grief. Crying, I ran across the hall and up the stairs. I cried for Michael, dutifully. The tears that hurt were for myself.

The official explanation came a week later. A shell had landed in the back of the open truck which a captain from Michael's

17

regiment was using as an auxiliary ambulance. He was carrying ten wounded men and one of them was my brother. The truck caught fire. The driver was the only one to survive and he had to watch them burning where they sat. He couldn't reach them through the flames.

Michael's death took whatever life there had been from our house and left it cold and empty as a church on weekdays. My father never came to my room again. Maybe he took it for a punishment; I wouldn't know. He retreated into his study, where he spent hours arranging books, poring over old letters and photographs and planning a history of the family in which, I am sure, Michael was intended to feature as a credit to his ancestors. My mother chose to obliterate grief in a fury of philanthropic activity which culminated in the stirring news that she intended to run as the first woman mayor of Boston.

I felt like a ghost. I was used to taking second place. But death raised Michael to a level with the angels. I could never match him now. I felt that the wrong child had died. I understood that what my father had done to me was done in indifference, because I was without worth. I was endured, not loved. At the beginning of each year, I started crossing off the days until I would go back to Point House, where Michael's name had no magic and where I, I myself, was loved.

Turning out a chest of oddments the other day, I came across a few yellowing copies of *Vanity Fair* magazine. Two were from 1925. It amused me to see how remote the world they presented was from the one I had inhabited and, good daughter of Brahmin Boston that I was, assumed to be invincibly superior.

Looking at *Vanity Fair* again, I wonder at my youthful arrogance. The experiences I missed! Mary Astor drooping backwards in John Barrymore's arms. Clara Bow showing off what it meant to have It with a shiny maroon pout. Tall Bill Tilden gracefully swooping to retrieve the wristwatch of an over-excited female spectator. Gershwin on the piano and W.C. Fields on the boards. Coca-Cola ('the charm of purity') soda fountains sneaking up on Coty's face powder direct from Fifth Avenue and the smartly gloved and hatted couple whose outstretched arms beckoned us to join them for the next crossing of the *Mauretania*.

I turned eighteen in the summer of 1925. Two years out of school, I felt no regret that I had not gone on to college like the rest of my class. I was torn two ways. I wanted to engage in noble acts of self-sacrifice which would win my mother's admiration, but I would also have liked to roll down my stockings and go dancing to a jazz piano. I was invited to dances, of course, by virtue of being my parents' only daughter. I had been given my inaugural tea at the Chilton Club and smiled upon by the mothers who mattered. But I was shy to the point of dumbness, and I had not inherited what my mother always referred to as 'the Armstrong face'. (An old family photograph can still astonish me with the porcelain delicacy of my mother and her sister Sarah, nestling together like swans in billows of pale organza.) Circling the dance floor, I often intercepted the frantic glances by which my partner beseeched his friends to rescue him, and saw from their smiles that they would not. Drowning in self-consciousness, I could take no comfort from the thought that I was probably the only girl in the room wearing a home-made dress, that the material had been cut from a silk remnant and that every girl there must be aware of it.

The nearest I had come to romance was a midnight drive along the banks of the Charles with a boy called Ned Shiplake, who, just as we came level with Harvard Bridge, pushed up my skirt and put his hand between my legs. I gripped his hand so hard that he yelped; I saw the white mark of my fingers on his skin. I told him to take me home and that was the last I ever saw of him. Alone in my bedroom, I touched my breasts and my hips and shivered at the passion with which I could kiss my own mirror lips. In May, when I went up to spend a month at Point

House with Uncle Caleb, a widower by then, I lay on my bed with the pink and white curtains blowing wide open to the sea wind. A love like the wind was what I wanted, free as the elements, a love that could carry me up to the sky and make me glorious, make me shine.

Caleb was lost without my aunt. He never smiled. Down in Falmouth harbour, the *Dryad* danced and chinked on her mooring, eager to be off, but her sides needed repainting and there was rust on the fittings. Once, I succeeded in persuading Caleb to come for a walk, when I told him that the gypsy-moth nests needed coating with creosote if the woods were not to be plagued with them. He left all the work to me and after a time I was so overcome by his sadness that I threw the brush down and told him we were going back to the house. He followed me back, unprotesting, shuffling his feet along the path.

That was the only summer when I looked wistfully at the life of the Gold Coast crowd. I fell into conversation one day with a black-eyed, black-haired stranger walking along our part of the shore in nothing but his scarlet bathing costume and a pair of patent leather shoes. He asked me to a party up at their house along the shore. I put on my best silk dress and went, but the room was full of naked backs and bird voices and cigarette smoke so sour it stung my eyes. I walked out through the open windows and down the wooden steps to the beach. Then I pulled off my evening shoes and ran home across the sand in my stockings.

What I craved most was not love but a purpose. My offers of assistance to my mother in her political campaign were firmly rejected, although no explanation was given. It may have been that the presence of a strapping eighteen-year-old was considered a disadvantage when she herself looked so slight and girlish. It may have been that my awkward ways would have made me an embarrassment. Denied a public role and informed that my uncle would prefer no visitors at Point House in the foreseeable future, I was at a loss as to how to entertain myself. A short spell of charitable work ended in disgrace when I was discovered to have been providing gin to a mother of six who had horrified me by admitting that she kept her spirits up on wood alcohol. Word got out that her new supplier was the daughter of our prospective mayor and my parents received a visit from a lady representing the charitable society. Shortly after her departure, my mother called me into the drawing-room.

Truly, you would have thought I was a criminal, to hear the way my mother spoke to me that evening. There was no respite to be gained from my father; he, as usual, had buried himself behind the paper, finding safety in detachment. Her voice went on like a funeral bell, tolling out my crimes as if they had no end. Taking gin from the cellar made me a thief. I had disgraced the family name. I had jeopardised my mother's hopes of becoming mayor and made a mockery of her prohibition work. Had it never occurred to me that alcohol induced apathy and bad habits and that this woman's job – she was a maker of lace inserts for blouses – was likely to be affected if she drank gin all day?

'And wouldn't you drink,' I said, 'if you lived in a North End tenement with a husband who beat you and six children under the age of eight? You'd need more than water to comfort you.'

My mother lifted her pretty oval face to smile at me like an angel from under the lamp where she was repairing the tattered cross and lilies in an altarcloth. 'If', she said, 'I found myself in such an unfortunate position, I would ask my husband to curb his appetite.'

I stared at her.

'His sexual appetite, Nancy.' A faint blush tinged her pale cheeks. 'I don't propose to go into details in your father's presence. You know perfectly well what I mean. Now, if you had really cared to help this poor woman, you should have reported her to the prohibition committee,' she went on, stitching away at her embroidery. 'It's the weak of spirit who need us most. You understand that now, don't you?'

I folded my arms. 'I understand that you're happy to have one law for them and another for us.'

Thrust and draw, thrust and draw, went my mother's small steel needle. 'Meaning what, Nancy? And do keep your voice down. We don't want the whole house listening.'

I took a short step towards her. 'Anything's better than telling the truth, isn't it, Mother?'

She was ready for my stare, but I saw her hand trembling as she drew up the red silk thread and snipped it off. 'I think', she said, 'you ought to go and lie down for half an hour. You're over-exciting yourself again. The best thing we can do now is to forget this incident ever took place.'

'Michael drank,' I said. 'He was drinking long before he went to France. And you knew. He wasn't so perfect. Not until he was dead and you could make a saint of him.'

My mother leaned forward over her embroidery. She made no sound, but I could see that she was weeping from the movement of her shoulders. The longcase clock sweetly chimed seven from the hall. My father laid his newspaper on his knees and carefully folded it to a quarter of its size. 'You owe your mother an apology,' he said.

I shook my head. 'I'm waiting for one.'

His eyes met mine. 'An apology, Nancy?' He dared me to say one dangerous word in that quiet, respectable room and he was right. I couldn't do it. Walking past me to the chair where my mother bravely hid her face from us, he laid a hand on her arm, excluding me. 'It's time for us to go upstairs and get tidied for dinner, my dear, don't you think?'

I went to the Athenaeum the following afternoon to collect some books for my mother. Standing near the entrance was a new and beautiful statue of a young girl holding a knife to her flowing hair. The librarian told me that it represented a young Carthaginian and that she was shearing her tresses to provide bowstrings for the warriors defending her city. Sitting in my room that night, I unpinned my hair and brushed it down to my waist, a shining auburn mass, my one true claim to beauty. Watching my eyes in the mirror, I chopped it until I stood in a waving sea of red. Scooping it up, I scattered it down the passage all the way to my parents' bedroom.

'A peace-offering,' I said in the morning when my mother, cold-eyed, asked if I had lost what remained of my wits.

Two days later, my father told me that they thought it would be better if I left town for a while. I was to go and stay with my mother's niece Kitty. Kitty had married a banker called Jim Archer. They lived in New York.

'New York?' I said. I had never travelled more than fifty miles from Boston. 'New York!'

I caught the trace of a smile on my father's face as he bent his head to polish his spectacles. 'Don't go getting ideas in your head, Nancy. You are not being rewarded for some act of virtue. Although, just between the two of us, I don't view your foolish behaviour in quite the same light as your mother. It seems to me that a little fun would do you no harm. A young girl shouldn't be too serious.'

He's sweetening me, I thought. He's afraid of what I might say. That's why he wants me out of the house.

'I haven't met Kitty since I was twelve. Why would she want to have me to stay?'

'She's looking forward to it,' he said calmly. 'We had a cablegram yesterday. Kitty has turned into a nice, sensible young woman. And she's made a good marriage. We all approve of Jim.' He glanced up at me. 'You might ask your cousin to recommend a hairdresser while you're there. The new cut doesn't do much for you.'

I looked at him thoughtfully, wondering why he should be so in favour of Kitty's husband, a man he had only shaken hands with at their wedding. It was, I realised, Jim Archer's status that commended him. Kitty had always been considered a little flighty and careless of the family name. A troublesome girl could always be brought into line by marriage to a Wall Street man, preferably from one of the old merchant-banking families of Boston. Jim's grandmother had been an Armstrong from New Hampshire, I remembered. Jim was one of us.

'So I'm to be found a suitable husband and taken off your hands?'

My father finished polishing his spectacles and replaced them on his long shiny nose. 'Your mother was just nineteen when we married,' he said. 'Girls shouldn't wait about. Waiting takes the bloom off them.'

Well, I thanked him for his concern and thanked him again for the news that I would be allowed twenty-five dollars a week on which to transform myself into marriageable material, although that was not quite how he expressed it.

I asked my mother for the money to buy myself a dashing cream hat with a spotted veil which I had seen in the display windows of Jordan Marsh. Instead, she gave me a lemon straw boater which had belonged to my great-aunt and which, she said, looked good as new now that she had stitched a fresh white ribbon to the crown.

'You'll get more wear out of that than from the rubbish they sell in Jordan's,' she said as she supervised the packing of my valise.

I didn't trouble myself finding an answer.

3

New York, 1925

I EMERGED FROM the echoing cathedral of the Grand Central Station concourse into sunshine bright as a sword and the sharp scent of a sea wind blustering hard enough to lift my grandmother's hat and send it bowling away over the roofs of a fleet of cars and out of sight. I took it for a sign of freedom. My cases had been sent on ahead. The Archers had been given the date but not the time of my arrival. A couple of hours would make no difference.

Turning the first corner, I found my way forward blocked by a swaying line of people in white robes and with bare feet. The ones at the front were blowing – or pretending to blow, for I remember no sound – brass trumpets, while those to the rear held seven-branched candlesticks which they brandished at us with mildly sinister smiles. Above them, sitting on a kitchen chair covered with gold wrapping paper, was a pale woman with heavy black hair hanging to her hips. She wore a purple dress and her mouth was painted as if it had been smeared with cochineal beetles, the scarlet of a fresh wound. Above her, on a flimsy banner, I made out the words 'Save yourself' and 'whore of . . .'

Hardened sinners walked off without a second glance, to be swallowed by the striped shadows cast by the track of the overhead elevator. The rest of us shuffled our feet and looked for escape routes as the angels moved among us, distributing eager

25

smiles and grubby scraps of paper. I looked down at the printed words 'Pray to be spared' and promptly handed it back to the nearest figure in white.

'You picked the wrong person. Sorry.'

The angel had a lean angry face and cold eyes. 'There is no wrong person for us,' he said. 'Only the chosen will be spared when the holocaust comes. And this is the city of hell.' He looked at me fiercely. 'Don't you feel the need to be saved?'

'Not until I've sinned a little more, thank you kindly,' I said and walked away before he could start arguing.

A new building was going up in the Forties on Madison Avenue. Up at the top of a black-and-gold wall, miniature figures in blue overalls jumped and swung and dived through an open forest of cable wires and girders. It was a high-wire act without the safety net. The audience ignored the hooting cars and moved out across the avenue for a better look. A couple of girls screamed encouragement. One of the workers waved back. I could smell the excitement as he leaned out over the edge of the building, one arm jauntily twisted around a cable wire. The side of the building creaked in a sudden gust of wind and the crowd sighed. They wanted him to fall. I could feel it. Scared by the yearning and the power in their need, I walked on.

The smell of gas which was everywhere, sweet and nauseating, drove me off the avenues and into the side streets. I was surprised to find myself back in Boston, standing on a cobbled street beside a small bow-fronted shop. The window caught my eye with a display of brightly coloured pamphlets and poetry magazines. As I peered in, a young man emerged from the door. Taking no more notice than if I had been a shadow on the cobbles, he pulled the leather satchel off his shoulder, stripped off his jacket and executed a neat somersault on the sidewalk, right there in front of me.

'Encore please,' I said, and blushed as he turned to look at me. He had curling light brown hair and the largest, most brilliant eyes I had ever seen.

'So you like circus acts,' he said. 'Good. Let's go somewhere and talk about them. I've just been reading the story about the trapeze artist in *Ein Hunger Künstler*. Criminal it hasn't been translated. Do you like Kafka?' His smile was so wide and disarming that I couldn't help returning it.

'I don't know who he is.'

'Never mind. What about Kilmer? He's written some marvellous stuff about the circus. Where shall we go?'

'I just liked the somersault,' I said weakly.

'*Saltus*, leap, spring, bound. *Supra*, over. Which suggests something more like leapfrog in its origin, wouldn't you say?' He picked up his satchel and swung it over his shoulder. 'Well?'

Not quite sane, I thought. What a pity. Smiling again, but in a cooler, more dismissive way, I walked on, fast. At the next turning, I thought I had never before seen such eyes or such a smile. I turned back. The street was empty of everything but sunlight.

Leaving Boston on a cloudy October day, I had worn my best serge coat. Two hundred miles south, New York was enjoying a freakish reminder of summer. My feet were tired and sweat was trickling down my sides. Since I knew no one in New York except Kitty, my social reputation was not going to suffer if I sat on a shady doorstep and took the coat off for a few minutes.

I must have been more exhausted from the journey and my walk than I had realised. When I opened my eyes, the weather had changed. The sky was grey as a saucepan lid and the sidewalk was flecked with drops. The coat, together with the handbag containing my month's allowance of a hundred dollars, had disappeared.

I felt like a drowned rat by the time I reached my destination on East 60th Street. It was not surprising that the tall butler who opened the door looked startled when I explained that I was Mrs Archer's cousin. Softened by a volley of sneezes, he showed me to a marble-tiled washroom and advised me to mop up the worst of the rain with a couple of my relative's monogrammed hand towels. A curt nod when I emerged indicated that I was looking presentable enough for escort to the first floor.

It was the kind of room I had seen in magazines, but never imagined that I would find myself standing in. The walls were white, the curtains of heavy apricot silk. Skins of wild animals mantled the floor so thoroughly that I was obliged to step on the flattened haunches of two cheetahs to get away from the door. My cousin lay before me, stretched on a chaise longue and turning the pages of a brochure while she addressed herself to the telephone. Still chilled from my soaking, I edged towards a chair by the fireplace.

'Not that one,' my cousin said sharply. 'Over there, on the white sofa.' She flashed a smile at me. 'Delicious with that marvellous-coloured hair. What was I saying? Oh, and then we went on to the Willow Room with the Schuylers.'

I sat where instructed, eyeing the pale bob which finished just on a line with Kitty's small, pretty ears. Above the fireplace, a ferocious woman with a riding-crop in her hand glared purposefully at the rugs, as if she intended to pulp any remaining shred of life out of the glass-eyed heads.

'Jim's mother,' Kitty said, finishing her conversation and following my gaze. 'Dreadful old tyrant. I can't think why we have to put up with that horror as well as seeing the original almost every week of the year. She only comes to check that I haven't had her image burned. How's Aunt Evelyn?' Her cheek brushed mine with the scent of jasmine and cigarettes.

'She's fine.'

'Well –' She looked me up and down, laughing and shaking her head. 'My very Bostonian cousin. Seeing you certainly brings it all back.'

I was mortified. My hair was a mess, but my dark blue suit had been specially purchased at R.H. Stearns, and my shoes were dyed to match. She gave my cheek a brisk pat with a hand as light and dry as an October leaf.

'Now don't sulk, it pulls your mouth down so, and you do

have a lovely mouth, Nancy. It's not your fault that you haven't had a chance to make the best of yourself. I remember the golden rule. Rouge your cheeks in Louisburg Square and you might as well call yourself a bride of the devil. Well, here I am, rouged to the hilt, and the devil hasn't paid one scrap of attention. I almost wish he would, just to liven things up.'

'Kitty, don't say such things!'

She gave me a comical look. 'I'm perfectly serious. I'd love the devil to come and carry me off. I'm as bored as I can be. Just imagine – three years of being a banker's wife! And it's been so tiresome this summer. Jim will go on about some stupid speculation in the Rockaways that went wrong. I keep telling him that it just makes my head ache, all that money talk. Does it show? Do I look terribly jaded?'

'You look lovely.' I had never heard a woman jabber so, and to so little consequence. Just listening to her made my head ache. 'Really lovely,' I said again, seeing that she appeared to be waiting for something more. But I had not convinced. Making a little pouting movement with her lips, she glanced at her watch, a delicate bracelet of gold.

'I have to join Jim at a party in one of the Cloud Clubs at six. I could take you, but I don't think you'd be happy dressed like that.'

'Oh I don't mind,' I said eagerly. 'I'd love to go in one of the new elevators, twenty floors up. I've heard it feels wonderful.' Fixed in my head was an ecstatic image of myself, lifted on wings of steel to dance among the rustling ferns of the Plaza Hotel Roof Garden, bathed in amber light as I whirled and spun. But Kitty shook her head.

'It does, and you shall, but not yet. We need to do some serious shopping before I take you anywhere, my sweet. I mean – that suit! I bet you got it at Stearns!'

I must have looked crestfallen for she patted my cheek again. 'Don't worry, you're going to look gorgeous. Now, let's have Crisp show you your bedroom.' She pressed an electric bell, then bent to whisper. 'Crisp used to be butler to the Duke of York. You should see how he sneers at the Vanderbilts for employing somebody who used to wash dishes for him at the castle. It's delirious! The man's an absolute goldmine of royal gossip.'

It seemed best to allow life to be arranged for me. Crisp, deeming me unworthy of his recollections, marched me to my room and expressed a chilly hope that I would find my valise within and everything to my satisfaction.

'I'd quite like something to eat, please,' I ventured. Crisp made a small head movement which might have been a nod.

'Mrs Archer will doubtless have informed the cook,' he said. 'Goodnight, Miss Parker.' And he stalked grandly away.

The drawing-room had been a shrine to spartan taste compared to the poodle's parlour in which I was expected to sleep. The dressing-table sagged under a pastel flurry of ruffles and pleats, while the bed defied me to make my way on to it through a mountain of fringed and tasselled cushions in every shade of pink. Even the ceiling had not escaped Kitty's attentions; white satin bows swung on cherry-coloured ribbons from every corner, lowered to just the height at which they could flutter around my face like outsize butterflies.

Unpacked and unfed – Kitty quite plainly had forgotten to mention my arrival to the cook – I crept into bed with one of the three books placed beside it for my entertainment, *Great Gardens of Virginia*, *Kidnapped* and *A Poet's Treasury*. Opening the last, I looked up Kafka. But this anthologist seemed to have no opinion of him and I fell asleep with Poe's raven croaking mournfully in my ear.

I woke with a start to find him flapping at my shoulder; one of Kitty's ceiling-strung bows had broken free of its ribbon and fallen on the bed. The building was silent, and the room was black as a vault, suffocating me with the darkness I still feared. Unable to find the bedside light, I stumbled to the window, dragged back the cold, heavy weight of the curtains and pushed up the sash. Gasping for air and light, I climbed out onto the precarious iron balcony, an ornament not meant for use.

It had stopped raining. A lavender fog hung round the street lamps and pressed against the walls. Above me, a green searchlight probed the sky like a giant's finger. Behind the whine and rattle of the Elevated and the squawking of horns, I heard the jangle of a jazz band, the sudden screech of a saxophone's climax. An open yellow car went quietly past. The driver's peaked cap hid his face. His passenger, laid out like a corpse across the back seat, was a girl in white satin with skin the colour of molasses. Her eyes were wide open and she was smiling up at the night sky as if each star extended a camera flash of acknowledgement.

A door suddenly opened across the street and two bodies plunged down the steps, locked in each other's arms. A crowd of party-goers clambered through the window onto the balcony opposite my own. The music was drowned out by shouts and whistles as the combatants shifted to my side of the street, up against the wall. I could see nothing, but I flinched as I heard something crack against stone. One of the observers leant forward, swaying over the rail.

'Twenty sees you on your feet again, thirty sees you through a couple of rounds. Whaddya say?'

Getting no answer, he shrugged and climbed back inside. The music overpowered the voices for a moment, then the window was slammed down and the curtains drawn. For a moment, there was a quiet so deep that I could hear the whistle and clang of a ferry as it sheered away from the docks. Bending over the balcony, I saw nothing but the white upward glare of a lamp.

'Are you all right? Shall I call for a doctor?'

One of the wrestlers came out to the middle of the street and looked up at me. 'I believe we already met,' he said. It was the somersaulter.

'Is he hurt?'

He smiled and folded his arms. 'No more than he needed to

be. But I doubt if he's up to greeting Juliet on the balcony just now.'

Blushing at the thought of what I must look like, I shrank back against the window. 'I don't know him. I was just getting some air. I'll go back inside now. So long as there isn't a corpse outside the door.'

His eyes opened very wide. 'A corpse? No, I wouldn't worry about that. He'll be back in there before I'm even out of sight. I just aimed to remind him of his priorities.'

'There's no crime in dancing.'

'There is when you've a meeting to attend.'

'About poetry?'

He narrowed his eyes a little. 'Among other things. Do you care about poetry, Miss –?'

'Nancy Parker. From Boston. I don't know very much about it. I like Whitman. And Tennyson.'

He nodded gravely. 'You could read a lot worse. Now back to bed with you before you catch your death, Miss Parker. That's an awfully skimpy nightdress you're wearing. You've done your duty and that nice Boston conscience can rest easy for the night.' Lifting his hand to an invisible hat, he raised it, bowed and sauntered away down the street. I hesitated for a moment before I decided to take the risk.

'Excuse me! You never told me your name. Perhaps we could –'

But, for the second time that day, I was too slow. He had turned the corner.

4

New York, 1925

KITTY NEVER WENT home to Vermont: society had become her family. The only relation I ever saw in her apartment was Jim's mother, a former Southern belle who had all of the steely will the portrait painter's brush had suggested by the whip in her hands. Even Kitty seemed subdued when Mary Lou Archer came to hold court for her weekly hour. I usually kept to my room.

My cousin was as busy as it is possible to be if you have nothing to live for but yourself. Even when, occasionally, she settled on a sofa to flip over the pages of a fashionable novel, I could see her tapping her fingers on the jacket, skimming the text like a starved heron in search of a juicy victim before she sprang up, declaring that she just didn't comprehend how other people found time to read. The days were given over to lunches, shopping and exhibition visiting, with the exception of Wednesdays. These were set aside for the telephone and beautification. Jim did not appear to mind that the masseur who visited her bedroom on Wednesday afternoons was a good-looking young Hungarian by whom Kitty allowed herself to be pummelled and stretched for a two-hour session before, rosy cheeked and freshly scented, she descended the stairs. I imagine that Jim looked on his wife's Wednesdays as an extension of the treatment which was meted out to his sleek, honey-seated sedan car.

In the evenings, we usually visited a hotel restaurant or one of the Harlem clubs at which Kitty would tell us how much she enjoyed mixing with real people. (Their uncommon reality lay in the colour of their skin. But she jumped as if she'd been shot when a Negro waiter happened to brush against her arm.) When we came home, Jim would pick out a few tunes on the piano, smirking at us in a way which suggested that he thought himself a regular king of the keys.

The evenings were busy. The days dragged. I filled them by wandering within the perimeter defined by Kitty as 'safe'. I looked at prints in the New York Public Library; I feasted my eyes on reptiles and the world's biggest elephant in the Museum of Natural History. (The Hall of Trees was my favourite place; reciting their names was curiously comforting.) When I tired of that, I loitered in the local shops, admiring the way their managers slid into a new voice and form of repartee with each fresh customer, flexible as comedians. A soft smile and a hand under the arm for a frail old lady, fishing in her purse for cents, a quick bit of banter with a tubby little blue-chinned man in a homburg hat who always blew cigar smoke over the apples when he stooped to pinch their sides. I could have watched all day, but Kitty disapproved. It was, she said sternly, just stupid to come all this way and hang around grocery stores. Hadn't I seen enough of them in Boston?

Often, dawdling in a side street, I caught myself looking for the somersaulter. Once or twice, I ran after a perfect stranger and had to apologise for my mistake. I never found him.

My escapes became increasingly rare. Kitty had run out of decoration projects; she lacked an occupation and I provided one by having arrived with what were deemed to be unwearable clothes. My mother, who saved her leather shoes by wearing galoshes from the first day of fall, would have been horrified by the ruthlessness with which my wardrobe was vetted and dismissed. I defended myself; Kitty's response was to parcel up my best skirts and jackets for the Salvation Army to collect on a day when I was out exploring the neighbourhood.

Kitty's dresses were Paris models. I, who did not even know what couture meant, was shown that a clever cut could make my chest look flatter, my legs longer and my hips, which would have delighted Rubens in those days, look almost narrow. I wrote home begging for an increase to my weekly stipend; my mother wrote back reminding me that I had already thrown away four weeks' money by carelessness. She added that she had no intention of supporting my wish to look like a salesgirl. She herself had never spent more than ten dollars on a new outfit. Her letter ended with a reminder that my own money was held in a trust until my marriage and, mercifully, could not be squandered on frippery.

'Mothers!' said Kitty, as I finished reading the letter out to her over the breakfast table. 'Well, I'll just have to see to you myself, shan't I?'

Giddy though Kitty was, I could never accuse her of being ungenerous. Jim, as she pointed out, often made more than a thousand dollars in a week. What else was money for if not to be enjoyed? Eyeing myself in a beaded shimmy with a rope of false pearls twisted round my neck, I was willing to agree with her.

'Hair next, Cinderella,' said Kitty. 'Then nails. There's a marvellous manicurist at the Plaza. The stories she tells about her other clients! You'll die!'

I looked at her uneasily. 'Won't Jim mind having to pay for all this?'

'Not when he sees you,' said Kitty. 'Jim likes girls to look good. You'll see.'

She was right, of course. She had her husband's measure.

Jim Archer was a pleasant featureless man with a slightly lost look around the eyes. As far as his wife was concerned, he could just as well have been a machine for printing dollar bills. When Kitty wanted a new dress or to lay a new zebra skin on the floor, she gave the machine a pat and a pleading look. If that failed, she sulked. The machine generally obliged at this point by spitting out the necessary number of notes. Jim's function was to admire and bestow, Kitty's to exhibit and arouse envy. This was the basis on which they had built what seemed to be a successful marriage, the example I was expected to follow.

I was grateful for their kindness. And yet, lying in my cushioned coffin at the end of another empty evening, I was ready to howl at the pointlessness of it all. Had I no purpose in life beyond the acquisition of a suitable husband? Was Kitty's life to become my goal, my marriage to be the domestic equivalent of living with a bank? Those were the times at which I felt ready to throw my new shoes and hats and cellophane-shrouded dresses out of the window and take myself back to Boston barefoot, if necessary. Anything, to escape.

I had brought with me my little watercolour of the shore below Point House, which I hung on the wall facing my bed. Looking at it, I could almost hear the hiss of waves along the sand, but I sometimes wondered if I would ever see it again. Uncle Caleb had admitted on my last visit that I reminded him too painfully of the past. Patting my hand apologetically, he told me that he felt easiest on his own, now that Louise had gone.

I wrote to him once from New York and told him I had been thinking about the old days. He sent back a long, rambling letter about an earthquake, the first anybody could remember in the area, which had destroyed the little summerhouse in which I used to preside over ceremonious teas with two china dolls which had once belonged to my aunt. I had nightmares after that letter about Point House slipping down from its precarious mooring on the cliff-tops. An analyst would probably have discovered that I was worrying about my own uncertain position.

What was it Caleb used to say about my mother? 'It's not that I don't like the dear woman, Nancy, it's just that I can't stand her.' I know what he meant. That was how I felt about Kitty. Poor Kitty. She was an advertiser's dream, the woman who believes in the transforming power of material possessions. And the crash of 1929 put an end to all that. Jim, like so many of his colleagues, grew reckless after seeing his investments treble and quadruple their value, month after month. Like every other banker in New York, he felt they were the chosen generation, the lucky ones. So he took what seemed to be a sound tip and put their considerable all into Sunshine Motors, panicked when the market dropped – and lost everything. The house went on the market. Jim was picked up by a trawler off the New Jersey shore a couple of months later. Kitty went down to Washington to identify the body. A year later, she found a new husband, a twice-divorced man who had made a fortune shipping bootleg liquor out of Cuba. She wrote letters to the family, but nobody replied. I expect she still had pretty clothes and silk stockings, but luxury would have been of little comfort to Kitty if society struck her off the list. And that was what I understand society did.

But I'm running ahead of myself, and past the three weeks of dinners at which the Archers handsomely exhibited me. Twice, I overheard Kitty talking about the Parker Trust Fund. Rather too often, she urged me to talk about Point House and Uncle Caleb. The house was valuable, and Caleb had no children. Knowing what she wanted me to say, I shook my head. Why should I only be lovable as a sound investment?

The candidates did not appeal. They were an amiable and courteous series of young brokers and bankers, pale as wax candles and with a conversational style as heavy as the plumped-up shoulders of their dinner suits. They swaggered about with hip-flasks of brandy in their pockets as though they were carrying Colt revolvers and boasted to each other about the number of speakeasies to which they knew the passwords. Their interests ranged all the way from which band was playing at the Plaza to whether they should invest in a weekend home on Long Island. Several already had. A few, aiming to show that they thought about culture just as much as any stuck-up Bostonian, asked what I thought of Ernest Hemingway and whether I cared for the poetry of Miss Millay. One of them, swelling up like a turkeycock, told me that he was planning to shake Gertrude

Stein by the hand when he visited Paris. He seemed to think that she would appreciate the honour he was conferring.

Bill Taylor promised to be just such another agreeable non-entity. Kitty, unusually, had decided to give a dinner at home in honour of this young man since, so one of her friends had told her, he was rich, well educated and unmarried.

I liked him at once. He was a little taller than me, heavily built, with rosy cheeks and blue eyes which sparkled with enjoyment and good humour as he looked about the room. I judged him to be in his mid twenties. His fair hair was slicked back from a centre parting; his arms were full of sunflowers, a gift which Kitty received with appreciative gurgles before relinquishing them to Crisp. (Sunflowers clashed with my cousin's apricot-and-white decor; I saw them upside down in the trash bin later that night.) At dinner, she placed Mr Taylor between herself and me and monopolised him for the first half of the meal. Conversation was ruled by the clock at Kitty's table, but she overran her time that night. It was well after nine when she glanced at me and gave Bill Taylor a little nod of dismissal. He turned obediently in his chair.

'And how are you enjoying your stay?'

Was this what I had waited for? But what else could a perfect stranger say? My smile was as warm as I could make it. 'Oh, tremendously.'

'Tremendously!' He spooned up a mouthful of baked alaska with relish, licking a dot of meringue from the corner of his mouth. 'My favourite. And what have you done which was so – tremendously enjoyable?'

The 'tremendously' was said with a friendly smile which suggested that I was being teased. I glanced at Kitty. She was deep in conversation.

'Nothing in particular. Nothing worth talking about. Truthfully', and I dropped my voice, 'I can't wait to leave.'

He raised his eyebrows. 'Sounds as though you haven't been doing the right things.'

'What are they, then? You tell me.' I watched him chase the last spoonful of ice cream round his plate and scoop it up. Most of Kitty's guests behaved as though a mouthful of food would be the death of them; it was pleasant to see a big man eating like a hungry schoolboy.

'Well, have you strayed below Fourteenth Street yet? Seen the Aquarium? The Brooklyn Bridge? No?' He shook his head. 'I'll bet you've had lunch at the Colony Club, though.'

Laughing, I nodded. 'Three times. Kitty's meant to be taking me there again tomorrow with some friends of hers.'

'And what about you? Don't you have any friends of your own?'

'I'm still a little lost,' I admitted. He looked at me thoughtfully. 'Not lost,' he said. 'Just different.'

By the end of the evening, I knew quite a bit about Bill Taylor. He had just returned from two years' study at Oxford University in England. He wanted to be a novelist, but had found nobody who would take him seriously. He had been given a part-time job at the *New Republic* magazine by Edmund Wilson, a name he spoke with considerable reverence. He was in love with a girl called Annie Goodhart whom he had known, off and on, for ten years. Finding that he had a sympathetic audience, he confided that he had made a mess of his time at Oxford by getting involved with a girl who 'belonged' to his best friend. Annie, who knew all about it, was ready to forgive and forget. His best friend, a colleague from their years together at Princeton, was still mad at him.

'Is that so surprising? I mean, if you took his girl from him –'

'He should have understood.' Bill Taylor's eyes fixed mine with a soft, entreating expression. 'Look, doesn't it seem possible to you that a man can love a girl just because she belongs to his best friend? Because it makes him feel even closer – no, don't answer. I know what you're going to say. I made a mistake, a bad one.'

I felt awfully sorry for him then; he looked so wretched.

'If he's a real friend, I expect he does understand.'

He shook his head. 'Chance isn't like other people. You can't question him. You can't judge him. He – he burns. He never went to lectures at college like the rest of us. He taught himself.' He looked quite touchingly joyful, as though he was relating a personal triumph. 'They didn't have a high enough commendation to give him when he left. He knew everything – everything.'

'And what has he done, this remarkable man?' I hadn't meant to mock, but he flushed.

'He'll conquer everything he turns to. Everybody who knows him recognises that.'

'You make me feel sorry for Annie. How can she hope to compete for you, with a friend like that?'

'There is no competition,' he said flatly. 'He won't see me. He won't even take a telephone call.'

'And it matters so much?' Was he in love with this strange friend of his, I wondered, to be in so tormented a state that he could confide in a perfect stranger at dinner?

'I feel – amputated.' He was looking not at me, but through me, as he spoke. Then he smiled and ran his finger around his collar. 'Phew, I'm hot. I hate being so emotional. I shouldn't have told you all that.'

'I thought it was rather flattering.'

'You did?' He gave an incredulous smile. 'No, you're being polite. Look, let me make up for it. I'm not needed after midday tomorrow. If you can make your excuses to your cousin, I'll give you lunch and a tour. I expect you want to see the Village.'

'Oh, I do!' I said, and felt my cheeks heat up as he laughed. 'Is it dangerous there? Kitty made me promise not to go on my own.'

'Very wise,' he said, still laughing. 'But don't worry. I'll protect you from all those bloodthirsty bohemians. They won't get so much as a nip at your ankles.'

'Well!' Kitty said after the guests had departed into the night.

'A success! I've at last found a man you don't look bored to death by. Isn't he charming? And awfully clever and interesting. He really liked you, Nancy. Didn't you think so, Jiminy Cricket?' (This was her pet name for the bank machine.) Jim Archer smothered a yawn.

'I don't have eyes for these things like you, Kitty. He was a bit on the serious side for my taste. Wanted to talk about the *New Republic* after dinner. I told him straight out that I don't care for the kind of reading on offer there. Nothing but opinions.'

I disliked the feeling that Kitty was already planning the engagement party. But I did want to see more of New York and this had been my only opportunity. I spoke abruptly. 'He asked if he could take me out for lunch tomorrow.'

'Did you hear that?' My cousin darted another significant glance at her husband. 'I'll ring the Colony in the morning and tell them we'll be one less. No, don't you dare apologise.' She clapped her hands over her ears although I had not said a word. 'It doesn't matter a scrap. Dear Nancy. You looked so happy.' She kissed me warmly, and unusually, on both cheeks. 'Don't stay up reading all night. We want to be sure those pretty eyes of yours are sparkling in the morning.'

Given Kitty's untrammelled jubilation, it seemed unkind to disclose that Bill Taylor had no matrimonial intentions towards me. I thanked them both for a delightful evening and went to my room. And, for the first time since my arrival, I fell asleep looking forward to the morning.

Bill Taylor telephoned at ten and called for me shortly after midday. Despite his friendly greeting, I sensed, far more strongly than the previous evening, that he was distracted and uneasy. I hardly cared. I was wearing a new merino coat with a velvet collar, a sea wind was blowing down the streets and I was free of Kitty's chatter for at least three hours.

'So where are we going to have lunch?'

'Lunch.' His stare was a little blank, but he recovered himself. 'Well, how about the Waldorf?'

I had been hoping for somewhere a little more adventurous. The Waldorf was a choice of which Kitty would have approved.

'How lovely!' I said.

The meal was awkward and felt slow on account of the way Bill Taylor kept fidgeting and snapping at the waiter for not serving us quickly enough. My happiness evaporated; it was clear that my companion was regretting his kind impulse.

'Cab, sir?' asked the doorman. I touched Bill's arm. 'I'm a little tired – would you mind if I just took a cab home?'

'Home?' His big blue eyes grew anxious. 'But it was all fixed. You wanted to go downtown. We're going to the Village.'

'If you're sure?' I still felt uncomfortable at the prospect of being treated as a troublesome obligation.

'I'm sure,' he said, and he put his hand on my arm. 'Please, Nancy. Don't start being difficult. Please say you'll come with me.'

Astonished, I stared at him. 'You have to,' he said. So I shrugged and said, 'Fine.'

The streets grew shabbier, the skyline lower as we bounced southward over cobbles and tarmac. 'Can't you ask him to drive slower? I do want to see everything, you know.' But Bill, if he heard me, paid no attention. Irritated, I pressed my nose to the window again.

When we arrived, I wanted to walk along slowly, taking in every window and bench. Instead, I was forced to run to keep up with Bill as he hurried along the sidewalks, hands thrust into his pockets.

'I thought this was a tour,' I said reproachfully. 'You haven't told me the name of a single building.'

'Well, that's Washington Square, and this is where we start.' He stopped outside a small, brightly painted house with a row of faded flowers drooping behind the bars which shielded the windows. 'The Pink Geranium.'

'I'm not thirsty,' I said. 'You've got me here under a false pretence, Bill Taylor. I never said I wanted to go touring speakeasies. You find yourself some other companion.'

'I'm not asking you to drink, just to come in,' he said. 'Well?'

'I'm not –' But he was through the door already and a cold wind was blowing against my back. I couldn't see a sign of a taxi. Reluctantly, I followed him.

It took a minute for my eyes to adjust from the afternoon glare to a sour-smelling darkness from which shapes swam slowly into focus – the broad curve of a man's shoulder, a lamp like a lily hanging from a brass chain. I started as if I had been struck when a hand grasped my sleeve. Looking down, I saw a hawk-like face and a pale helmet of hair the colour of wood ash.

'Why the hurry?' the woman said in a low, slightly foreign accent. 'Stop and talk to me. He won't mind.'

I tried to pull away, but she had my arm in a vice. 'Better watch out, little lady,' one of her companions said, grinning up at me. 'Don't let the witch of the east get her nails into you.'

'Sit yourself down, tiger-face,' the woman said. 'Right here on my knee, if you're feeling friendly. Have yourself a drink and tell us about life in the hungle-jungle. What's it like out there?'

I found myself laughing. 'I don't know any jungles. I wish I did.'

'I'm talking, my darling,' she said, 'about the jungle of the soul.' She opened her eyes at me, wide as the blind blue stare of a summer morning. Bill's hand descended heavily on my shoulder, pulling me forward.

'We aren't stopping,' he said. 'Nothing to interest you here, not unless you happen to enjoy the company of degenerates and drunks.'

'Speak for yourself, fish-face!' the woman called after him as he escorted me briskly away. She had a point: Bill Taylor did bear a faint resemblance to a handsome, well-nourished fish, a halibut, perhaps, or a fine white turbot.

He led me up a flight of stairs at the back of the shop and

stopped at a brown, painted door. A sign on the wall informed me that we had arrived at the offices of Wide Sky Press.

'This is where my friend lives,' Bill said in a low hurried voice. 'That's why we came here. I thought if you could say you were interested in seeing the Press, having something published –'

I didn't say a word.

'You'll understand when you've met him,' he said. 'You'll feel it too. Everybody does. Please, Nancy. Just for me. Just this once.'

I stared at one of his eyes as hard as I could, in the way that makes people start shifting their feet. 'Who gave you the right to use people like this? Telling me you were going to give me a tour. Making out you felt sorry for me.'

'Well, are you coming or not?' I don't think he'd listened to a word. His hands were shaking.

What sort of man could it be who had such an effect, I wondered, and I did, I have to admit it, feel a little curious now to set eyes on him myself. 'Well,' I said, 'unless the door's locked, we may as well just walk in.'

I could see nothing at first but the bulky shape of a machine crouched on a dusty wooden floor. Book-lined walls became dimly visible. There was a divan in one corner and a table which had recently been used for a meal. Nothing else. I watched Bill pull down some books from the shelves.

'Well, that's something. He's still got the Shelley I gave him last year.'

'An oversight.'

I recognised the quiet laconic voice even before the man walked through a doorway at the side of the room. He must have come straight from a shower, for he was wearing nothing but a pair of trousers and a towel draped over his shoulders. He took the book from Bill's hands, walked over to a log-basket crammed with waste paper and dropped it in.

'Now get out,' he said. 'And take your lady friend with you.'

'She wants to see the Press,' Bill gabbled. 'I swear, Chance, I wouldn't have come here otherwise.'

'Out,' the man said again. 'You heard me.'

I stepped forward, almost up to his side.

'We've met before. Don't you remember?'

The room felt very still. He looked at me with a frown and then his face cleared. It made me think of the sea when a storm cloud sweeps over it ahead of the sun. 'Why, if it isn't the lady of the balcony! Miss Parker of Boston!' He shook his head and laughed. Bill, while evidently confused, decided to join in the joke.

'Why didn't you tell me you knew Chance? And there I was –'

'And just what have you heard to interest you in the Wide Sky Press?' His eyes were fixed on me, bright and intent. 'I seem to remember your saying you weren't much of a one for poetry.'

'I never heard of the Press until five minutes ago,' I said. 'But I do know that Mr Taylor is pretty unhappy about the way you've treated him.'

'Two sides to every story, Miss Parker, as I'm sure you know,' Chance murmured.

I glanced at Bill. He was scarlet and I could see that his long eyelashes were wet with tears. He looked like a large, unhappy child.

'I just wanted to give it one more shot,' he said mournfully. 'No reason to think it was going to work. Hell, you're right to hate me. I'm the worst friend a man ever had. I'll go.' He looked at the door, but he didn't move. I saw a faint smile, quick as a passing shadow, cross Chance's face.

'No reason for you to talk like a bad play,' he said. 'I'm not telling you to go now, am I?'

Bill lifted his head. 'You mean – I'll make it up to you. You just tell me what you want to do, Chance. I swear to God. Anything.'

'Anything?' He laughed, looked at Bill, walked back to the

Press and stood there, drumming his fingers on the iron side. 'All right,' he said suddenly and held out a sheaf of papers. 'See if you can persuade your friend Mr Wilson to print this in his literary pages. *The Dial* are willing, but I want a wider audience. It's too good for them, anyway.'

'Poems?' Bill asked as he folded the sheaf carefully into his pocket.

Chance's smile was the wide sudden grin I had liked when I first saw him. 'Better than poems. A statement on their behalf.' He flung his arms wide. 'A creed for poets, the few real ones who are still out there, waiting to be found.'

'You'll find them.' Bill had begun to look more cheerful. He gave himself a little shake, brushed an invisible fleck of dirt off his lapel. 'Speaking of poets, I wanted to ask you –'

'Going somewhere in particular, Miss Parker?' He must have been watching me all the time. At the door, I turned my head.

'You two have things to talk about. I'm fine. I'll find my way home.'

Chance shook his head. 'No need for you to leave. Aren't you still owed a tour of the city? Bill, I'll be eating at Marini's on Friday evening. You can tell me anything else then, if you must.' He held out his hand. 'Dorry'll call a cab for you downstairs if you ask her nicely.'

'Fine, Chance, fine.' Bill loitered, twisting his hat in his hands and eyeing me. 'Coming then, Nancy?'

I shook my head.

'Friday, nine o'clock,' Chance said and shut the door on him before he turned to face me. 'You looked just like an angel,' he said. 'Standing up there in your white nightgown. I kept thinking about you. A red-haired angel. It's quite a colour, you know.' I stood as still as if he'd hypnotised me while he lifted a strand from my shoulder and let it drop. 'You must grow it. Down to your hips. Now, can you manage to keep yourself busy for half an hour? I've some work to finish on the press. Make yourself at home on the sofa. Take your shoes off if you like. You can read this.' He dropped a book into my lap as I sat down. 'And if you don't care for it, you needn't trouble to tell me.'

I stared up at him. 'Do you always talk like this?'

He laughed. 'Only to people I like. And I do like you, Miss Nancy Parker. I like your spirit and I like your red hair.'

I leaned back against the torn tablecloth which covered the threadbare end of the sofa. 'I feel quite at home myself.'

And it was true.

It was dark when I woke. I looked up for the familiar, sinister shapes of the satin bows, mothlike, fluttering. Instead, I saw Chance. He had pulled up a chair and was sitting at the side of the sofa, staring at my face. He was wearing a shirt now, and he was so close that I could smell lavender starch on it.

'You've been asleep for an hour,' he said. 'You looked so pretty and restful that I decided to let you alone. I was just going to find a blanket in case you decided to drop out for the rest of the evening.' He picked up the book from where it had fallen on the floor. 'You didn't get far.'

'I told you before. I'm not much of a reader.' I looked up at him. 'Does that bother you?'

His smile was slow and thoughtful. I could not look away from his mouth. 'No,' he said at last. 'I don't think it bothers me at all. So, are you ready to go adventuring?'

He took my hand to help me up and I felt myself tremble suddenly. Isn't it strange, how we never forget these things? The unexpected softness of his palm, the watchful tender look in his eyes.

'I'm ready.'

'Good.' Distantly, I could hear the laughter of the people in the room below, the clink of glasses. Another world. 'I'd like to bring you back here, later,' he said quietly. 'I'll take care of things. Will you come? Would you like to?'

My lips were so near to his that I could imagine the sweetness I would taste if he kissed me, the feeling of his hands on my skin. I had never in my life wanted anything so much as I wanted to hold on to the sense of strangeness and longing I felt just then. 'Let's see how it goes,' I said. I knew from his eyes that I had already given him the answer.

What did we do all the rest of that long evening until he brought me back, what did we talk about? The words have gone. But I remember being so glad that it was Chance and not Bill Taylor who was walking beside me and laughing and spinning stories out of every shady corner and steely edifice until it seemed that I was being led along the corridors of a palace of secrets. He helped me scramble through a gap in the iron fence that railed off the devastated site of Madison Square Garden. He told me how, if things went the way they should, the ghostly desert of broken stones and tumbled bricks was going to rise again as a cathedral of learning, a college to be bestowed on the poor at the expense of the wealthy. And I looked beyond his big glowing eyes to the cranes rearing giraffe necks at the stars. I kept on listening and not really hearing until he said, quite suddenly: 'Now put your arms around my neck.'

So I did. And I kept on looking into his eyes as he carried me over the rubble. 'Don't look until I tell you,' he said. And then he swung me up until I was sitting free of the ground on what felt like a big silver trumpet.

'Open your eyes,' he said, 'and mind you take hold as soon as you do.'

Well, I opened my eyes and nearly rolled down to the ground with fright. He'd perched me on the outstretched arm of a bronze archer, a woman the size of a giantess. Close up, she was a stranger, fierce, inaccessible. I only recognised her when Chance jumped me down to look at her.

'The Diana,' I said. 'Of course, I should have known. There's a little plaster cast of her in my uncle's house. I never dreamed she'd be so lovely.'

'No match for you,' he said, and I quivered as he trailed his finger around the curve of my cheek and down the length of my throat. If he had stroked my breast, it would have felt no more intimate.

And sometime later, near to dawn, we stood side by side on the narrow walkway of Brooklyn Bridge, staring up into a sky so full of lights that I could fancy a ship of stars had weighed anchor above the harbour waters. I spun round to look at the Statue of Liberty raising her arm towards Brooklyn, and almost slipped.

'Careful,' Chance said and he wrapped his arms around me and turned me gently to face him. That was the moment when he bent his head to mine. Our two halves found each other. I am not a poet. I can only say that is how it was for me, then and always. My one, my only love.

It was past nine in the morning when I telephoned Kitty to apologise for having caused her unnecessary worry and to tell her that I intended to marry Chance Brewster as soon as I could obtain the consent of my parents. It was the first time that I had ever managed to silence Kitty and it didn't last longer than ten seconds. She asked whether we planned to live near the Park and sighed when I said no. She wasn't in the least interested to know whether we loved each other. But I told her anyway. I told everybody I met. I lived from day to day in a state of unbelieving joy.

'We will help you when we approve of what you do but we will not help you to do things of which we do not approve.' This was the extract from my parents' letter which I read out to Uncle Caleb as we walked up and down the long corridors at Point House. (The wind was blowing too fiercely for a walk in the neglected garden.)

'I always knew your father would grow into a pompous prig,' Caleb said, stabbing his cane at a hole in the rug. 'He used to write sermons when he was ten years old, y'know. Should have been a minister. And Evelyn always gives me the feeling that she's only happy when she's preaching. Just as well she didn't become the mayor. There'd have been no stopping the woman.'

'Do you think I'm acting crazily? They certainly do.'

He shook his head. 'You needed to escape. We used to worry about you, you know. Louise was –' He broke off and shook his head. 'Sorry. I still can't seem quite able to –'

'It doesn't matter.' I squeezed his arm.

We sat down on the sofa which Louise had lovingly covered with petit-point roses in the years when she had the eyes for such delicate work.

'You can be married from here, if you don't mind the weather,' Caleb said. 'Time for another bride in the house. But I'd like to know a little more about your Chance before I start choosing presents. How's he expecting to keep you clothed and fed? You say he runs a publishing company? What do you know about it? Annual profits?'

I laughed. 'I'm not sure there are any. Not yet. Chance is only interested in helping poets who haven't yet been discovered. Nobody well known.'

'High minded,' Caleb said with a nod. 'Well, I like a man of principle. But he won't get rich on it. Private income, now. Anything you can tell me?'

'I don't think he has one.'

My uncle stabbed at the floor while I told him all I knew. Chance's father had shot himself after being outwitted by a business partner. His mother, an Englishwoman, had gone back to her own family somewhere near London. Chance had heard nothing of her for over six years. Caleb shook his head.

'He's in need of money then. And you come into your trust when you marry. I don't expect he's unaware of that.'

'I told him. He never asked. He doesn't think about money.' I pulled away from him, holding myself stiff. 'I thought you'd be pleased for me.'

He took my hand in his and squeezed it. 'Look, Nancy, I realize you haven't had an easy life at home. Are you sure, absolutely sure, that you know what you're doing? You're not just running away?'

I leant forward and kissed his withered cheek, paper white from the months he had locked himself away inside the house. 'Be pleased for me,' I said. 'I am so happy.'

He nodded. 'And why shouldn't you be? Now, what do you want for a present?'

We were married at the beginning of December. A good many guests kept away, not relishing the prospect of a trip up to the North Shore when most of the summer people had gone and the winds had begun to bite. Bill Taylor, who planned to marry his Annie the following year, was the best man. My parents hid their displeasure well enough to convince at least half the guests that Chance Brewster was a successful New York banker who dabbled in literary matters as a pastime. A few eyebrows were raised when Chance declined to make a wedding speech of thanks on the grounds of nerves. Later, Bill told me that he had been too intoxicated to string more than half a dozen words together. And I never even noticed. The day was like a dream to me, a prelude to what I imagined as endless happiness. My marriage was like a talisman. I had put myself beyond the reach of harm.

PART TWO

5

June, 1980

THE MONTH OF love – and who is there to love a wild old woman who talks to herself from habit and doesn't bother to change her clothes from one week to the next. A rhetorical question, and why worry? I care for nobody, no, not I, and nobody cares for me. Nobody, nobodaddy, none but daddy, no, not that line of thought today when the sea and the sky are a glitter in my dazzled eyes, when every rose in the garden has unfolded its petals.

He's gone. He's dead. Twin crosses mark their graves. I pay an annual hundred dollars to see no weeds grow over them, but you won't find me chilling my knees on the grass in prayer. I am what I am. I owe them nothing.

I was twenty-six when they died, he first, she a month later. Of grief, they said. I doubted that. Control was what my mother thrived on, not love. Cancer got him. Pincer claws, pinching pain into his cheeks and hollows between his ribs until all that was left on the bed was a shrivelled doll, yellow as custard, smelling faintly of rotting flowers.

I had no wish to be there when he died, but my Aunt Sarah, Kitty's mother, wrote to tell me that the family thought I had a duty to fulfil. She didn't fulfil hers. Never left Vermont. But she was right. I didn't care to think of him being rolled and turned and cleaned and babied by those starch-faced nurses who fatten on the deaths of the prosperous. Ministering angels! Ministering their bank accounts!

So I left Chance to care for the child, bought myself a black linen coat and travelled back across the scrub fields and thorn thickets, staring at the reflection of my face in a misted window, gliding like a ghost through branches, ponds and stone walls. The phantom faded in the brash orange and yellow hoardings which threw their shadows across the tracks as we came towards Boston.

Back, then, to a house of whispers where the blinds were already down; to a reek of disinfectant as if death could be driven off by a good dousing of Lysol or a swill of the mouthwash my brother used to mask the smell of drink on his breath when he went girl-hunting. The smell brought him back so powerfully when I arrived that I stood gasping in the hallway, my hands at my throat.

I had not seen either of them since my wedding eight years earlier. My mother's youthful looks had gone. The straight-backed pillar of the community had become a bent old lady with not a strand of auburn left in her white hair. Bending to kiss her cheek, I saw the sockets and promontories her skull would expose.

'You took your time,' she said. 'I had lunch cleared.'

'I had soup on the train.' I tried to sound gentle, daughterly. 'What would you like to do, Mother? Shall we go in together?'

She shook her head, looked away towards the door to the drawing-room. 'I've some sewing to be finished.'

'Can't it wait?'

'You go in.' Her thin hand patted my cheek. 'It's good that you came, Nancy. Your father was always so fond of you.'

'Fond!' I didn't mean to sound violent, but the word came spitting out of my mouth like a hot pepper. She gave me a small wintry smile.

'Sit with him for a while. Read to him. Do what you think best.'

What's best for death? Whatever you think, that's my view. I ignored the nurse, snapped up the blinds, filled the room with light and the blue of a spring sky. I rifled the shelves of his study for books to read to him, books I had not opened myself since my schooldays. Dickens, Longfellow, Thoreau, Melville, Twain – scraps and patches. Whatever caught my eye. Whatever kept my gaze from his face, from his swivelling, terrified eyes. If I met them, they became imploring. What right had he to expect my love? I was willing to do my duty, no more. Dreamily, I sprayed my throat and shoulders with scent, wrapping myself in a cloud of protection, keeping out the smell of dissolution.

Morphine and jaundice had blurred his mind, but he frowned and shook his head when I asked if he wanted to see my mother. The nurse sighed and said you never could tell the way it would take them, nothing personal.

'Mr Parker!' She shook his arm. 'There's no cause to be naughty, you know. There's your poor wife wanting to sit with you. You're not going to tell me you don't want to see her?'

Obstinately, he shook his head. She gave a smile like a grimace at me. 'Leave it alone, dear. We don't want to upset anyone, do we? It's you he wants to see. Look at the smile on his face now!'

I looked, and silently admired the power of her imagination.

Soon, I forgot to look at my watch, or to listen for the distant chime of a clock. Time was present only in the passage of small, fairly regular events. Movement. Sound. Need. Frequently, my father parted his furred lips for air and then pursed them into a brown cherry. Terminally, the two ends are as one. Another thing I hadn't known. Empty, inattentive, I stared at the open book on my lap, blocking the silent pressure of his eyes when he turned his beseeching gaze on me.

Sometimes, struggling with the nurse to lift him onto the commode, I almost smiled at the tricks life plays. Was my unwilling voyeurism the price to be paid for those stealthy visits to my room, those few guilty seconds of relief? I looked away as we hauled him up again. The nurse wiped him clean and pulled forward a pillow to ease the pressure on the drooping yellow buttocks. Helping her, I stared at the grey worm of flesh nestling between his thighs. The nurse caught my eye.

'Better you than your mother,' she said. 'It's not easy for a wife, remembering.'

'We all have our memories,' I said and left her to make of that what she liked.

I tried to talk about it to my mother one evening after we had finished eating supper together. She walked towards the door, away from me, moving just fast enough to show a dread of intimate conversation. She hadn't once asked after her granddaughter, never mind my husband.

'There are questions that need answers,' I said, and I took hold of her arm, obliging her to turn. Calmly, she faced me. The eyes that had subdued a thousand in the lecture halls had no trouble in confronting my nervous stare.

'Well then, Nancy?'

'You must have known.' I felt the blood flaming into my cheeks. 'You sent me away to Point House that summer. You knew. You must have known what he had done?'

'Done?' Her eyes were cold as stone. 'What do you mean – "done"?'

'That he ... that he –' It was no use. I felt as if I was profaning the sanctuary of some holy place.

'Your father loved you,' she said. 'Can't you even wait for his death to start defiling him?'

Tears flooded my throat. Shaking my head, I went back up the staircase, to sit by his bed. The nurse had drawn the curtains and darkened the room, except for a table lamp which made a small harbour of warmth beside the bed. As mine had once, until a hand stifled it. He was unusually tranquil. His eyes were open, but I think he was sleeping. They held none of the usual mute appeal.

Their room, technically. Her room, in everything but name.

Her spotless dressing-table, robbed of the tray of hairpins, the brush and pot of cold cream which were her only concessions to vanity. (She had moved into my brother's old room, cradling herself in another past.) Her family photographs and portraits. Her drab wooden boxes containing letters, cards, a faded flower or two. Her indifference to colour and beauty, reflected in the beige paper on the walls, the sensible oilcloth flooring on which my father's leather slippers still clung together in forlorn anticipation. I could read twenty years of desolate nights into those slippers. And, sitting there, I was wrapped in an over-powering sadness. For a life lost, a life barely lived. An existence of stolen moments, profound guilts. What kind of despair or hunger had possessed him, to send him seeking ease in his daughter's bed?

His breathing was so quiet that I thought for a moment it had stopped. Leaning over the bed, I looked down at his face. His eyes winked open, red veined, fearful. His hand moved on the quilt, searching for contact.

'No,' I said. 'No forgiveness.' I bent lower. 'It can't be earned.' But I filled a glass of water and held it to his lips. He was so weak that I had to cradle his head while he drank.

I was there, waiting, for three weeks, April into May, chafing at the feeble thread of energy by which he clung to life. My mother had not yet given up her good works in the city. Every morning, shortly after breakfast, she took herself off to the Gardens which, in those early years of the Depression, had become the unofficial dormitory for the homeless. It was, as my mother saw it, a useful public duty to gather and carry home the newspaper sheets the vagrants used for bedding.

'What, exactly, is the point?' I asked when I found her on her knees, tidily folding and parcelling the sheets with string before she carried another armful down to the cellar. She said that it was perfectly obvious what the point was. The Gardens had never been designed to become a public doss house. Cleaning them up might get those hoboes back to work.

'But there aren't any jobs, Mother,' I said. 'There's nowhere else for them to sleep. It's the same in New York.'

'I know what I'm doing,' she said.

I left her to it.

The telephone in my parents' house had always been reserved for emergencies. Polished and attentive, it waited in the hall for such a situation to arise. I felt quite bewildered when, hearing the clamour of its bells late one evening, I picked the receiver up to hear Chance's warm voice against my cheek.

'Where are you?' I sounded nervous, more accusing than I intended.

'With Bill. Eleanor's sleeping over with Annie's parents tonight. She's fine,' he said hastily, reading my thoughts. 'No trouble. Missing you. We both are.' His words were slurred. I held the receiver closer, leaning forward over it as I saw my mother coming out of the drawing-room. She looked towards me, and stopped. 'I think of you every day,' I said. 'Tell me what you're doing. How is everything?'

I wanted to pour all the love I felt into the void of the mouthpiece. It was impossible. We spoke from different worlds. I had nothing to communicate but the state of life arrested, held at gunpoint while the clock ticked relentlessly at the chiming of the hour.

'You're doing well,' Chance said as my voice trailed into silence. 'You are so brave. Shall I come? Would it help?'

My mother had never moved from the doorway. I was frozen with self-consciousness, walled in ice. 'No,' I said. 'Just write me letters. Tell me things.'

He answered, as so often, indirectly. 'Sweetheart. Sweet girl. You'll come through shining. Shine on, Nancy Jane.'

God knows where he got the Jane from, but I warmed to the 'shining'. That generous word gave me an image of myself to hang my hopes on, an armoured queen, a scourge of grief, an Amazon, a Boadicea. Shining through, come wind, come rain. Chance always knew what to say.

60

'I wish,' I said, weeping. 'I wish . . .'

'That it was over?'

'That it wasn't so slow.'

I put the receiver down. 'So you can't even give him time to die,' my mother said. 'Oh Nancy, after all we did for you.'

I turned on her, trembling. 'What? What was it you did for me? Well? I'm listening.'

'Gracious, if you don't know by now!' she said. 'Ask your husband. He'll give you an answer.'

I ran after her as she turned away. 'What? What answer?'

She let her glance go down to where my hands grasped her shoulders. 'That you aren't like other people,' she said. 'Now please let go of me.'

There was little communication between us for the next two days. And on the third, with one strange cry, more like a bird than a human being, my father left us.

My new black coat was a good investment. Two funerals in six weeks. After the second service, squeezing my hand and pressing damson-veined cheeks to mine, several well-meaning old women told me how brave I was being. I wanted to burst out laughing. Brave? When my spirit was, for the first time in years, light as a leaf? The past was done with, ready to be buried, shovelled underground, dismissed. I had nothing to hold me back and money to speed us forward. May all bereavements be so lightly worn.

From my mother's little box of ornaments, I took one necklace of hard shiny stones and hung it round my neck for luck. Obliging ladies came in to bag up the contents of clothes-chests and outdated armoires for charity. The furniture signalled its value to me in dollars, not in sentimental worth. I had only to glance at the polished dining-table, the stiff-armed chairs, the subdued lamps with their tasselled shades, to feel the claws of the past at my throat. I wanted none of it.

It was fortunate that I had no sentimental yearnings, for I could not have afforded to indulge them. My parents, Uncle

Caleb even, had foolishly allowed themselves to be caught up in the game of speculation which ran like a contagion through even the most sober families in the late twenties. Having entrusted their modest wealth to Jim Archer, they shared in his downfall. Caleb was spry enough when we talked after my father's funeral – he did not attend my mother's – but a family friend told me Point House was going to ruin and that the two gardeners who used to tend my aunt's pergolas and pleached alleys had been paid off. The front rooms were boarded up; my uncle lived between the kitchen and the old cook's bedroom at the back. Even the *Dryad* had been sold.

When the lawyers had finished their explanations, the way forward was clear. I took the first reasonable offer I got for the house and its contents and went back to New York with what was left after the lawyers themselves had taken their cut. For all of a year, Chance and I were quite a wealthy couple.

So, June it is. The love month. And all the love I showered on Chance is poured into a garden by the sea, two acres of sandy ground. Has it taken me so long to realise that I am simply replaying the role of my aunt, whose yearbooks are here just as she left them, a row of red-bound booklets recording her plans and defeats, her substitute for the journal she never troubled to keep? Plants came before people in Louise's life: she was no fool.

Would she have been pleased by the wilder paradise I have created here? I doubt it. Her taste was formed by another age. I have a photograph of her taken just before her wedding to Caleb. The frame is tortoiseshell, heartshaped. She looks glancingly at the photographer, her eyes large and questioning. She is wearing a simple pearl necklace. Her hair is pinned up and, I am almost sure, plumped out with hairpieces to present a becoming cloud.

My aunt grew up in a Normandy manor house. Perhaps that

was what she was making here, a château garden, a civilising imposition of geometric paths, manicured privet hedges, pale visions of pink, lavender, and rose.

Why wonder? It is likely that she, as I have done, took refuge from an unpredictable and violent world in the blind consistency of nature. I know how she felt. Like her, I take a quiet pleasure in recording each month's tasks, in seeing the years replicate themselves in flowers. Where you plant a rose, there a rose will grow, and stay. And that, in my experience, is more than we can expect of each other, even of those we love best.

June, in my personal circumstances, has not always been a time of joy. June was the month in which they drove me out, shuttered the windows against my frantic hands. In June, 1939, I entered another world, of bells and echoes and unexpected laughter. And strapped flesh, and silence. But here, in the garden, I have made June mine again. Here, I can play God. All, here, is under my control.

Spectacles off, squinting between the sun-spattered leaves, I see it as a dance of colour, bursts of flame, foaming whiteness, inky purple shading into blood red. The clematis montana has climbed free of the pergola, winding its sinews over the lowest branches of the elms; oriental poppies set fire to the grass; staring at the hot flowers of the marigolds, a trick of vision turns their leaves to cobalt. I have made a living *jubilate*, a murmurous light-filled harbour. I have driven out the ghosts of grief.

Spectacles on, it pleases me less. A little of Aunt Louise still loiters in those tidy paths, those neat borders of pinks. I know who to blame. I told Joe Finnis what I wanted. But he had to know best. 'You've the eye of a city planner,' I told him, and he just grinned.

'Why worry if you're so sure it won't outlast you? If you are still sure of that.'

'Don't rile me,' I said. 'I know what I know.' I tapped my head. 'It's in here. And we'll be going with it, Joe, so you be sure you have your affairs tidied up when the time comes.'

'When,' he said, mocking me. 'And in the meantime, where do you want the cyclamen setting?'

After twenty-five years of working on the garden together, Joe and I still have our arguments. He tells me it's my own fault that Eleanor never comes up here: I am too difficult and critical. I've even had him lecturing me on my duty to consider the family and the future of Point House. I don't let him get under my skin. I simply make it clear that I see no reason yet to start making plans. Let them show an interest. They show none.

You could say that it's all for the best, given the likelihood that there will be no property here for them to inherit. Even my uncle and aunt were aware of a problem when Caleb inherited this palace of dreams, this terminal reverie. The cliff is slipping shorewards, not so much that a visitor or a short-term resident would notice, but enough for the signs to be visible to a sharp pair of eyes. Sure, or should I say unsure as the San Andreas fault, the earth under Point House is working its own quiet course of shifting and settling, slipping and dropping. Biding its time for the weeks, the months and years it needs. And then down we all go without a dime in our pockets, rattling into extinction, rocketing down to emptiness in a blaze of glory.

I like to think of it. All gone. Lilies drifting on the waves. Rose briars tangled on the rocks. And the slow sea surging in to take the land back into itself. There are worse endings.

That's why I don't trouble myself with wills, selfish though that may seem. You are welcome to enjoy what is here, my dears, and if you aren't permitted, well, so life is. Blame your mother, not me. I collaborate with nature now, not people.

6

New York, 1926

CHANCE AND I lived over the Pink Geranium for the first four years of our marriage. I don't think any woman had spent more than an hour's stretch in those dusty rooms until then. If she had, I would have known about it. Chance still kept most of his clothes in a battered schoolboy's trunk used to prop open the kitchen door. When I asked where I was going to hang my dresses, he showed me the shower rail.

'I'm going to have to change things here a little,' I said one day after the rail snapped and dropped my best skirt in a puddle of rust and caked soap.

Chance was reading some new submissions for the Press. His eyes were half shut and his long legs were propped on the table at the window where we ate all our meals. Reaching forward, he curled his fingers around a fork and wielded it dreamily over the pages.

'It's still got egg on it,' I said. 'Your pen's behind your ear.' Pulling up the chair so I could stare straight at him, I waved a hand. 'Chance! There's life out here! Hello!'

'Listen to this, Nancy.' He leaned forward, holding up the papers in one hand and extending the other over my head as if he was giving a blessing.

> *Be warned. Be warned against joy*
> *Draw your blinds against ancient moon-fear*

65

Or be mocked by the morning star
Be torn by the carrion, the vulture bird
Of hope.
Hear. This. Or dwell in darkness.

'Well, that's cheerful,' I said.

'Isn't it! *And* he wants me to pay him fifty dollars for the privilege of printing it.'

I stared. 'You're not going to?'

'I'll give him ten dollars and tell him I'll do what I can. The ancient moon-fear's a good touch,' he said as I opened my mouth to protest. 'Now what were you saying?'

It took me a moment to remember; Chance's eyes still had that effect on me.

'Change! Aren't we happy just like this?' He stared around the room. 'I know what you need – a reading chair! I'll get them to sell us one from downstairs. And we'll find you a lamp, a good strong one. Bright enough to keep the spooks off you at night.'

I caught his hand as he reached for the papers he had laid on the table. 'That's a wonderful idea,' I said. 'But it was decoration I was thinking about. I bet these rooms haven't had a lick of paint since the building went up. Hasn't it ever struck you that the brown and yellow together are a little bit depressing?'

He screwed up his eyes. 'It's all right. Kind of a library colour scheme.'

I shook my fist at him. 'Chance – don't you ever, ever think about anything but books?'

'I think of you,' he said. 'And I notice a lot more than you give me credit for. That's a new blouse, isn't it?'

His smile was so pleased that I didn't have the heart to remind him I'd worn it at Bill and Annie's wedding two weeks earlier, and that he had remarked on it then with just the same sweet grin. I pushed the chair back and stood up.

'Come on. No more Press work today. You've been at it long enough. We're going shopping.'

He dropped his gaze like a guilty child. 'You know I haven't any money to spare, Nancy. I'm glad we gave the Taylors a good present and a dinner, but it cleaned me right out. And I can't ask any of these new poets for contributions.'

I felt disappointment rise in my throat like bile. 'They can't all be broke. Why shouldn't they contribute?'

'Principle,' he said. 'Have you heard about principles, Nancy?'

I made a face at him. 'Don't lecture – the weather's too nice. I'll pay.' I picked up his hands and swung them as if I meant to start dancing. 'Just this once – we haven't taken a stroll together since the day we got married.'

'I can think of better ways to take an afternoon off,' he murmured. And he tilted his head back and looked up at me until I couldn't do anything but just drown in his eyes.

There never was any point in trying to push Chance in a direction he didn't want to take. He was willing to let me do as I pleased with the rooms – so long as I didn't ask him to involve himself or to relinquish an inch of space which could be used for bookshelves. Granted those limitations, I was a free woman. I hung white curtains in the windows, scattered the floor with Persian cushions and brightly patterned rugs. I painted the deal doors green and filled in the panels with poor attempts at landscapes: fields and hills under deep blue skies.

'More!' Chance said as I came through the door with my arms full of flowers from the Washington Market. 'What about all those roses?'

'That was two weeks ago. And these weren't expensive.' I poked one of the carnation stems through the top buttonhole of his shirt. 'There, now you look ready for lunch with Bill and Annie – or had you forgotten they came back from Italy yesterday?'

'Nothing wrong with my memory,' Chance said. 'Where is it we're having lunch?'

Was that the day he told us all that he was going to use the Press to publish a new kind of dictionary, more precise than any yet in existence?

'Greatest dictionary the world's ever seen,' Bill shouted to a room full of bored businessmen. 'And my friend Chance Brewster's the man who's going to write it. You know what we ought to do? Celebrate!'

The birth of the world's greatest dictionary, that bane of my early married life, was welcomed at a sleek new speakeasy near the old Brevoort Hotel on Eighth Street, where we drank ourselves into such a stupor that we ended up cutting our arms with Chance's penknife and swearing we were all going to live in bloodbrothership until the end of our days.

Can you imagine anyone wanting to celebrate the prospect of redefining more than four hundred thousand words? But that was the kind of effect Chance had on us all. We would have followed him anywhere, trusted him with our lives. The future seemed to be there in his hands.

I've never had much of a gift for making friends, but I can't look back to a time in our married life when we weren't close to Bill and Annie. It was easy to see why Bill had set his heart on her. Annie Goodhart like me was eighteen when they married. She had curling black hair and a skin like milk and roses. Her cornflower eyes were fringed by the longest, darkest lashes I have ever seen and a new puppy couldn't have gazed at Bill with more adoration than she did, all the time. Her parents' only concern when Bill married her was that he might not be able to afford the kind of life to which they felt their beautiful daughter had a right. When Bill, whom they knew only as a struggling journalist on a paper which was not famous for paying large salaries, told them that his parents were ready to buy Annie and him an apartment near Gramercy Square and to make over a considerable sum as their wedding gift, the Goodharts were reassured. They decided that it befitted them to be equally generous. In order to keep Annie near them, they offered to pay for the building of a second home in Princeton.

The wonder of it was that in the years when we were struggling to survive, and Annie and Bill were shopping at Tiffanys and holidaying in Europe, there was so little sense of competition or jealousy. We all knew that Chance was the genius among us. And I was Chance's wife. Curiously, that seemed to even things out.

I never fooled myself into supposing that life with a genius was going to make me into an intellectual. Still, it was a measure of my love or of Chance's skill as an educator that I did find myself beginning to care about things I'd never troubled to think about before. I didn't always follow what my brilliant husband said, but I loved the sound of his voice and the ringing tones in which, like a knight in armour riding out to save a beautiful princess, he spoke of defending language from the barbarians.

'Do you realise that we don't have a trace of the Celtic language left in our vocabulary?' he asked when I came in with the shopping one morning. 'Not a single word left.' And, as I came towards him, I saw that his cheeks were wet with tears. I took him in my arms and held him close, but I couldn't comfort him. I was only his love; language was his passion.

What comes back to me most strongly when I think of him then is the way we never stopped talking. I told Chance things I have never spoken about to anybody else. He had all my secrets, except for the one which might have saved us.

'Why is it you have this horror about making love?' he asked one night when I had pushed his body away from me with a violence that left us both shaking. 'Why can't you tell me?'

'I've told you. I just need to have the light on. That's all it is.'

He pulled the cord and his familiar features came free of the shadows and the terror. 'You look terrible,' he said. 'As if you

69

thought I was going to murder you. Look at your hands. You're sick, Nancy.'

I hunched forward, rocking my head on my knees. 'You think I'm crazy. Go on. Say it.'

He pushed my hair back. 'Nobody's saying anything. Just tell me. Talk to me. Don't we know each other well enough to share a few private things, Nancy? Nancy? Sweetheart?'

I turned away and stretched out with my face to the wall, not speaking. I couldn't share that one. I kept it deep inside me, a black dirty scuttling thing that thrived in darkness. My love for Chance belonged to the light. Telling would bring it down into the shadows, and I wasn't able to take that risk.

Sometimes, when we had shared a bottle or maybe two – for I often drank to keep him company in those early days when alcohol seemed to heighten our sense of intimacy – we would start wondering what miracle it was that had brought us together. Not God, for sure.

'When my father died,' Chance said, 'he chose to commit the ultimate crime against his religion. My mother thought he did it from despair. It wasn't that. He was daring God to do his worst. He died knowing he was going to hell for it. That was the day I stopped believing it all, the day of the funeral.'

I held the bottle towards him. 'To hell with God,' I said. 'To hell with religion. It's all phoney.'

Chance looked at me and laughed. 'If you could see yourself! You're red as a beet! Nobody's going to jump out of the cupboard and call you a blasphemer, Nancy. You just said what you felt. And that's fine. But you can't settle for nothing. You don't want to be a nihilist.'

'I don't need to be. I've settled for you.' I put my arms round his neck, nestling into his lap. 'You and the language of truth.'

He stroked my hair, twisting strands of it around his long fingers and holding them up to his face. 'Trust the language,' he said. 'Not me. I'm not the kind to be a leader or a visionary. That's the mistake Bill keeps making.'

'You're the nearest thing to a god I'd want to find,' I said. 'My own golden saint.' I shrieked as he pushed me off his lap and struck me to the floor.

'Don't ever say that again,' he said in a low voice. 'I'm a sinner, Nancy, same as you and Bill and Annie and every other dirty human being you can name. Maybe there are saints in the world, but I'm not one of them. You put your crown of thorns on someone else's head. Not this one.'

We made it up later. He carried me to the bed and dried the tears from my eyes and said he didn't know what had come over him. But I didn't forget the way I'd seen anger turn my dreamy, loving husband into a violent stranger. Just for a moment, I'd been given a peek into an abyss, a well of emptiness and mystery and rage. And it scared me.

I was invited to lunch by Kitty three or four times during the second year of our marriage. (She left me in peace for the first year, excusing herself by saying that she didn't want to break up the honeymoon. I think she was still angry with me for having failed to fall in with her plans for my future.) Hatted and gloved, I sat opposite her in hotel dining-rooms, idly imagining the life I, too, might have led as a silk-stockinged, Paris-suited banker's wife, spicing the empty midday hours with malice.

It was Kitty's idea that we should all go out together one evening and that Chance should be put in charge of the entertainment. She didn't, as she put it, know many literary types. Chance had not published a book, but if having read them made one literary, he qualified with gold medals. I suspected, knowing the magazine columns Kitty liked to read, that she was imagining a riotous evening of the stars during which she would swap a few witticisms with Scott and Zelda before Ernest Hemingway gave a quick bull-fighting display with a knife and tablecloth.

'I don't know if you'd be interested by the writers Chance

71

knows,' I said cautiously. 'They aren't exactly household names.'

'Try some on me. I bet I'll surprise you,' Kitty sparkled. 'I don't just sit looking at my nails all day, you know!'

This ludicrous conversation took place in the elaborate, gleaming dining-room of the old Waldorf Astoria, where I had first lunched with Bill Taylor in the fall of 1925. The prices were even more exorbitant than I remembered.

'The amount of breakfast I ate!' I said, staring at the cost of eating a bowl of soup.

Kitty darted a sharp glance at me. 'My treat,' she said. 'The sole's always delicious here. Names now, Nancy.' And she tapped her fingernails on the edge of the menu.

Dutifully, I rehearsed the list of those poets whom Chance was still endeavouring to bring before the attention of the world.

'Paul Hammer,' Kitty said thoughtfully. 'I wonder if he's related to the Hammer who gave a ball at the Plaza last week? It was a frightful evening. Fancy dress. I went as Pocahontas, and, would you believe it, Mary Winchell, you must remember her, was there in exactly, but exactly, the same costume. And there were five Al Jolsons! Poor Jim. People kept coming up to him and asking when the minstrel show was starting.'

Half an hour later, setting down her coffee cup with a little moue of displeasure to the waiter at its over-boiled taste, Kitty returned to the attack.

'How would it be if Jim and I come along one night next week and we all go somewhere amusing to eat? Chance could show us some of the places he knows.' She smiled upwards as the waiter began to reset the entire table for her fresh cup of coffee. That was how they did it then, if you paid enough.

'Places?'

'You know.' She smiled brightly. 'Where things happen. Heavens, Nancy, you needn't look quite so dumb. We've all read about the kind of things that go on in the Village at night. Now,

I know we're pretty free on Wednesday and Thursday. Unless, of course, your husband's too busy to see us.' She twisted up her lipstick and nibbled it into the corners of her smile to present an upward curve. 'That's better. God!' She peered into her mirror, dabbed at her nose. 'Bags under the eyes again. Oh, I do hate looking at myself this early!' She snapped the compact shut before fixing me with an accusing stare. 'You're very quiet. I do believe you don't want us to meet your precious husband. You think we'll embarrass you!'

She was right on target, bull's-eye, but I saw no escape. Kitty's little jaw was thrust out at an angle which did not allow for excuses. In a spirit of adventure or self-sacrifice – it was difficult to guess which governed her mood that day – she awaited consent.

'Wednesday then,' I said and smiled gratefully as she raised her hand for the check. The famous Parker Trust Fund had been smaller than I had imagined; at the end of a year, I was becoming aware of the cost of keeping Chance.

At a restaurant chosen by my husband for its unusual menu – he seemed to have taken to heart my instructions to give Kitty an evening to remember – the two of us sat listening to the Archers' indignant accounts of how their English butler had betrayed them by going off to work for a Hungarian cosmetics queen.

'After all we did for him!' Kitty wailed. 'I even gave the man a gold watch for his birthday! And he seemed so grateful!'

The waiter loitered.

'I do wish they'd print these things in a language we could understand,' Kitty said. 'What's the Italian for veal?'

Chance leaned forward. 'Why don't we have the specialty? *Capozzelle* is the dish they recommend.'

'Well, if that's what they do best,' Jim said. '*Capozzelle* for everyone, Johnny.' All waiters were Johnny to Jim. It was his way of showing that he was at ease.

Capozzelle, as Chance had surely known, were pieces of

sheep's head, served in a pale sauce with the lungs and tripe. Kitty took one look at her bowl and asked for it to be replaced by a plain green salad. Jim, bravely, said that he liked home cooking.

'Of course it's the atmosphere that matters,' Kitty said in a voice that had become unnaturally high. She waved at a poster of a smirking gondolier, guiding his craft through a haze of grease-spots. 'I've always adored Venice. My first fiancé used to say that he thought I must have been Botticelli's *Primavera* in one of my previous incarnations.'

Chance said it was an interesting line of thought because Botticelli had never been to Venice. I knew that he was not going to be any nicer than that for the rest of the meal. His long fingers kept fiddling with the cutlery; it was always a bad sign. Sure enough, when Kitty asked what he thought of the new film version of *The Great Gatsby*, Chance said that he didn't imagine it could be worse than any other adaptation he had seen. Kitty looked stricken: it had, she said, been commended by her favourite critic as film of the year. Jim, launched on a monologue about Wall Street practices, was brought down in mid-sentence when Chance leaned towards Kitty and asked if bankers always talked trade at dinner.

Kitty straightened up as if he had dropped a poker down her back. 'At least Jim has a profession to talk about.'

Chance gave her one of his widest smiles. 'I love talking about books to people who read them. Do you read much, Kitty?'

Sensing an insult, Jim leaned forward. 'Are you trying to suggest that she doesn't?'

Chance's hands went back to arranging knives and forks. 'Just curious. You see, Jim, my impression is that elegant women – like your beautiful wife – prefer reading the reviews to the books. I can understand that. They don't have much time to waste. Am I right, Kitty?'

'I don't care to talk about it,' she said in a cold little voice. 'Of course I read books. We have several friends who are authors, if you must know.' She stabbed at a shred of lettuce. 'And at least people have heard of them. Nancy was telling me about your poetry list and I must say –'

'So where are you going to for the summer?' I plunged in, gabbling. 'Didn't you mention Europe? I suppose you'll cross on the *Paris*?' I raced on, pouring questions over them until, sullenly, Jim offered some kind of response and the dangerous moment had been averted. Knowing how irresistible Chance could make himself when he was in the mood, I felt angry and humiliated. But my anger was stronger against them for having imposed themselves on us. We lived in separate worlds; it was absurd to pretend that being in the same city made us all part of the same group, committed to common interests.

'So?' said Kitty, touching up her powder with quick little pats as Jim paid for the meal. 'What's the plan? Where does it all go on?'

Standing, Chance towered over the table. 'Out there,' he said, waving at the door. 'Come on. I'll lead the way.'

It took me a while to understand why he was looking so cheerful. Asked to show off his city, he supplied an honest answer. He was a man who loved to walk. Sometimes, he would disappear after dinner and come back exhilarated by some wonderful new idea after wandering five miles along the Hudson or up to Harlem. Taking no account of Kitty's tight-fitting evening shoes, that was exactly what he was offering as the evening's entertainment. As a guarantee of the project's success, he started off with a stroll through the stinking back streets of the deserted fish market down by Brooklyn Bridge. He told me afterwards that he had intended to terminate the promenade at Corlears Hook, where the lower side of Manhattan leans out into the East River.

'But that's a two-hour walk! And you saw her shoes!'

'Gold kid, weren't they?' he said.

I don't think my poor cousin had even driven through Lower East Side before and she certainly didn't seem charmed to find herself walking along South Street. Chance kept talking away about what the steamship hotels, built in rosy old Hudson River brick, must have looked like in their glory days before they had their windows boarded up and their façades scratched with initials and obscenities. He seemed to be off in a world of his own.

'Just rats,' he said when a line of heavy grey bodies glided across our path and vanished over the waterside wall. 'Nothing to worry about. One of the old boys who still lives down here took me out to Ellis Island last week. Showed me where the oyster beds were. Did you know it was called Oyster Island once, Kitty? Did anybody ever tell you that some of those oysters live to almost twenty? You can read their age from the ridges on their backs.'

But Kitty had endured enough. Her sharp eyes had caught sight of a distant taxi.

'Get it,' she snapped at Jim. 'And hurry!'

Chance was all surprise. 'On such a fine night? I thought you'd enjoy a stroll by the water. Look at the moon!'

Kitty was past being polite about the way her literary evening had turned out. 'You're as crazy as she is,' she said. 'I suppose that's why you married her. Just as well. None of us could imagine who was going to do it.' Jim had the cab standing by with the door open, but his wife wasn't finished yet. 'Do you realise why I took you in?' she asked, her face so close to mine that I could smell her body under the scent of gardenias. 'Because I was sorry for you. I thought it was your parents' fault you'd turned peculiar. I wanted to help. And look at you now, thinking an evening in the fish market is some kind of a treat! You did do well for yourself, Nancy dear!'

We watched the cab rumble out of sight before turning to each other.

'Don't be sorry,' he said. 'You don't owe that spoilt bitch anything and neither do I.'

'That's right.' But I felt queer and sick. Peculiar? What did she mean? What had she heard?

'Here, you're shivering.'

'I'm not cold.' But he pulled off his coat and wrapped it round me. 'Poor Nancy. I didn't mean you to suffer.' Stroking my hair back from my face, he bent to kiss me. 'I got so irritated by all that stupid talk at dinner. You know what I'm like. You must have known it wouldn't work.'

I shrugged my shoulders. 'One evening. It didn't seem so much to ask. I do things for you. All those dinners with Bill and Annie –'

'But you like Bill and Annie. Look,' he said, reluctantly, 'if it's going to make you happy, I'll write and apologise. We'll ask them to something she'll like.'

'God, no! I don't care if I never see the Archers again.'

'Well, then? Are you still worrying about what she said?'

I pulled his hands towards my face, warming my cheeks in the hollows of his palms. 'You don't think I'm peculiar, do you?'

'You're Nancy and I love you,' he said.

'Peculiar Nancy.'

'Lovely Nancy. Different Nancy. The Nancy I love. Now stop fretting about it.' He was walking me backwards as he spoke, until my shoulders pressed against a wall of brick.

The street was empty and the night was quiet and the full moon was hanging like a lantern over the East River, spilling its whiteness down into the shadows between the buildings. I still couldn't stand to be touched in the dark. The other time always came back, making me gasp and twist away from him. But there, safe in his visible arms, in the pale glow of the moon, I felt nothing but love.

Afterwards, when I had pulled my skirt down, I slipped my hand into his, inviting confidences. 'Tell me something – was it, was doing this different when you were with the other girl? With Beth?'

His fingers loosened at once, easing themselves away from mine. His voice came from a distance, a breath of cool air blowing past.

'Let's not get into that, Nancy. We're fine together. Now, shall we walk home or go wandering?'

It was Annie who had stirred up my unease. Most weekends, Chance and I joined the Taylors at the house where Annie had grown up and where her parents still lived, a pleasant old farm about ten minutes' drive from the centre of Princeton. Here, while Bill and Chance set off on day-long walks to discuss the meaning of life or some such important matter, Annie and I helped her mother in the kitchen or went with Mr Goodhart to inspect the progress of the new house in Princeton. They were pleasant times and Chance surprised me by the interest he took in the workings of the farm. We began to talk about moving out of the city, something we didn't achieve until 1929.

I wonder now how much Annie ever really liked me. At the time, she always seemed affectionate and easy, but that was Annie's way with everybody she met. It was no wonder that charming was the word people always used when her name came up. But charm is a defence and Annie was a girl who always succeeded in keeping her private thoughts to herself. I was fond of her, but I never felt sure that I knew her.

I was lying in a hammock on the Goodharts' farm porch one afternoon when Annie asked if Chance ever talked about Beth. It was a hot bright day with a sky as blue as if it had just been painted. I was sniffing that faint, lemony scent in the air you only find when you go south of New York. Below us, Mrs Goodhart was scolding a cat away from two of the hens, flapping her skirt at it.

'Beth?' I said, blank.

'Elizabeth Lawrence. His girl.' She leaned out of her chair to look at me. In outline, I could see the swell of her stomach and her hand resting placidly on the mound. Almost unconsciously, I smoothed the folds of my cotton skirt over my own flat belly. Annie caught the gesture and shook her head at me.

'You wouldn't want to be pregnant in this weather. It's no fun. I can't even get my rings off, I'm so bloated.'

'It suits you. You look lovely. But you always do.' I lay back, staring along the lines of the wooden roof to where a spider's web furred a corner. 'I don't see why he should talk about her. It was a while ago. And she'd moved on.'

'Oh, she never cared for Bill,' Annie said eagerly. 'Not in the way she did for Chance. She was still crazy about him when he left Oxford and he – well, you must know how he reacted when Bill took up with her.' She sighed. 'Poor Bill. He did make such a fool of himself. Beth Lawrence must have laughed herself sick. Still, water under the bridge. Maybe you're right not to worry.'

Beyond her, walking along the edge of the stockyard towards the henhouse, I could see Bill, his feet moving at a run to keep up with Chance's easy stride. Why had she mentioned it? Curiosity? Thoughtlessness? I couldn't guess.

'Do you think he married me on the rebound?'

'Nancy!' Her eyes were wide with astonishment. 'What an awful thing to say!'

My fingers plucked at the hammock strings. 'I know. But do you?'

Mrs Goodhart, plump and panting, came up the steps, still clucking at the miscreant cat. Looking at her, it was possible to catch a glimpse of Annie thirty years on. 'Now which of you girls is going to help me turn the cakes out? Not you, Annie – you just lie there and rest yourself. Doesn't she look gorgeous?' She smiled at me. 'It does seem to suit some women so. Come on then, Nancy.'

I lingered behind her. 'Why did you mention it? Does he still talk about her?'

'Not to me,' she said, closing her eyes.

'To Bill, then?'

'Nancy!' Mrs Goodhart called.

'Sometimes,' she murmured, as though she was already half-asleep. 'But I'm sure it doesn't mean anything. You'd better go in.'

I wish this was a nice story. I wish I could just write about the good times. But then none of it would make sense, and making sense of things is the purpose of it all.

At least, that's what Chance used to say. That was his reason for amassing all that information for the book he was forever preparing to write. Pico della Mirandola was his hero, a prodigy who had conquered all knowledge by the age of twenty-four. So Chance said. I didn't understand. What is the point of trying to know everything? Does it make you happier? Does it bring you peace?

There was an old man who haunted the streets of the Village in those days. He was called Tommy Sanders. I never spoke to him but I sometimes watched him shuffling into one of the restaurants with the bag of papers which, we all knew, was the book he had been writing for the last thirty years. People were always kind to him. The restaurant owners used to give Tommy free coffee, soup and bread because he kept guests amused with the stories he told. Every now and then, some young editor would be said to be trying to publish the book. Everybody laughed. We all knew what would happen. Tommy would panic at the thought of his words finally appearing in print. He would tell the young editor that he needed time for a major revision and then he would simply disappear for six months or more, leaving no address. By the time he came back, the editor had moved on to another project and Tommy was free to sit in restaurants again and talk about the great work, safe in the knowledge that it would stay in his possession.

I tell you this because sometimes, in moments of despair, I would see a little of Tommy Sanders in Chance. I think, in some strange way, he was terrified by the act of completion. He wrote, endlessly, with no thought of publication. He used the Press to draw young poets in, but himself never went beyond publishing a few slim pamphlets on language which were distributed to friends. Success frightened him. He wanted to be in a state of perpetual progress towards it.

Lying on one of the jetties in Falmouth harbour when I was a child, I could look down through the water and see everything that moved. The bodies of tiny transparent creatures were visible, close enough to touch. I could slide my hand into the water and fish out a mother-of-pearl button from where it lay in a tangle of weeds. It wasn't the way of Louisburg Square. Here, nothing was hidden. I could look for something and find it lying just where I expected. I knew where I was, I knew how things ought to be.

In the first years of my married life, I lived in a state of constant uncertainty. I could be happy, radiant even, as if I stood inside some great chorus of music swelling up to the sky and I was one perfect note with my own place, my own right to joy. Other times, there was no coherence at all, just a sense of bewilderment and loss that set Chance and me on the opposite sides of a sheet of plate glass. And you could walk beside it for a whole day and never find a splinter or a crack. There were times when I lay at the bottom of a well of sorrow and couldn't even give it a name.

And what, I wonder, would a psychiatrist have to say about my suddenly writing all of this down, after so long?

Dr Storrow, I feel fairly sure, would have told me that I was doing the best thing possible. If I had listened to him, I would have done it twenty years ago. I should have listened.

When Dr Storrow joined the staff of the State Hospital, I had been there for eight years. Sedated with insulin to such an extent that I had only the faintest awareness of which end of the day was morning, I had been promoted to the freedom of one of the open wards. Had I wished, I could have roamed up and down the overheated passages, taken my turn to thump my fists on the keys of a piano in the chapel or glued my ear to the gold-flexed front of my own radio set.

Dancing was the big thing on the women's wards. When the patients became obstreperous, the staff would flick a switch connected to the loudspeakers hanging from the ceiling at either end of the room, drowning the howls in the smooth and steady beat of the big-time swing bands, to which, after a while, the rebels succumbed, stumbling to and fro between the beds with their faces turned up towards the ceiling, heads nodding and bobbing like corks on water under the refreshing downpour of noise.

I didn't dance. Later, Dr Storrow told me that when he first saw me, I sat in a chair by a window all day, half-asleep. (If I kept my eyes closed, I could make other people disappear.) He stopped the insulin injections and had me moved to a smaller ward in which the patients were quiet and kept to their beds. The only treatment I received during that period was a weekly visit to his room during which he encouraged me to talk about myself.

'I'm not mad, you know,' I told him at the end of every session. 'I could leave here tomorrow, if you'd sign the papers. I have so much to do. Please, Dr Storrow. Please don't make me stay here any longer.' Often, I cried. Dignity doesn't survive well in such conditions.

Dr Storrow was always sympathetic. He said that, although I clearly couldn't remember it, I had done some pretty bad things at the hospital in my first years there. It wasn't going to be a simple matter of arranging a release.

'I have friends who'll help,' I said. 'I can give you names.'

He looked down at his notes. 'We have their names, Mrs Brewster,' he said, a courtesy which never failed to please me in an institution where even the women who came in to mop the floors called me Nancy, though I gave them no permission to do so. 'They aren't willing to take the responsibility.'

'They took the responsibility for condemning me to a living death.'

'You had to be restrained when you were brought in,' he said mildly. 'And, if the notes are accurate, you were in a condition of toxic exhaustive psychosis. You refused to eat. You weighed less than a hundred and ten pounds. There was concern about threats you had made.' At which point, Dr Storrow hesitated. 'You know the history, Mrs Brewster. We don't need to discuss the details again.'

'I know what they thought,' I said. 'And I know I was innocent. I could never have done it. Can't you understand that, doctor? Can't you see how impossible it would have been for me to have done what they supposed?'

I have no idea whether he believed me, but he was kind. He did his best. It was his intention to support my appeal for release in 1949, after ten years. But he was a busy, hard-working man. The relevant papers still hadn't been completed when, early in 1949, he died of a brain haemorrhage. Dr Baird, who took his place, was not so sympathetic. My case notes convinced him that I ought to be kept in hospital on an indefinite basis. All things considered, I was lucky to be discharged in 1954.

Fifteen years. One year more than the whole of my married life. A price exacted for every moment of my life with Chance. But if I started thinking along those lines, I would indeed go mad. Better not to think. Better to be glad that, unlike some of my fellow inmates, I had known what it was to belong to the real world, to be loved.

It hadn't, until my conversation with Annie, ever occurred to me to wonder what Beth Lawrence looked like. I found a photograph of her tucked away at the bottom of one of Chance's packing cases. It showed a good-looking girl with intense eyes and straight dark hair held back by a ribbon. On the back, Chance had scribbled her name, a date and an address in New York. Everyone had told me she lived in England. I looked at her face again, and pushed the photograph away from me, out of sight.

I had never questioned Chance's right to a separate life. I knew he had meetings and lectures to attend, poets to visit, friendships that needed maintenance. Even when he didn't come back to me all night, I accepted the explanations he gave. One of the poets he was trying to help worked as a night porter at a shady hotel in the Upper Eighties. Chance often told me that he had taken the offer of a free bed there, rather than wake me. It hadn't seemed strange; plenty of couples lived that way.

But now, I had cause to wonder. Who was to say that his poet friend wasn't in on the secret, providing him and his girl with a room where they could make love all night in the velvet dark? Did they laugh at me for being such a sucker as they clung together? Imagination isn't only granted to the creative; suppositions twisted and stirred like a nest of snakes in my mind.

A month had passed since I found the photograph. Chance told me he was going to a reading – I think he mentioned Hart Crane. He said he would be back by ten.

'No later,' I said, and I reached up to ruffle my hand through his hair. 'A girl gets lonely.'

He looked down at me and smiled so lovingly that I found it hard to believe he could be cheating on me. 'I'll be back before you know I've gone,' he said.

I turned on the radio – a luxury I never enjoyed when Chance was around – and took a long, indolent soaking. That took me to nine o'clock. I rinsed out some stockings and put on the silk pyjamas which Annie had brought me as a present from her honeymoon. I dabbed a little scent behind my ears and brushed down my hair. Chance liked it long and loose; he said it made me look like a Celtic queen. Then I hung a pink towel over the bedside lamp to soften its glare and stretched myself out on the clean cotton sheet.

I woke, coughing, to a smell of burning. The towel had fallen onto the bulb and the shade was crackling like a camp-fire. I snatched up the bed cover and threw it over the flames before dousing the charred mess with a bowl of water.

Smoke curled past me in a bitter wreath as I pushed open the window. A rattle of shutters going up at the bakery opposite told me the time – six in the morning. Dawn rain greyed the sky and spattered the empty street. I could have burned to death for all he cared. Shaking, I leaned on the grimy sill and drew the damp city air deep into my lungs.

It was past seven when the door finally opened. Not a word of apology. Only a quick glance at the open window and the mess of burned material still lying on the floor by the bed.

'Just a towel that got singed. I dealt with it already, all right? All right?' I heard my voice slide upwards, out of control. 'You told me you'd be home by ten. You promised.'

He sat down opposite me at the table. 'I know. But I couldn't get away. There was a situation.'

'Is that what it's called?' I sat as my mother might have done, stiff as if my back had been roped to the chair. 'Well,' I said, 'and isn't it time you told me about Elizabeth Lawrence?'

'About Beth?' He looked bewildered. 'I don't think there's anything to say. Especially not when you're in this kind of mood.'

'You really ought to have married her instead of carrying on like this,' I said. 'Or wasn't she rich enough to keep you?' I flinched as he raised his arm. 'You keep your hands off me!'

'I wasn't going to hit you,' he said quietly. 'But my God, I am tempted. Do you begin to know what you sound like?'

I was past caring. 'I've seen the photograph. Oh yes, and the address. Maybe I'll pay you both a visit one of these nights. Bring round some flowers – why not?'

Chance dropped his head on his hands. 'Beth Lawrence came

here to New York on a visit just over three years ago,' he said. 'To break off her relationship with Bill and to see if she and I could get together again. It didn't work out. I haven't seen her since. Does that answer your question?'

'Annie said you still talk about her,' I mumbled.

'Annie talks a lot of nonsense,' he said. 'But you! Do you really think I'm capable of that kind of behaviour? Doesn't the word trust mean anything to you at all?'

'It would, if you were ever here.' I felt my face beginning to crumple and pucker when he came round the table and took me gently in his arms.

'Let's stop this right now, Nancy. You mustn't get into one of your states.'

Silently, I pressed my head into the cradling warmth, holding still so that I could feel the low steady pumping of his heart. 'I love you so much it hurts,' I whispered. 'I can't bear to think of you with anyone else, but I'm no good. I'm no use to you.'

He didn't trouble to answer me. Instead, he lifted me up in his arms and carried me over to the bed. He unbuttoned the pyjamas and folded them back. His eyes looked down at me as he moved his hands across my breasts and over my stomach, light as feathers on the down of my skin, stroking me until I turned to him, trembling, crying for him to enter me and give me peace.

'Nancy,' he murmured into my hair as he covered me with a sigh. 'Oh, Nancy.'

And I haven't said anything at all to make you understand how sweet he could be to me. I haven't written a word about the poems I'd find lying by my plate when he cooked dinner. About the time I thought he'd forgotten our anniversary and came home to find that he'd scattered roses all the way up the stairs to our apartment and hung a great stuffed satin heart outside on the door for everyone to see. I haven't told you about how, after the one time he did strike me, he touched nothing but water for a whole two months. I haven't written about the patience he showed for my ignorance, or about the hours he spent teaching me how to lay type for the Press, so that we could work at it together.

He did love me. And I wasn't worthy of him. I never lost my sense of wonder that such a brilliant and remarkable man as Chance Brewster should have picked me to be his wife.

The rooms above ours belonged to Dinah, the smokey-voiced woman I had encountered on my first visit with Bill. The couple who ran the Pink Geranium and owned the building warned me away from her. They said that she was trouble. They said they only let her keep the rooms because she was prompt with the rent. When I asked what was so bad about her, they said she was a devil with women. So I kept my distance and took care always to be looking in another direction when I passed her in the street. Meeting her as I came out of our apartment one day, I ducked my head and tried to hurry past. Smiling, she stretched her arms across the stairway, blocking my passage. 'I don't bite,' she said. 'Dinah the pusscat, that's me.'

The way she said it, with a laugh in her voice, made me smile in response. She was dressed in narrow trousers, a white blouse and a cream-coloured jacket. A hat with a spotted veil just covering her eyes was a perfect match to her gloves. Even my mother would have acknowledged that she looked like a lady.

'And how long do neighbours have to wait before they're allowed to call on each other?' She put a hand under my chin. 'Or even to know each other's names? I only know you as the girl with the sad eyes.'

I let that pass. 'My name's Nancy,' I said. 'And visits would be fun. Only my husband works at home and –'

'And leaves you alone at nights.' Her smile broadened. 'Oh,

we all know about Mr Brewster's night walks. Don't think I mean anything by mentioning them. Still, a girl shouldn't be shy about calling. You'll find me home any time after six. It's open house on Sundays and Fridays.'

I took the offer up the following week. Dinah's front door was painted green and gold with the black branches of a blasted tree stretching out across the lintel. Somebody – Dinah, perhaps – had covered it with tiny skulls in the place of leaves. Behind it I could hear the muffled sound of laughter and rumba music. Too late, I looked down at my brown-and-white sports shoes and a tweed skirt which I sometimes wore when we visited the Goodharts' farm. The door was open and a very tall, whey-faced young man was ushering me in, folding himself almost in two with entreating gestures as I muttered an apology and turned to bolt back down the stairs.

'You're frightening her, Stefan. Nancy! And you've brought flowers! How sweet. Take them in the kitchen, Stefan, and get Nancy something to drink. You do drink, don't you, darling?'

Mute before the vision of Dinah in clinging white silk and a scarlet turban, I allowed myself to be led forward and introduced. I saw a birdcage painted in turquoise and gold, a bowl of brightly coloured wooden fruit, curtains of crimson velvet weighed down with faded brocade. Two tall girls were dancing slowly around the room, mouths glued together as if they meant to suck each other's blood out. Hastily, I swallowed down the fiery, transparent liquid which had been handed to me.

'That's how to do it, darling,' Dinah said and she handed me another. 'Come and sit beside me. Don't look so frightened. Nobody's going to eat you. You just walk back down those stairs whenever you feel like leaving.'

But I stayed.

Each time I visited the upstairs rooms, she told me a little more about herself.

Her real name was Dunyasha and she was a White Russian who had left Moscow with her parents in 1917. Her story was one of those odd romantic ones which were not unusual in the decade following the Revolution, of midnight escapes, jewels stuffed in boots and hats, bribed porters, moments of terror. Dinah was a good storyteller; it was impossible to sift fiction from truth in her tales. She told me that her family fled to Paris, where her parents still lived. But Dinah had been oppressed by life in cramped rooms where her mother and father clung to their traditions and constantly lamented the past. She found a rich young American who fell in love with her and brought her back to be a Southern belle and rule over an old plantation house near New Orleans.

'The past all over again,' she said. 'I felt I had never left Russia. The proprieties, you know. So I came to New York. And here I aim to stay, drinking, writing and falling in love with tall red-haired girls.' And she burst out laughing as I blushed and looked primly down at my knees. 'Nancy, Nancy, do you really think I couldn't seduce you if I tried?'

'Well, I certainly hope you won't or we can't be friends any more,' I said. 'Tell me stories about Moscow.'

'No. I'm bored of talking about myself.' She fitted a cigarette into an amber holder and drew on the smoke as she reached over me – I am sure the way her breasts brushed against mine was no accident – for a little yellow box. 'I'm going to read the cards,' she said. 'I want to take a look at this elusive husband of yours.'

I had never seen tarot cards before and this was an old pack, handed down, so Dinah said, from a Hungarian grandmother. She picked out a handsome fellow in a green tunic and a red plumed hat.

'That's our man – the poet himself. Now let's see what the cards have to tell us about him.'

'Well?' I said impatiently as she shuffled the pack a second time and spread a circle of cards around the central figure. 'And what's the great revelation?' I couldn't help feeling a little curious. 'Can you see a move of home? Travel?' I wanted to ask

89

about children, but Dinah didn't seem the kind of woman to care about babies.

'I see wasted gifts and passionate regrets,' she said. 'That's all. Poor Mr Brewster. And my poor Nancy.' She lifted her eyes. Hooding them against the smoke, she looked like a beautiful predatory bird. 'Tell me,' she said, 'are you really going to let a man like this sponge off you for the rest of your life? Is he worth it?'

I stood up then and walked back down the stairs. I didn't visit her again until she sent me a written apology and invited us both to dinner.

Chance didn't go, of course. He couldn't stand to be in the same room as Dinah.

What she had said was almost unforgivable. Almost, because there was a germ of truth in it. The money from my trust fund had been used up. I had been married for just over three years. And I had no idea of what our future was to be.

7

December, 1980

OTHER FAMILIES, EVEN if they don't much care for each other, make a point of getting together at Thanksgiving and Christmas. Not ours. I don't mind missing Thanksgiving – I'd rather see a turkey gobbling in a yard than stuffed on a table – but the winters at Point House are the bleakest season of the year.

Every November, first of the month, I write to Eleanor, suggesting that she might like to bring the girls and, if she must, her lover, for a visit. Every year, Eleanor writes back to explain that this will not be possible and to invite me to remember – could I forget! – that they see themselves as a nuclear family. As an extra-nuclear relation, I am bidden, if I wish, to join them in their festivities. Stalemate. The trouble with Eleanor and myself is that we are both stubborn women. So – she does whatever she does to keep those poor, neglected girls entertained and I do what I've been doing for more years than I can count.

Round about seven o'clock on Christmas Eve, I put on my galoshes and walk down the drive to Joe Finnis's cottage with a pumpkin pie I have baked earlier in the week. Joe makes a chicken dinner, nothing complicated. We talk about the garden and the woods and then, like an old married couple, we toast each other with a dram of brandy. It helps warm me up for the thirty-minute walk down to Falmouth for the midnight service.

91

Joe always offers to drive me, but I prefer to go at my own pace. I like walking under the trees at night. It takes my mind back to the only Christmas I spent here with Caleb and Louise, marching between them in a high-buttoned coat with my hands snug and hidden in the brown satin lining of an ermine muff loaned by my aunt. There's still a dry ache in my throat when I pass the old cemetery where they lie under tall stone crosses, high on the crest of the hill which separates Point House from the town. Looking down on the tall wedding-cake steeple and the windows below it, bright as golden coins in the dark, I'm back watching the *Dryad* glide home across the bay at dusk, carrying her head as high as a young queen.

I only come the once each year, but I have my place. You'll find plenty of Parkers in the memorial book which records every donation made since 1809, when they built this church on the site of Falmouth meeting-house. (Here, four hundred years ago, the good people of Falmouth, like their neighbours in the place we now call Danvers, were willing to damn honest women for trafficking with the devil.) I am aware that Aunt Louise gave the two handsome high-backed chairs which sit by the entrance, and that Caleb paid for the replacement of three windows when they were blown out by a winter storm. My own name is not mentioned. I'm under no burden of obligation or gratitude to this community.

I sit at the back in my own tall white pew and leave just before the service ends. By the time they're trooping through the door, kissing and hollering goodwill at each other, I'm off up the road, out of reach.

Joe comes up here early on Christmas morning to light the fire and lay the table while I get to work on a chicken with all the fixings. Glazed sweet potatoes, green beans, gravy, cranberry sauce, followed by a big mince pie and hard sauce. This is the one occasion in the year when I find that the skill I once possessed hasn't entirely left me. We munch fortune cookies and wince at the jokes before exchanging presents, usually a new pair of rose-clippers for me and a tin caddy of Earl Grey tea for Joe.

After lunch, if the weather permits, we take a long stroll along the shore. I love it down there on a fine December day when the surf is snappy and clean as torn white paper and the sky so bright and hard you could rap your fingernails on its surface.

This year, however, we had quite a surprise.

I don't have a television and I never can be bothered to listen to the news. I was unaware that any event of earth-shaking importance had occurred since November, when a hick cowboy actor came riding in on a landslide and swept poor President Carter clean out of the White House. Joe and I were sitting over a pine-cone fire in the cottage on Christmas Eve and discussing this depressing turn of events when we heard a knock at the door.

'Carol singers,' I said. 'Let them be. They'll go if we keep quiet.' I sat still, holding my hands out to the sweet-smelling blaze while he went off to the door with a plate of cookies for the children, as I'd known he would. I couldn't hear any carols, just a girl's voice, babbling. She sounded hysterical.

'Tell her it's private property,' I called out. 'No room at the inn.' And then, ashamed of myself: 'Give her five dollars and I'll pay you back.'

I didn't hear any answer. Joe came back into the room and gave me a look I couldn't interpret. 'Company,' he said and went out to the kitchen.

I saw a tall skinny girl in jeans and the kind of boots a Texan cowgirl might wear. The hood of her duffel coat was pulled forward, but I could see the jut of her chin in the shadow and a few loose strands of light brown hair, enough to know her for my granddaughter. But what on earth could have brought her visiting at this hour, all the way from New York? A thought struck me hard enough to make my heart jump. 'It's not Eleanor? Is your mother hurt?'

'She's fine.' Judith's voice was low and stifled, as though she was suppressing tears. 'I called,' she said. 'I rang your phone all morning. It's been taken off the hook, they said. So I came up on the bus and hitched a ride into Salem from the station.'

'You walked here from Salem? Fifteen miles?' She nodded. I glanced at Joe, who was loitering in the doorway and rubbing his hands. 'Get the child a chair and some coffee. She must be off her feet with exhaustion.'

We fed her some pie and cheese and crackers, all of which she wolfed down as though she hadn't seen food for a week. I watched her hands tremble as she took the coffee mug from Joe. Drugs? Drink? I couldn't puzzle it out. She looked dreadful, so thin that I could see the hollows in her hips denting her black jeans like moon craters.

'Judith, dear.' I pushed back the hood so that I could get a proper look at her face. 'Tell me what it's all about. Does El – does your mother know . . . ?'

She wrapped her thin arms round me, burying her face in my shoulder. Her hair smelt of smoke and the city. 'Don't tell her,' she murmured. 'I don't want anybody to know where I am, please, please don't –'

'Now, Judith,' I started. Joe caught my eye and shook his head. I loosened her arms and sat her down. We sat in silence for a bit, listening to the snap of the fire and the stutter of rain on the roof. Surreptitiously, I glanced at my watch. Eleven o'clock. No midnight service for me this year.

'He's dead,' she said in a trembling voice. 'They shot him. It's the sign.'

I could feel a headache coming on and I had to stop myself wishing she could have taken her troubles elsewhere. Hadn't I been complaining for years that Eleanor never allowed the girls to visit?

'Judith, can you please tell us who's been shot before you start talking about signs?' I felt a sudden moment of hope. Was it possible that somebody had shot our new President before he succeeded in making his inaugural speech? A good Democrat could celebrate that.

94

'John Lennon,' Joe muttered at me over her head. 'It was on the news last night.'

'Well, that is something,' I said, stroking her hair. 'John Lennon.' The name was certainly familiar, but I couldn't see that anybody's death except her mother's or her sister's was sufficient reason to come haring up to Massachusetts in the middle of the night. 'You poor child.'

'I knew you'd understand,' she said eagerly, and rather pathetically, considering my ignorance. 'Ma and Cathy couldn't get it. And I couldn't stand the thought of dressing up the rooms and opening the presents like nothing had happened. I had to get away and all my friends were out of town with their families. I didn't know where to go.' Her big dark eyes stared up at me. 'It's so sick! The world's just so terrible! I know it's the sign! It's got to be!'

'What you need is a good night's sleep,' I said, but she shook her head and started sobbing.

Joe put her in the back of his car and we drove her up to the house. She cried the whole way.

I felt bad about lying when Eleanor rang the next afternoon to ask if Judith had been in touch, but I had given my word and the poor girl was so insistent that I didn't have the heart to go against her. (No: let me be honest. I took pleasure in the thought that she had chosen to be with me, not her mother.) I had fixed up the least cold of the spare rooms and made it look more welcoming with some bright cushions and a pink and green quilt. She seemed quite pleased by my efforts, but I couldn't get her to eat after that first night. She stayed in her room for the whole of Christmas Day. I took her up some mince pie and cheese on a tray, but she didn't even make a pretence of dirtying the fork. She did, however, ask if I could lend her a Bible. I felt a jolt of alarm when she told me that it was the only book she felt safe to read.

Joe made more progress with her than I had done. The fact that he's a good-looking man may have helped. A couple of days after her arrival, Judith told me she was going down to the cottage to see him. Naturally, I wanted to know what they had talked about when she returned after midnight.

'Ants,' she said.

And she started telling me a whole crowd of things Joe had told her about ant colonies. Frankly, I was astonished. I had never seen Joe show an interest in anything beyond the vegetable level, and here was Judith asking if I appreciated what a truly remarkable and even great man he was. I thanked her for sharing that insight with me and asked what she wanted for breakfast. It troubled me that she still wasn't eating.

'Well, you certainly have made an impression on my granddaughter,' I said when Joe came up to the house the following day. 'When you've finished introducing her to the wonder of life among the weaver ants, maybe you could get her to take an interest in food.'

'I doubt it,' he said. 'Can we talk? Out in the garden?' He glanced up the stairs and I realised that he did not want Judith to overhear.

I was glad to get out before the weather changed again. Just then, it was glorious. The wind was like champagne, making the waves scud and froth all the way out to the horizon under a vast pale sky. Standing with my back to the house, I could feel the sun like a warm hand on my face.

'You have to tell her mother where she is,' he said abruptly. 'Otherwise she'll be calling the police in.' He looked away from me. 'Newspapermen do have long memories, Mrs Brewster. You don't want them dragging up the past.'

I felt another kind of heat in my face, the sort I hadn't experienced for twenty years. 'What past?'

He looked down. 'It's pretty common knowledge around here, Mrs Brewster. You can't stop people talking.' There was a long pause. He was right, of course. I hadn't thought it through.

'You've talked to Judith more than I have,' I said. 'What's going on? And why does she keep talking about signs?'

He took a deep breath. 'Well –'

Judith, it seemed, had been introduced by a friend to a man who called himself the Baptist. His followers were known as the Children of Heaven. The Baptist, who had set up a community on the West Coast, not far from San Francisco, had told them to expect a sign towards the end of the year. Judith's friend had already left her family to join him. Judith was convinced that the shooting of John Lennon was the sign they had been told to wait for.

'So why did she come here? I'm pleased she did, of course – but why?'

He looked me in the face. 'Can't you guess?'

I shook my head. 'To get away from Eleanor? To get money?'

'That's part of it, I think,' he said. 'But it's more than that. She thinks you'll understand. Her mother has told her what happened here in 1939. She knows all about Isabel March.'

'All! She must know a great deal more than I ever did!' I turned away from him, staring out to sea, closing my mind against a sudden invasion of images, voices. 'I'm sorry,' I said. 'I don't mean to sound bitter. So, I'm supposed to help. What do you suggest I do? Send her back to New York? She's obviously miserable there. And she's old enough to make choices.'

'You can't let family feelings interfere,' he said abruptly. 'She's not your child.'

I turned around. 'She might as well be, don't you think? It was me she came to, not her mother. Don't forget that.'

He shrugged his shoulders. 'Do as you think best. I'm only telling you what she said.'

I walked for a long way along the shore by myself that morning, thinking about the past. This is what I did when I got back. I telephoned my daughter and told her that Judith was visiting. I didn't mention the Baptist or the Children of Heaven. Then I went up to the room where Judith was sitting with the

Bible on her lap, staring at the wall as if she hoped to find a picture in its blank whiteness. She looked so forlorn that I wanted to cry. I sat down beside her and told her that I had talked to Joe.

'You can stay here for as long as you like,' I said, stroking her cold clasped hands. 'It's good for me to have company. We can get to know each other again. There are a lot of things to talk about, aren't there?'

Her face lit up at that. 'I've read Isabel's books,' she said. 'Some of the things she says are just amazing!'

'Like the Baptist?' I said gently and she nodded.

'Listen to this,' she said. '"Let us not think that hope is dead. Let us stand together, watchful –"'

I let the words slide past me as I watched her expression change.

'"– for those who fail to read my message clear."' She was staring at the wall with such passionate intensity that I could almost believe Isabel was back, her hands raised to bless a new disciple. A new victim.

'There are no saviours in the end,' I said. 'Just us. Your grandfather and I didn't understand that. If we had, our lives wouldn't have gone so terribly wrong.'

She twisted round to look at me. She has lovely eyes, Judith, big and bright and shining. Just then, they reminded me almost unbearably of Chance. 'I'm not going to listen,' she said. 'You're just like my mother. You want me to be damned. Well, I'm not going to let it happen. Isabel would have understood. There's a place for me with the Children and I'm going to take it. I thought you'd understand. I thought you'd help.'

I sat back. 'You want money.'

'Five hundred dollars,' she said. 'They said it had to be a thousand, but I can't ask you for that.'

Tears were still streaming down her face. She looked so young, such a child. I felt heavy with sadness at the thought of the fear, the loneliness she must have suffered. 'Well, I'll tell you

98

this,' I said slowly. 'There's a desk in the big room downstairs and I don't always lock it. That's all I'll say. But stay here for a while and let's see if we can't straighten things out. You'll be safe. Nothing's going to come to an end this week, whatever your Children of Heaven say.'

'Whatever *He* says.' Unexpectedly, she put her arms round me. I felt the softness of her hair against my face, the thinness of her body. 'I'm going to be so happy,' she said. 'I wish I could take you with me.'

Her bed was empty the next morning. The money I kept in my desk for emergencies, four hundred dollars, had gone. I telephoned Eleanor that evening. She told me that Judith had not returned. Then she put down the telephone.

I know I had told Judith about the desk, but I still wish she had come and asked me. I can't rid myself of the picture of her turning over my papers and letters, searching through the drawers like a thief.

And at the same time I wish there had been more for her to take. Four hundred dollars might cover her journey to the West Coast, but it won't keep her where she most wants to be.

Perhaps I should have done more for her. All such journeys are worth while, even if they sometimes lead into blind alleys. I know, none better, how it feels to find a saviour.

8

New York, 1928

JUDITH'S VISIT STARTED me thinking of saviours and charlatans. I wouldn't be telling the story right if I suggested that we walked straight into the open arms of Miss Isabel March. That wasn't how it was, not at all.

It was Dinah, quite inadvertently, who started us off on our first search of that kind. One evening she asked me to do her a favour. She had been instructed to cover an event at a dance hall high up on the East Side and she didn't want to go alone. The newspaper clipping which she pushed in front of me announced an evening of spiritual revelation in the presence of a Monsieur Gurdjieff, recently arrived from Paris. The photograph showed a broad, powerful face. The eyes, dark and deepset, looked directly at the camera. I couldn't make out the shape of the mouth behind the moustaches drooping over his lips like a couple of lovesick leeches. 'Any village in Russia, you'll find a man like this,' Dinah said. 'Making out he's holy. Holy as a hole in the head.'

'I like his eyes,' I said, studying the picture more closely. 'I'd put my trust in him.'

'You! You'd put your trust in a gypsy who told you she'd seen sickness coming to you from your money,' Dinah said, stroking my arm. 'But I love you for it. I never knew such a girl for believing in cheats and liars.'

I gave her a warning look.

'I say nothing,' she said, holding up her hand as if she was taking an oath. 'Not another word. Bring him along if you like. They won't be short of seats.'

'You can't have forgotten we were going round to Bill and Annie,' Chance said when I asked if he wanted to come. 'Tell her you're busy.'

'They might like to see this man, too,' I said. 'And we weren't going to do anything special. Suit yourselves, but I'm curious.'

It ended with the three of us going along for drinks with Bill and Annie before we all squeezed into a cab and headed for the Nineties on the East Side. It was probably as well that none of us was entirely sober when we found our destination and took our seats. The hall reminded me of the chilly Boston rooms in which I had spent so many hours listening to my mother extol the joys of a pure body and a clear mind. Behind an upright piano on the platform, a red cord curtain billowed forward from its rail every time the street door was opened. The air smelt sad and damp; the audience, sitting in the first ten of some thirty rows of empty chairs, were huddled in scarves and winter coats. I saw Bill and Annie looking at their watches; Chance had his nose in a book. Dinah, exuberantly overdressed in a red velvet cloak with a black beret tilted sideways on her ashy bob, took a flask from her pocket and held it out to me.

'Do you think he's cancelled?' I whispered as Bill shifted restlessly on the slippery seat of a fold-up chair. 'Maybe we ought to give up.'

Dinah shook her head. 'And you were the one all ready to put your trust in him.' Seeing Chance watching her, she stroked my hand. 'Gurdjieff's always late. Famous for it. Adds to the sense of mystery.'

Twenty minutes later, Bill and Annie had just told me they were going to head home when the door behind us opened. A tall, loose-limbed man in a three-piece tweed suit strode past us, paused to crush the smoking butt of his cigarette under his heel and then climbed onto the stage. 'Alfred Orage,' I saw Dinah writing in her rapid journalist's scrawl as he started to speak. 'Six years working with G. at Institute for the Harmonious Development of Man. Query: who funds IHDM and what does it do?'

Orage talked for about forty minutes. Chance started taking down notes, but I couldn't entirely follow what we were being told. The gist of it seemed to be that we were all capable of teaching ourselves. 'We do not propose to reveal any wonderful secrets,' Orage said towards the end. 'The secret is the buried treasure inside each of you, of us. None of us can grow until we have uncovered that treasure. The teaching is only the spade with which you can start to dig.'

'Look left,' Chance murmured. 'Front of the piano.'

The audience gave a little gasp; it really did seem as though he had performed some illusionist's trick, to be standing there in front of us when nobody had seen him walk on to the stage. He was wearing a dark trilby hat which he removed with a slight bow as he faced us. I saw powerful shoulders, a square head with the grey hair cropped close to the skull. But it was the eyes above the thick and flourishing moustache which mesmerised me. I couldn't, even now, tell you what colour Gurdjieff's eyes were; what struck me then was the warm intensity of their stare. I felt as if he was looking into each of us and knowing just how we felt. Not judging; just knowing. Glancing along the row, I saw Bill lean forward and prop his elbows on the chairback in the next row.

'We will start with some movements,' Gurdjieff said in a low, wonderfully rich voice. 'Then there will be tests of memory. Not all of these will be genuine.' He smiled. 'And I am afraid there will be no prizes for guessing the truth.'

102

'Just contributions to the Institute, and make them generous,' I heard Dinah mutter. I wished she would stop being so cynical; it damped down the sense of excitement which was making my stomach flutter with anticipation.

The dances were faintly absurd – they carried me back to the classes at which, as a child, I had been expected to throw myself into interpreting wind-blown branches or drooping flowers. The most striking aspect of them was the way the performers responded to Gurdjieff. He never appeared to move or to be aware of anything beyond their presence on the stage; they, in turn, were evidently dancing not for us but for their master, and with a pleasure which made up for the stilted nature of the choreography. I didn't bother to look at their movements after a time; what made the spectacle so attractive and unusual was the confident happiness in their faces. Looking from the performers to the audience, I thought Gurdjieff had chosen a good way to advertise his school. I doubt if a person there was unaware of the contrast we presented.

It was the same with the memory tests. We have all seen such mental tricks performed and wondered about the time and skill required to produce feats which seem effortless. But what affected me again was the sense that I was watching a group of people who had discovered how to enjoy life. It was their happiness, not the exercises they were demonstrating with such ease, which had changed the atmosphere in that dreary room. And, looking at Gurdjieff's warm bright eyes and the way he watched over his followers with such affection and tenderness, I wanted a share of it. I wanted to be like them.

'Well, thank God for that,' I heard Dinah say as the performers filed off stage, leaving Gurdjieff alone. 'Just time to get out before the purse-squeezing.'

I heard her as if through a mist. 'I'm not leaving,' Annie said. And I saw Chance lean back in his chair to hold a whispered exchange with Bill. Dinah slid her arm around my waist. 'Coming?' I shook my head. 'I'll talk to you tomorrow.'

103

She looked as if I'd struck her. 'You're staying? After watching that?'

Gurdjieff had been standing on the platform watching us while the other members of the audience turned and tried to hush us up with reproachful stares. Now, quite suddenly, he lifted his arm and pointed it at Dinah.

'You leave now,' he said. 'You go, please.'

I thought that was pretty clever of him. Dinah's exit was turned from a show of contempt into something altogether more shameful, more along the lines of Eve being told by God that she wasn't fit to stroll around the Garden of Eden any more.

She was wrong about the purse-squeezing; Gurdjieff didn't even mention money. Instead, after telling us all to move up closer to the stage so he didn't have to strain his voice shouting, he told us about a book. Or rather, The Book.

I have never read more than a few pages of the great work. Gurdjieff was not a writer by instinct and his fondness for talking in parables worked more effectively in speech than on paper. Still, what he told us that evening made it sound as though this book was going to be of major importance. It would, he said, offer people something that was not available to them through religion. *All and Everything* was what he planned to call it, because that was what it was going to be about.

'But I have a difficulty,' he said, and I saw his eyes lock onto Chance. 'English is not my language. I have all the ideas, the thoughts, in here.' (He patted his chest.) 'But I have to find somebody willing to help. I think we have somebody here who will show his friendship.'

'What about the Dictionary?' I whispered as I saw Chance's hand shoot up like a bright schoolboy's. 'Why not let Bill do it?'

But I was too late. Gurdjieff was nodding and Orage was walking down the aisle towards us. 'You'd better come and join us afterwards,' he said to Chance. 'We're going to the Child's on 86th.' His eyes glanced over the rest of us. 'You're together?'

'We've a date at Delmonico's.' Bill's announcement was news to me.

'You were impressed though?' I asked Bill as we took our places at the corner table which was always kept for the Taylors. A friend came up to congratulate Bill on a piece he had written for *World News*, the new outfit he had recently joined. Annie patted my hand.

'Don't look so anxious, Nancy. Couldn't you see for yourself? It's just that Bill didn't want to stand in Chance's limelight. I mean, if Mr Gurdjieff had realised he had a writer like Bill sitting there in the audience!' She gave her husband an adoring look. 'You know they've just made him the deputy books editor?'

'They have? Oh Annie, that's wonderful.' I spoke with additional warmth, to hide the fact that I was a little embarrassed for them both. Did they really suppose that Gurdjieff would have preferred to work with a man as ordinary as Bill Taylor when he could have my husband for the asking?

I talked to Bill a little more plainly on the way home, when we had worn ourselves out in exclamations at the feelings the evening had aroused in us.

'You're sure you don't mind? About Chance and the book?'

'Mind!' He put his arm round my shoulder and gave me a hug. 'Hell, no! Haven't I spent every year since college aching for Chance to find a project he could carry through? And Nancy, I do believe he may have found it.'

'And you do think Gurdjieff's the real thing?'

'Chance and I both went in for Buchman a while back,' he said pensively. 'Well, Buchman was a ranting fraud in my opinion. Hollow as a sucked egg. But Gurdjieff – he's the genuine article. Good connections, too. Jane Heap – *Little Review*? Mean anything to you? Never mind. Just take my word for it, this move won't do Chance's career any harm at all.'

It didn't seem the moment to say that I didn't believe Chance was thinking about his career. Bill was being happy for him in his own way. He really did love my husband. That, in all the confusion of my life, is one thing of which I have never been in doubt.

Gurdjieff returned to France the following week, leaving Orage and Chance in charge of the revision of his book. The discussions often took place at our apartment and that, so far as I can recall, was when I began to develop an interest in cooking. Orage was a man who could easily have developed an entirely separate career as a chef; often, while Chance was writing out a new section, his colleague and I would mess up a few pans trying out some gorgeous new concoction he just thought might work.

I liked Orage. He didn't make me feel conscious of being undereducated the way Bill and Chance sometimes did. He made me feel my opinions were worth something. I could talk to him about my dreams of getting away from the city, of living somewhere I could look at greenery and smell air that didn't make me feel I was choking. Of raising a family. Little dreams. The only time I saw him get angry was when I spoke about my parents. Grating orange rind for a sauce one evening, I told Orage the one thing I had kept back from my husband.

'Well,' he said after a long pause, 'you're not the only one to have been through a bad time. That Russian woman upstairs, for example. Are you telling me you've suffered more hardship than her because your father may have done more than he should?'

'Not more,' I said. 'As much. It's pretty hard to grow up carrying a secret like that inside you.'

He glanced up at me. 'But it isn't a secret now. And you're an independent woman, living a free life in another city. If you feel harmed, it's because you aren't trying to put it behind you.'

I felt my face harden. 'Perhaps I don't want to.'

'Then you can't be free of it,' he said, taking the bowl from my hands. 'But that's your choice, not anybody else's. You can offer your forgiveness any time you choose.'

'Mind the sugar doesn't boil,' I said. He just gave me a look and set down the bowl.

'We haven't had this conversation,' he said. 'I'm going to check the pages with Chance now.'

An ordinary man would have been content to think he had two brilliant followers devoting themselves to his service in such a selfless way. But Mr Gurdjieff was not an ordinary man. He had, for example, an extraordinary passion for the telephone; I cannot imagine what the cost to the Institute must have been of the transatlantic calls on which he would talk with as much leisure as though he had just dropped in for supper. His mind seldom stooped to such trivial matters as variations in time. For Gurdjieff, there was only one time, the moment in which he was presently dwelling. The rest of the world was expected to accommodate itself and usually, finding his manner pretty well irresistible, did so.

Chance had been working on the revisions with Orage for a little over two months when we received the most eccentric of his calls. It came at four in the morning, an hour when a sudden awakening causes you to expect disaster. I sat up, hands locked round trembling knees to keep myself still.

'I'll take it,' he said.

He was on the telephone for an hour and he came back shaking his head with a look somewhere between astonishment and despair.

'Gurdjieff?'

'Who else calls at this time?'

I slid back under the quilt. 'Anything in particular on his mind this time?'

'You could say so.' Chance wandered over to his work-table and stared down at the pile of papers. 'All of this has to go.'

'Go? Go where?'

'Back to Orage's apartment,' he said. 'Gurdjieff's already talked to him and set up the new arrangement.'

'And what's that?'

Chance sat down on the edge of the bed, pulling his slippers off. 'The book lives in Orage's study. Anytime I, or anybody else visits him, the study will be unlocked for thirty minutes. And, if we care to place ten dollars on his desk, we'll be at liberty to study one page, no more, of the book. And to copy it out, if we want.' He dropped the slippers on the floor and, taking careful aim, kicked one of them across the room to score a goal against the table leg. 'Bingo. Oh, and one other thing. You know the pages aren't numbered yet? Well, they're now going to be rearranged, out of order.'

'What for?' I stared at him in dismay. 'After all you've done – Chance, you can't go on with this. It's mad. You'll never reach the end.'

'Twelve hundred pages,' he said dreamily. 'Quite a task, wouldn't you say? Still, I can see the point. By doing this, he's making the book belong in exactly the same way to each of us. It's a perfect gesture towards intellectual equality.'

'Ten dollars a page!' I shook him. 'You can't do it. We don't have the money and you don't have the time.'

Looking down at me, he grinned and pinched my cheek. 'Come on, Nancy – where's your faith? Haven't you got any? Gurdjieff has, or he wouldn't have thought this up. It's a challenge!'

'You could', I said after a long pause, 'break the rules. I mean, he doesn't have to know whether you pay every time or whether the door's locked.'

I was wasting my breath. Not even his worst enemy could ever have accused Chance Brewster of a lack of integrity.

9

Red Road Farm, 1929

YOU'LL KNOW 1929 as the year of the Wall Street crash. But, for every high-flyer like Jim Archer, there were twenty like Bill Taylor, shrewd men who kept half their wealth fluid and never risked a cent they couldn't afford to do without. So the Taylors survived and we – well, we had nothing left to lose. Subsidising the Press and keeping up our rent payments when they were climbing month by month had left me with less than three hundred dollars by the fall of '29.

What that year marked for me was our escape from the city. There was no option; even Dinah, defeated by three rent rises in a year, quit the city and took a train west. (Where, I understand, she made quite a success out of acting as a consultant on historical films with an aristocratic flavour.) We, too, could no longer afford the fashionable indulgence of life in the Village and Chance wouldn't consider living anywhere else.

It was the Taylors, as so often, who came to our rescue. Annie's parents had decided to rent a house next to their daughter's new home in Princeton. They were old and they wanted to enjoy every moment of their two little grandsons' childhood. They offered to let us stay in the farmhouse as its caretakers. It was not, as they explained in their kindly, confused way, a place which offered much in the way of opportunity to youngsters like ourselves, but it did mean that we could survive, and comfortably.

109

We sold the Press. Bill Taylor found a man who was trying to set up a collection of movable-type machines and he offered to take it away for two hundred dollars in cash. Chance hadn't published anything for over a year and Bill reckoned that the financial climate wasn't going to help his kind of poetry to flourish. Chance didn't argue. He wasn't in a position to do so. Speaking personally, I was glad to see the back of the Wide Sky Press.

Red Road Farm was our home for the next three years. It was a ramshackle old place, lying at the end of a red dirt track and overlooking, beyond the yard and an empty barn, a lush green field bordered by flowering hedges. Annie, who had spent all her childhood summers there, loved it, but the farm was no paradise. The screens had shrunk too severely to fit the window frames; I spent whole afternoons swatting flies out of a kitchen where the only form of refrigeration was a manhole over the water tank, in which our supply of milk and butter floated in muslin bags let down on strings. (Kneeling on the floor above the dark water, I sometimes shuddered at the resemblance between a long white butter-bag and a severed arm, bobbing on liquid blackness.) From fall to late spring, the wind whistled through the cracks in the windows and shook the shutters; there were nights when we seemed to be sharing the house with an entire army of ghosts. Coming home from an early evening walk across the fields, I would rattle the key in the lock, giving the phantoms time to slip out over the weathered windowsills into the night. Sitting alone, when the wind whistled down the lonely track, I kept my eyes away from the glitter of the moon stalking me from window to window.

Still, when the oil lamps were lit and a fire was poked into redness out of the grey ashes, the farm was cheerful enough. I do not remember this as an unhappy period, perhaps because Chance was in such a state of radiant energy and excitement about his grand and seemingly never-ending project. During all the time that we stayed at Red Road Farm, I never once had the sense that I was being betrayed or neglected. It was, I can say with confidence, a time when love was strong between us.

Lack of money kept us quiet. Chance applied for several openings as an editor, but none of the companies he approached was willing to give him the right to choose his own authors. And a man of his intelligence could not be expected to confine himself to the kind of work they offered, rewriting the lazy plots of cheap romances and crime novels. I started making lampshades, gluing on prints and maps cut from the pages of old books. Sold through a friend of Annie's who ran a decorating shop in Princeton, they brought in enough to keep us fed. The life of Chance's old suits, made by an English tailor during his Oxford days, could be prolonged if I used my mother's trick of mending holes with threads pulled from the seams. Economy was the one skill in which I had undergone a splendid education.

My parents, at irregular intervals, sent me their prayers. Uncle Caleb, twice, sent me a cheque for a hundred dollars. I gave the money to Chance, easing my guilt at having helped Bill Taylor to dispose of his beloved Press.

'Be careful how you spend it,' I said. But I didn't have the heart to reproach him when he came back from his next visit to the city with a sackful of poetry books and a bottle of wine that he had bought for our dinner under some counter in the Village.

Chance's energy had always been phenomenal, but now, with nothing to interrupt him, he seemed to have lost all need for sleep. It was not unusual for me to wake at four in the morning and go downstairs to find him bent over a book at the kitchen table. Orage, a voracious reader, had refuelled his intellectual curiosity; during our first year at the farm he was studying, in tandem, a Russian grammar, a Hebrew Bible, Dante and a whole collection of books relating to cabbalistic doctrine. When he discovered that he had left his carefully copied manuscript of Gurdjieff's book on a bench at Penn station – it was never recovered – he simply shrugged and said that he would have to start again. Nothing, then, was beyond his reach.

Except, perhaps, humility. And that brought about an unfortunate incident which still makes me laugh at the recollection.

Bill and Annie had been going on at us for the past three years about the fine thing it would be if they could introduce Chance to their friend Edmund Wilson. But Chance was a proud man. He didn't care to be helped and the occasion had not presented itself until we left New York. Wilson was giving an afternoon talk to some Princeton students and he invited himself to stay the night with the Taylors. The perfect excuse! Annie drove out to inform me that they would be bringing him over for dinner and that I was, if necessary, to chain my husband to the stove. Anything, to make sure he didn't disappear.

'I'm not disappearing,' Chance said. 'So long as nobody imagines I'm going to start complimenting him on his style and so forth. My home. My views.'

Nobody pointed out that it was not, in fact, our home; the Taylors were always beautiful in their manners. But, truly, the fuss they made about that visit! You would have thought we were getting ready to entertain the President. Bill came to the farm at least three times to tell Chance what an opportunity for his literary career this was and to hint that I should take especial care with my dinner preparations. I wasn't having any of that.

'We have soup and roast chicken on Saturdays,' I said. 'And that's what I'm making.' All the same, I put on lipstick and powder and checked the seams of my stockings before going to the door.

The Taylors came in first, wearing the pink excited glow of people bestowing a lavish gift. Mr Wilson came up behind them, shaking the snow from his shoulders in a quick, petulant way. Small and heavy bellied, he had a square, imperious face and pale eyes. Seeing how they appraised me, I guessed that he was performing a mental striptease on the low bodice of my old black satin dress. Half a head taller than he, I was tempted to bend down and give him the privilege of an honest stare instead of a voyeur's fantasy.

112

'Enchanté, Mrs Brewster,' he said, kissing the tips of my fingers and sniffing them like a woman smelling fruit at the grocer's.

'Oh, me too,' I said, pulling my hand away. 'Well, if you'll excuse me, I have food to prepare.'

I brought in the soup; Chance produced a bottle of red wine which he had been keeping for a special occasion. Mr Wilson sipped at his glass like a bee and recalled in a shrill, stammering voice that the last occasion on which he had drunk such a p-perfect claret had been when Scott and Zelda were giving a di-dinner for his birthday at the Plaza. Then he started to talk about literature in a high-flown kind of way. He shook his head over what he called the maudlin quality of Proust's presentation of unrequited love and clucked like a laying hen when Chance said it was no more sentimental than any of the medieval romances. I asked him what he thought of Willa Cather and he said he didn't have much time for p-popular authors. The word 'popular' was accompanied by a small pinched smile which made me wonder if I had put salt in the soup.

'Do you have to be unpopular to be a genius, then?'

'Oh goodness,' he said. 'Well, if you want to think of poor Willa as a genius, I have nothing to say on the matter.' But he did, and on he went. He was like a little turkeycock, all strut and gobble, pecking away at the reputations of the great so that he could stand over them, swollen with self-assurance. I wondered at Bill and Annie for holding him in such high esteem; he had none of Chance's eloquence and passion. Across the table, I could see that Chance was fiddling with his knife, twisting it in his hand. Our evening with Jim and Kitty came back to me in a rush. Something bad was about to happen.

'Well, I'd better heat the plates up,' I said, looking for an opportunity to get out of the room. When I came back in with the vegetable dishes, Wilson was on his feet. Chance was leaning back in his chair and sipping his claret. He looked flushed and cheerful.

'No need to bring that in, Nancy,' he said. 'Mr Wilson won't be staying. He seems to think I've insulted him.'

'Oh, but I'm sure you didn't mean to,' I said, setting down the dishes in a hurry. 'It's just the way Chance talks, Mr Wilson. You mustn't take any notice. Can I give you a chicken leg, or would you rather –'

'I'm sorry to spoil the evening, my dear,' he said. 'But your husband must take the blame. Bill? Annie? Shall we find our coats?'

'For God's sake, Chance,' Bill muttered. 'Just apologise.'

Chance traced a circle on the table with the blade of his knife. 'All right,' he said. 'I apologise for thinking your friend had a sense of humour. It never occurred to me that anybody could talk so much nonsense about poetry and expect to be taken seriously.'

Wilson gave him a look which was both startled and contemptuous. Then he walked out of the room.

Standing in the lamplit hall as our three visitors turned their faces towards the sharp whip of the night wind and a flurry of snow, I pitied them all, Bill and Annie for being forced to miss their dinner, Mr Wilson for letting himself be so easily offended.

'You shouldn't have let him upset you,' I said impulsively as his small, gentlemanly hands tucked a cream silk scarf into the high collar of his coat. 'I'm sure he didn't set out to annoy you. He always gets so carried away when he's talking about books.'

'In that case, you have my sympathy, Mrs Brewster,' he said. 'You had my admiration already. Auburn hair is a particular weakness of mine.' The way he eyed me then, I wondered just which area of my body was preying on his mind. Not my head, for certain.

'It's brown,' I said, giving him stare for stare. 'Just ordinary old brown hair with a speck of red in it.'

'It looks auburn from where I am standing, Mrs Brewster,' he said. 'I'm sorry we should m-meet under such circumstances.'

Coming closer, he said: 'Perhaps we might lunch one day?' He lifted my hand to his lips and I felt a thick, wet muscle probe out to taste my skin. 'I like to spoil my women,' he said.

I pulled my arm away, thankful for the sound of Bill's car horn.

'Please, do go. You've made our friends leave – don't make them wait as well.' I pushed him away from me, just hard enough to make him gasp as he struggled for his balance on the icy steps. 'Go on,' I said. 'You get out of our home, you snaky-tongued thing.'

He gave me a startled, round-eyed look. Then he shook his head, clapped his hands across his chest to keep the cold out and hurried on down to the car. Watching the headlights sweep over the old barn and down to the ridges of the frostbitten track, I rubbed the back of my hand against my skirt, blotting the wetness from my skin.

I never did get Chance to explain what had been considered so offensive. Annie said that he had described Wilson as a creature of fashion, incapable of literary integrity. If his manner towards me was anything to go by, I think my husband had his measure.

I found myself pregnant in the summer of 1930. I never had a moment's doubt that I would have a girl. I told Chance that we were going to call her Eleanor. In the bedroom, as the summer reached its height, I drew the flowery yellow curtains shut and stretched out naked in a temple of gold. I was serene as a ship in harbour, floating but anchored in a state of dreaming attendance. I had never felt so easy in my mind, so entirely free of confusion.

I remember one soft October afternoon when I led Chance away from the farm, to a little meadow with a shady river bank where I loved to sit and dream in the tall grass.

'Sit yourself down and turn your back,' I said and walked a

little further up the slope. I stood in the dappled shade of a walnut tree and stripped off every scrap of clothing I had on before I walked back down the bank.

'You can look now,' I said and watched him turn to stare up at me, my arms raised and my belly all rounded and pretty, like a queen of the harvest.

Dum Dianae vitrea sero lampas oritur ... I'm pretty sure that was what he said. I ought to know, because I made him say it over until I had it off by heart. Diana lighting her golden lamp to shine across the fields. But he didn't need to say a word; it was there in his eyes.

We stayed there all afternoon, stroking each other in the long grass, rolling on our backs to lose ourselves in the calm unwinking stare of the sky, idling the hours away until we heard a farmer whistling to his dog in the lane above the meadow. Giggling like children, we flattened ourselves, waiting for him to pass, fingers against each other's mouths, eyes shut tight with laughter.

The smell of warm earth still brings that day back to me, the comfort of lying so close to the soil, like gentle animals.

And that was supposed to be one of the proofs of my madness, a demonstration of my taste for evil rituals. Witchcraft, even, I heard it pronounced.

Witchcraft!

Maybe it was partly because the Taylors were away that I remember the last months of my pregnancy as being a period of especial freedom and intimacy. Or maybe it was because Chance had a proper job for the first time.

We owed that, as it sometimes seemed we owed just about everything, to Bill and Annie. Bill, who took his literary career very seriously, had asked for a six-month sabbatical to travel to France and work there on a biography of Gurdjieff. He drove out to the farm one day to say that he had talked to the books editor at *World News* about the possibility of Chance standing in as his deputy.

'I know you don't think much of our little outfit,' Bill said, dipping his finger in my cakemix bowl. 'This is gorgeous, Nancy – you'll have to give Annie the recipe. But the pay's good and nobody's going to dictate what books you review. Now's your chance to push some of those lame dog poets of yours. Not too many, though – *World News* isn't known as a literary journal.'

'It isn't?' Chance said with a grin. 'I'm shocked!'

'Don't mess about,' Bill said, licking his fingers. 'Do you want it or not?'

Publicly, Chance had always scoffed at *World News* for the means by which it sought to reach as large an audience as possible. Privately, in common with almost every high-minded writer I have met, he longed for any opportunity to broadcast his views. 'Oh Chance, of course you have to say you'll do it,' I said as he glanced towards me.

'What about Orage? What about the book?'

'I never heard Gurdjieff deny a man his right to earn money,' Bill said, so glibly that I suspected he'd planned his words already. 'It's just for a few months, Chance. Just to help me out.'

'Is that what it is?' I asked Bill when Chance had gone to bring in some wood for the fire. 'Or is this another of your charitable acts?'

'It's a fill-in,' Bill said. 'Don't let him get his hopes up, Nancy. This isn't going to lead anywhere.'

I found myself looking away from him; I suddenly felt very angry. 'You don't think Chance is capable of doing a desk job just as well as you?'

'Chance isn't like the rest of us. You know that. He's a dreamer.'

I stared at him. 'So why take him on?'

Bill shrugged. 'I'd hate for them not to miss me. And believe me they will after Chance has done a winter's worth of book issues.' He kissed my averted cheek. 'Don't get me wrong. I want Chance to have the time of his life and be paid for it. But it won't last.'

He was right on both counts.

10

Red Road Farm, 1931

'STALIN'S MOUSTACHE . . . STALIN'S moustache . . .'

That phrase has been clicking around in my head like a cracked record for the past three days; I'm going mad trying to place it. Did Gurdjieff's moustache resemble Stalin's? Did somebody tell me that? Could I have thought it myself? What would I have thought about Stalin anyway, back in 1931, when we knew so much less?

They said I was like this in the early years at the hospital. I don't remember those times, but notes were made. Dr Storrow knew all about my peculiarities, and that was eight years later. I'd have a phrase, sometimes as much as a couple of sentences, fixed in place so that nothing else could find a way in. I wonder now if I used them as a block, as a way of not thinking about the things that were too dreadful to remember.

'Stalin's moustache' was one of those phrases; I never expected it to pop up again with the same awful insistence, flickering its letters at me like a Times Square slogan.

I'm upset, that's the cause of it. Cooped up in the house for too long. I need to get out in the garden or the woods, to be busy again, to use my hands. Every time I put down my pen, I catch myself twisting and knotting them in my lap, pulling at my fingers until the bones crack.

Occupational therapy wasn't such a bad thing, though I

always drew the line at basket weaving. It kept my hands active, the way they need to be. Weeding's my secret vice. I like to think, as I work the roots loose from the gravel and earth, that I'm pulling out the bad things, the memories I want to put on paper and then let slip out of sight, out of reach, to where they can harm me no more.

I was not in a good state after Eleanor's birth. I had seen Annie pregnant and nursing, swollen, beatific, hormone-gorged. I thought it was like that for everybody, an instant route into sleepy contentment, unquestioning pleasure.

Not for me. Everything disgusted me. Lying with my legs branching high in stirrups, exposed to the murmur of voices, the clink of instruments, I thought of what they were seeing which I could not, and was sick with shame. I turned my head away when my screams turned to its wails and a moist, shrivelled fish creature was placed in my arms. Holding it to an iron pillow of aching flesh, I felt my stomach heave as its head moved over my skin, seeking, like a blind worm.

'You'll soon get the hang of it,' said the breezy English nurse, pausing on her passage through the ward to clamp the sucking mouth in place. 'Just relax.'

It hung there on me like a limpet on a rock, this thing I had carried inside me with such wondering tenderness and pride until its weight pulled me downwards and it shifted and kicked for attention. I stared away from it at a pea-green wall, listening to the soft mumbling sounds by which nature was attempting to reward me. I carefully avoided meeting the eyes of any other mothers at these times; I was too scared of letting my thoughts show.

But Chance was happy. You never saw a more devoted father. He'd play with its hands for hours, tickling the palms with the tip of a finger, stroking the creases in its arms. The baby never screamed when he took it in his arms and rocked it.

If I had been given a syringe of morphine that year, I would have plunged the needle into my arm and never woken up.

One night at Red Road Farm, when Chance was working late at the *World News* offices, I took the baby out of her cot and rocked her to stop the crying. She yelled so loud that I thought she might choke and I almost wished she would. There was a full moon hanging over the fields and a warm smell of smoke and dry grass. I wrapped her in a shawl and carried her up the hill. I sat there for three hours, staring at the moon while she screamed and then whimpered and, finally, fell asleep in my arms.

Chance was sitting up waiting for me in the kitchen when I came back.

'She's quiet now,' I said. 'She liked looking at the moon.' He didn't say anything, just took the baby from me and stroked her cheeks with the tips of his fingers.

The next day, he took me to visit Mr and Mrs Goodhart and they told me that I was to call them right away whenever things got too much for me with the baby.

'Dear little Ellie, it'll be a real pleasure for us, Nancy,' Mrs Goodhart said. 'I do so wish Annie had given us a grand-daughter.' She smiled at me. 'You aren't the only one, you know. My sister Hilary couldn't stand the sight of her little girl for the first year.'

I sat beside her on the sofa, leaning close so that Chance couldn't hear me. I picked at the pleats in my skirt.

'Mrs Goodhart, you don't think I'm crazy?'

'Try not to care about things so much, that's all you need to do, my dear,' she said.

I wasn't sure she had given me an answer.

In the summer of 1931, when Eleanor was three months old, Bill and Annie came back from Europe. They waited a tactful fortnight for Chance to get used to rejoining the ranks of the unemployed. I assumed that they were trying to sweeten the abruptness of his dismissal when they asked us to come and have lunch at Bill's favourite restaurant.

'You go. I'll stay here,' I said. 'I don't feel like getting dressed up.'

Chance disappeared for most of the next day and returned carrying a khaki-coloured linen dress with a white starched collar, the kind of thing you'd expect to see a nurse wearing.

'Macy's,' he said. 'The girl there said you'd be sure to like it.'

Putting it on, I wondered how it was that a girl I had never met could despise me enough to recommend such a costume. Or that a husband could care so little as to think I looked pretty in it.

'The colour's really unusual. But you've lost so much weight, Nancy!' Annie said as we sat down. 'I don't know how you did it – I took six months to get back in shape after Jay was born.'

'Pretty good shape now, honey,' Bill said, pinching her cheek. 'Nancy's too thin.'

I didn't bother to argue; I could see my face, bloated as a milk cheese, bobbing and leering at me from the mirror behind his head. I shifted sideways, blocking the reflection.

'So how was Provence?'

This was evidently the right thing to ask. Bill swelled up like a ship under sail, bursting with his tidings.

'A revelation,' he said. 'That's what I'd have to call it, wouldn't you say so, Annie?'

She dabbed a little sauce from the corner of his mouth in a wifely way. 'I'm not saying anything, sweetheart. I'm just going to sit here and listen.'

It was just as well that we were fond of Bill and used to the way his stories ambled and digressed; twenty minutes later, we were still waiting for him to reach the point.

The account began, so far as I can remember, with their visiting Gertrude Stein (Bill could never bear to go anywhere without investigating the local celebrities). Miss Stein had given them tea and biscuits and suggested that they pay a visit to an

English poet called Charles Neville who lived in the next-door village. Bill paused to give Chance a significant look.

'*The* Charles Neville.'

This was wasted on me, but Chance seemed interested.

'And? What was he like?'

I was surprised when Annie tapped her fingernails on Bill's forearm and told him to hurry along with the story.

'You don't need to bother them with Charles.'

'Yes, I do, honey,' Bill said. 'Trust me. So, anyhow, we went to the next village – walked there, in fact, although – do you have any idea how hot a Provençal afternoon can be?'

'I truly thought I was going to pass out,' Annie said.

I chewed on a little sore area of skin inside my lower lip and watched my face forming interested expressions in the mirror. Then I narrowed my eyes until I could make the shadows on the glass turn into waves. If I were at Falmouth now, I could be sailing a tall ship across a glassy sea, with the gulls crying and swooping round my head.

'Nancy,' Chance said softly. 'Stop making faces.'

Back in the room again, I smiled at him.

Bill was telling us how they had called on Charles Neville and almost been sent away again by the woman they mistook for his housekeeper. 'All I did was ask if Mr Neville could spare a few minutes to talk to an admirer.' He laughed and shook his head. 'Boy, did I say the wrong thing to the wrong woman!'

'You mean she was his mistress?' I asked.

'Worse than that!' But he looked more amused than disconsolate. 'She sat us down in the front room and informed us that this was her house and that she was entitled to every bit as much recognition as Mr Neville and so of course Annie had to go and address her as Mrs Neville. And that tore it! Why, the two of them practically ripped our throats out!'

'You're telling it all wrong,' Annie said. 'Making them out to be monsters. Tell Nancy how Isabel found us the cottage to rent and gave us the camp-beds for the boys to use.'

'Isabel's a nice name,' I said. I made a picture for it, a tall smiling woman with her arms full of flowers and hair falling down over her breasts like spilled corn.

'No, Nancy, not nice,' Bill said with a solemn look that didn't go too well with the fact that he had a forkful of peas balanced in front of his mouth. 'The plain truth of the matter is – well, she's the one. She's it.'

'It?' At last, they had all of our attention. Annie gave a satisfied little nod.

'We kept saying to each other how we wished you could have been there. I mean, the whole thing was so transforming. She puts you through things that – well, we just see everything in a different way now, don't we?'

And Bill, his peas safely swallowed, nodded. 'No question. I'd follow Isabel March to the ends of the earth. So would Annie. That's the kind of woman she is.'

I didn't dare to look at Chance in case I laughed. I had suddenly seen the Taylors marching across a desert with a train of bearers staggering under the weight of all Annie's new French dresses.

'And Gurdjieff?' Chance said at last. 'The book you were going to write about him? Did Miss March have anything useful to contribute?'

Bill and Annie looked at each other. 'Now you've got to understand this clearly,' Bill said. 'Isabel isn't the kind of person to dismiss anybody without good reason.'

'Has she ever set eyes on him?'

'Didn't need to.' Bill took out a cigar and tidily clipped the end. 'She wrote him a letter, asking him to set out his arguments and to explain the principles of the Institute.'

'And?' Chance's voice was astonishingly calm.

'It's immoral,' said Annie. Bill shook his head. 'That's not the point, honey. I saw his letter myself. Chance, the man's practically illiterate. I'm not surprised he picked on you and Orage to write his book for him. We're not blaming you – why, he took us

124

in every bit as much. But your Mr Gurdjieff is just a Russian peasant who's picked up a few conjuring tricks. That's all there is to him.'

I put the picture of the beautiful corn goddess out of my mind. This Isabel March was like her name, a cold spiteful wind blowing out of Europe.

'It doesn't have to be true,' I said. 'Why should she be right?'

My voice was high and shaky. 'Here,' Chance said quietly, and he lit a cigarette and passed it to me. 'And take a sip of water.'

But Bill seemed oblivious to my distress. 'You'll think like us when you get to know her,' he said. 'Believe in yourself, Nancy. That's the key.'

Our hints that other subjects would be welcome did not cause the Taylors to slacken in their crusade for our conversion. The next time they visited Red Road Farm, they brought along a letter.

'It's from Isabel to both of you,' Bill said with the beam of a man who had come to us directly from God's right hand. 'It's her welcome.' He held it towards me. 'Well – aren't you going to read it?'

I stared at him. 'Now? Aloud?'

The Taylors smiled at each other like a couple of conspiring priests. 'You'll want to,' Annie said. 'She does write so beautifully.'

'Dear Brewsters!' the letter began in an oddly exclamatory way before informing us that our friendship with the Taylors had already bound us together. Bill, it seemed, had been through a hard struggle to find himself – Bill chuckled and nodded his head in agreement – while Annie's happy disposition and readiness to explore new ideas had already left a gap in the lives of her new friends. (The taste of bitterness made me swallow and pause in my reading; why should it be given to Annie, who lacked for nothing, always to please people and to be happy, while sacrificing nothing?)

'You've certainly made a hit!' I said, to hide the pause. Bill waved the words away. 'Go on! There's more!'

Turning the page over, I learned that Chance and I were expected – 'we count on you' was the phrase – to visit the village of Lavalle and help Isabel and 'my colleague', by which I supposed she meant Mr Neville, to recreate its state of former glory. Bill interrupted to explain that Lavalle had once been a centre of medieval scholarship and that Isabel was going to revive it as a university for – they exchanged another look – 'right-minded people'.

'Right-minded?'

'People who think like us,' Annie said. 'People who want to change themselves. To make things better.'

'And Isabel's to be the president?' I smiled. 'Of course she is – what a stupid question. We couldn't all decide just what right-minded meant, could we?'

'There's no disagreement,' Bill said quickly. 'Isabel says what we all feel. Only she puts it better.'

'Let her come here,' I said. 'To America. She is American, isn't she? God knows, we need someone to follow.' My mind held a picture of the pinched face of a child who had come to the farm the previous day, offering himself as a bird-scarer. He picked up a stone when I told him we had no work to give him. I thought he was going to throw it in my face, but he swung his arm back and sent it up at a tree, to bring a couple of jays screaming and chattering out of the leaves.

'I'd scare them good, see,' he said before he turned to walk away down the red track. My misery seemed like the country's mirror on days like that. On days like this. Let the corn-haired queen of Provence come down from her mountain and see what had happened to her homeland instead of dreaming up her castles in the air.

'Eleanor needs changing,' I said as I heard the start of a thin screaming noise.

'She's sleeping,' Chance said. 'I checked.' So the noise was in

my head again. I put my hand up, rubbing it against my forehead.

'She's been suffering from migraine,' Chance said softly.
'Since the baby.'

The Taylors looked at him, not at me; I felt the flutter of a silent
exchange go past me like a cloud of moths. 'No need to be so
upset, Nancy,' Bill said slowly. 'Nobody's making you do anything you don't want to. Although you might be interested in
making a donation to the university – it's an awfully good cause.
Annie and I are giving a thousand dollars.'

'And my parents are going to make a loan of five hundred
towards building a library,' Annie said.

'Well!' The screaming had stopped again. I handed back the
letter. 'Hurrah for you! I wish I had as much money to throw out
of the window. If I did, I'm sure your friend Isabel would be
standing outside with her hands open.'

I could see that Bill was doing his best to keep his temper.
'Now, I know you don't mean that –' he started; out of the corner
of my eye, I saw Chance shake his head at him. I smiled, a small
fierce smile.

'Let's drop the subject of Isabel, shall we? Just for today. If we
could just talk about something else, we'd have no need to
quarrel.'

'Who's quarrelling?' Chance asked and he started winding up
the gramophone. 'Kick the rug back under the table, Bill. Annie?
Care to dance?' And he started twirling her around the room,
holding his head back and kicking his long legs out like a
nervous, elegant colt. A woman's voice spilled moonlight and
roses into the brightness of the kitchen at midday until my mind
started to feel gentle and syrupy. I wished Chance had taken me
in his arms; I loved the way he held me and swung me out and
back to him while he looked into my eyes. It made me feel so
safe. Watching him across the room, I remembered that first
time I saw him turning a decorous somersault on a New York
sidewalk. His hair had streaks of grey now and his neck had

thickened a little, but he still looked like a boy when he was laughing, as he was laughing with Annie now.

'Ready to come out of your dreams yet?' Bill asked, holding his arm towards me. A little clumsily, we circled the table, concentrating on the steps.

I thanked Isabel March for her letter and said that we didn't see much opportunity to visit Provence in the near future, but that we wished her the best of luck with her projects and that I was hers very sincerely.

That could have been the end of it. But the Taylors were in regular touch with Isabel and she always had a friendly message to be passed on to us. (We never heard another word from Gurdjieff, or even from Orage, after Chance wrote to explain that he was abandoning the revision.) Pressed by Bill, Chance read some of Isabel's poems and wrote a review for *World News*, in which he said that she was as good as Emily Dickinson, maybe better.

Poetry aside, Chance seemed to feel no need to share the Taylors' almost reverent awe. But I looked at Bill and Annie and their children, their easy smiles, their comfortable air of assurance and I longed to be like them. Might their Isabel March bring me back to peace? I read her weekly letters to the Taylors and struggled to understand her poems. Sometimes, in the dark unpredictable moments of despair, I murmured her name to myself.

April, 1981

I had a visit from Eleanor last weekend. She flew up to Boston and came out to Falmouth in a hired Mercedes. Money to burn.

'I can't see why you don't just take a sack of dollars and drop it off the cliff,' I said. 'Isn't a regular train service good enough for you?'

She smiled, that small knowing smile which had always

made me want to shake her. 'You haven't changed, Mother,' she said. 'Look – I've brought some of those old albums you were asking about. Shall we go through them together?'

She was doing her best to be pleasant; I could see that. Nicely dressed, too, nothing too smart, but good material and a skirt that covered her knees. Not a word about Judith. We just sat and looked at photographs for the first hour. I showed her some of herself as a toddler in 1932 at Red Road Farm, sitting out on the porch in a little flowered dress and bonnet I made myself, and at Appledown, our home for the next two years. She needed spectacles to take a closer look at herself.

'There,' I said. 'That's where you spent most of your time at Appledown, playing on a scrap of grass outside the kitchen window. We dug a sandpit for you and your father made a fence with the palings painted all in different colours – remember?'

She started leafing ahead through the pages. 'How could I? I was only four when we left. Where's Tom? You must have some photographs of him.'

'Tom was only a baby.'

('Look at his little legs – oh, couldn't you just eat him!' Annie shrieked at me over a chasm of nearly fifty years. 'Oh, Nancy, he's the sweetest thing!')

I snapped the thick pages shut. 'Let's take a look at your albums, then.'

Eleanor's two books covered the period from when she was nine until her graduation from Bryn Mawr. 'Do you really want to do this?' she asked as she lifted them onto her lap. 'You're sure it won't set you off?'

My smile was tight with control. 'Don't be silly.'

She was right, of course. How could I take pleasure in seeing Annie's tidy inscriptions under every picture? Eleanor standing between the Taylor boys, each of them clasping one of her hands; Eleanor having her Christmas party hat set straight by dear old Mrs Goodhart; Eleanor squashed up against Annie's shoulder on a Ferris wheel ride; Eleanor smiling up into Bill's eyes in her flirty chiffon dance-dress with a sweetheart neckline and a nipped-in waist.

'They always did want a daughter,' I said as she closed the book. 'And I guess it didn't trouble you too much having those handsome boys of theirs around you. It never did trouble you. Anything to do with sex –'

'Stop that right now, Mother,' she said. 'We don't need to hurt each other.' I shrugged, annoyed by the sense that she had somehow got the upper hand of me without my knowing how she had done it. That's an attorney for you.

'Have you heard anything from Judith yet?' I asked. 'That must have shaken the happy family up a bit, her running along to Grandma for help. Couldn't get any help from you and your fancy man, poor girl. She looked half starved when she turned up here.'

I heard the hiss as she sucked in her breath, but her smile stayed in place. I have never been able to accuse my daughter of lacking self-control. 'Joel and I have been together for over seven years,' she said. 'The fact that we are not married does not give you the right to call him a fancy man. He contributes. He pays his share of the girls' education, and that's more than you ever offered to do.'

'You didn't ask,' I said. 'And I'm sure he's willing to pay. Buying his way into their affection and I wouldn't want to say what else. Very nice. Very considerate.'

That was when she slapped me, hard enough to leave a sting on my cheek. I was about to give her a few hints on treatment of the elderly and infirm (my knees always suffer at the end of a long winter) when she whipped out her handkerchief and started dabbing the corners of her eyes.

'Oh, for goodness' sakes!' I said. 'Don't start on that. I'm sorry if I hurt you. I won't mention Joel again.'

'It doesn't matter.' Wiping her eyes, she slid down to the floor, crossing her legs like an Indian. She does have a lovely figure, and I noticed a new auburn tint in the sheen of her hair.

'Why is it that we can't ever get along, you and I?' she asked.
'I came here with the sole intention of making our peace. I was
going to show you the albums, tell you that I'd got Judith home
again, thank God, and then see if we couldn't talk over the idea
of having you looked after a little better.'

I stared down at her. 'Slowly, Eleanor. Judith's back with you?'

She nodded; I thought I saw a trace of smugness in her smile.
'Joel fixed it. He flew out there. She hadn't been involved long
enough to be totally beyond reach, but we still had to find a
deprogrammer. She was full of crazy ideas at first, but she's
starting to quieten down. I'm paying for her to have full-time
treatment.'

Deprogramming was not a technique with which I was familiar, but the image it evoked sent a chill of recognition through
my bones. It suggested that when someone's ideas don't quite
fit the normal pattern, you just bring in a mental mechanic, a
deprogrammer, to fuse the circuits. As simple as the wiping out
of memory with the application of jelly on the forehead and two
small electric buttons. I lay back on the sofa, remembering the
cheerful voice counting down from ten, the humming in my
brain before the explosion of white light, the light-hearted
moment of waking. And then, the moment when I met my first
question and knew that I was lost, a little lost sailboat floating
on a broad sea of meaningless blue.

'We couldn't let her throw herself away, you know,' my daughter said. 'But everything's fine now. We saved her.' Looking at
Eleanor's competent, well-manicured hands, the neat pearl
drops in her ears, I felt the anger flooding up my body in a tide.

'How do you know she was throwing herself away?' I asked.
'Did it never occur to you and your Joel that Judith might have
known what she wanted?'

Our eyes locked. 'Never,' she said. 'Especially when I knew
she'd been here and talked to you. I'm sorry.'

'You're not,' I said. 'And you're wrong. She was going there
anyway.'

She folded her arms; for a moment, I could see that she would have an intimidating manner in a courtroom. 'You didn't try to stop her,' she said.

'I could have tried harder.'

'Why didn't you?'

I wanted to say the truth, which was that I thought the more distance Judith put between herself and her mother, the higher the walls of the community behind which she took refuge, the better her opportunity for survival would have been. Wasn't that what I had done myself at Judith's age, plunging into a marriage which I knew would free me from my parents and their expectations?

I pushed the albums to the other end of the sofa and stood up.

'Let's go for a walk along the shore, shall we? Blow the cobwebs away.'

It was a beautiful afternoon. Baby gulls stalked in front of us on the water's edge, dowdy little brown birds hopping behind their stately mothers. Sandpipers ran on light red legs over a mirror of wet sand; frills of foam scalloped the shoreline into a bridal train and the wind tugged at our hair, whipping it across our cheeks as we trudged towards the distant granite cliffs.

'Look!' I pointed ahead of us. 'Do you see the cormorant standing on the buoy out there? Ten years now, every April. It can't be the same one, can it?'

Eleanor didn't even trouble to turn her head towards the water. 'Nature's your province, not mine,' she said.

'When I've been free to look at it,' I said and bit my mouth shut before I said something to spoil the pleasure of losing myself in the roar of the sea and the harsh cry and chatter of the gulls. The sound of permanence.

'So what did you mean about getting me looked after?' I asked the next day as we cleared up after breakfast in the kitchen. 'Are you planning on putting me in a home? Is that it?'

'You're seventy-four,' she said, holding the plate I had already wiped dry under the tap. 'And nobody in their right mind would stay here all year round.'

'I've managed fine for a quarter of a century,' I said. 'No thanks to you.'

'I'd have come more often if you didn't make life so imposs-ible,' she said. 'Insulting me. Treating me as though I hadn't progressed beyond being ten years old. Have you realised that I'm past forty-five?'

'You're fifty,' I said. 'And you've never liked coming here. You're a city woman. Look at your hands. White as satin. Catch you caring for this garden.'

'I've never been given the opportunity,' she said. 'You're too afraid of losing control.'

I nodded at the silver bulk of her smart hired car, blocking my view of the lower lawn. 'That's yours? Well, let's get this over with. I'll put my coat on and we'll drive up to The Towers, since I imagine that's where you've reserved a place for me.'

'Stop that! Just stop it,' she said and I saw that her face was white as the wall. For a moment, I felt stricken. Then I reminded myself of the agenda to my loving daughter's visit. It was clear enough: get Mother in The Towers and the old house on the market. I couldn't blame her. I wouldn't have treated my seventy-four-year-old mother any differently if she had lived that long, and nobody could have raised money on a property with more alacrity than I had when I sold the house in Louisburg Square. I hadn't even allowed a day to elapse after my mother's funeral. As you have done to others, so shall it be done to you. And that is how it is, how it goes on.

The Towers used to be Falmouth's smartest hotel at the begin-ning of the century. Whitneys and Astors used to stay there; the children of Vanderbilts and Morgans were coached by former tennis stars on courts as smoothly striped as satin hat-boxes. I hadn't visited the place since I was a girl. The conversion was blandly tasteful and handsome flower arrangements almost obscured the odour of incontinent senility.

'We think we've succeeded in retaining a gracious atmosphere,' the superintendent simpered as she showed us around. 'And the views are beautiful.'

'Not so beautiful as mine,' I said. 'But they're pretty enough. I don't see any –'

'Guests?' She smiled. 'We have no patients here, Mrs Brewster. We are all friends, all one happy family.'

'How delightful,' I said. 'And such a quiet family, too.'

'Most of our guests keep to their rooms,' she said, smiling a little harder. 'Not all of them are so agile as you, Mrs Brewster.' She asked us to wait while she fetched one of the daily menus for us to inspect. The moment she was out of sight, I picked up my bag.

'No,' I said. 'I'm sure I ought to be grateful for your concern and foresight, but no. You take me home, and you take me now.'

'I can't understand you,' Eleanor said as she drove past the porter's gate and turned onto the coast road. 'How can you possibly prefer freezing and half starving yourself in a house where you never see a soul to being warm, well fed and with plenty of kind, civilised people around you?'

'Independence,' I said. 'I've made my declaration and I'm not changing it.' I wound down the window and leaned out, drawing the salty sea-wind into my lungs until I started to cough.

'There!' Eleanor said. 'You're so childish, Mother.' And she sighed loudly, meaning me to hear.

'Anyway,' I said as we reached home, 'I've got Joe Finnis to help me. And it might interest you to know that he works here in exchange for his lodging and twenty dollars a week. You could learn a lot from Joe, Eleanor. You could think of what pleased me instead of laying plans to put me out of the house. Well, it's not for sale yet, not until I'm finished.'

'With what?' Standing on the other side of the car, she glared at me. No, I'm exaggerating. Eleanor does not glare. She gave me a meditative look. 'With the book? I wonder what version of the past you're going to offer, Mother. How, for example, do you explain what happened when I was eight? You never told me.'

I felt a little giddy when she said that. 'I never mentioned a book to Judith. Who told you?'

'Ask Joe Finnis who pays the rest of his wages,' she said, and she laughed with the first look of real pleasure I had seen since her arrival. 'Independent! Did you really think you could live here, unguarded, after what happened? After fifteen years of being locked away?' She leaned across the hood. 'Joe worked at the hospital. He's experienced. So, you see, I do care about you, Mother.'

She left that afternoon. Later, I went down to the shore. I swam straight out, cutting through the icy waves, emptying my mind of anger with every long, level stroke. I filled my head with images of night and water, the long and liquid lines of sea and sky.

I have always thought of Joe Finnis as a boy, comparing him to myself. His face is square, his eyes are pale blue and full of light. He could, I suppose, be fifty, old enough to have cared for me when I was at the last hospital. I took him on as an untrained gardener. I only asked for a character reference. Could she be telling the truth?

I told him, quite casually, one day the following week, that Judith had gone home to her mother.

'I'm glad,' he said.

'She told me about the study you've made of ants,' I said. 'You never told me.'

'You never asked,' he said. 'It's a hobby. I like to keep myself occupied.'

I had nothing to keep me where he was digging over the flower bed, but I lingered. 'Anything else I should know?'

He lifted his head for a moment. 'I don't think so, Mrs Brewster. We're two of a kind, you and I. We both like our privacy.'

I felt awkward about pressing him, but I decided to make one more attempt. 'I've been trying to remember what it was you did before you came here. I'm sure you told me.'

He has a good smile, Joe, wide and guileless. 'I think I'll start spraying the fruit trees this afternoon, if the weather holds,' he said. 'The forecast's good.'

I didn't resume the conversation. And now, at the end of another week, I'm ready to believe Eleanor made a story up to spite me for not complying with her wishes.

She is capable of that.

I've never trusted her.

11

New Jersey, 1931–1935

WE LIVED ON a farm, but it wasn't ours. We couldn't do a thing to it without old Mrs Goodhart reminding us, ever so kindly, that they wanted to come back from the Princeton house and find everything just as it had been. That was what we were there for, to preserve, not innovate. The nearest we had come to proper farming at Red Road was to care for the Goodharts' little flock of bantams. But farming was the way of life I settled on for us, nothing too ambitious, but a comfortable, regular existence.

Nothing could bring my spirits down faster than a mention by Chance of the fact that he was missing the Village. Isabel wrote me that the life of people in cities is like that of animals caged in a zoo; even the highest windows, she wrote, offer you nothing but a way out. I shivered when I read that. Isabel had fallen from a window and nearly killed herself a few years earlier – Bill said that only a miracle had saved her life. I could imagine myself doing something like that, ending life as easily as by the crack of a pane of glass.

The country would keep me safe, wrap me in routine, plait me in a ring of fat green hills, docile as a cow in a well-fenced field. I knew the prison I wanted.

My parents died in the summer of 1933. And with the closing of that part of my life, my funny moods slipped away.

I waited until October, when the renewal of the lease on Red Road Farm came up, to discuss the future with Chance. I hadn't told him until then just how much money had been raised by the Boston house sale; I wanted to have my own mind clear before he could crush me with the steamroller of his own determination. 'It's not as much as it might have been,' I said, 'but enough for a new start.'

I saw the glint in his eyes and knew he was thinking of a new printing press, an apartment, a little brownstone even, back in New York. I felt sorry for him, but not sorry enough to sacrifice myself.

'Most of all,' I told him, 'I'd like to go back up to the Cape, to live by the sea again. But I know you wouldn't want to be too far from Bill and Annie, and from the city. It wouldn't be fair on you.'

'All right,' he said. 'What's the plan?'

All the time I was telling him, I could see him twisting a yellow pencil in his fingers, winding it in and out, pressing the stub into his palm. His face was blank as a wall; everything he thought was in the working of his hand. I imagined that I was the pencil as I saw it snap.

'You'll still have plenty of time to read and write,' I said. 'But it's not practical for us to rely on your literary interests to do anything more than drain our resources. Dreaming won't pay the food bills.'

'You want us to be like the Taylors,' he said.

I folded my arms. 'They're your friends. And what's wrong with living like other people? Anyhow, Isabel says –'

'Don't,' he said, and he held his hand up as if he was warding me off. 'I'm not interested in hearing Isabel March's views on our marriage. She's a great poet. Apart from that, she doesn't have an opinion worth a cent.'

'You don't like Isabel because she's cleverer than you,' I said. 'You're jealous. That's why you liked Gurdjieff. You could patronise him. He wasn't so bright.'

A line of blood flamed along Chance's high cheekbones, thin as a knifeline of blood. 'I didn't mean it,' I said.

'Didn't you?' He looked down for a moment or two, then shook his head and went towards the door. 'Your money,' he said as he walked out. 'My life.'

'Mine too!' I shouted. 'And mine!' But he was gone.

The house I found for us was in west New Jersey, looking across the broad grey snake of the Delaware to the fields of Bucks County, smooth and bright as squares in a paintbox. Driving to it from Princeton, we came through a winding green valley before the road narrowed to a track and started to climb the hill.

Appledown – its name spelled a circle around a picture of a plump red apple glued to the porch door – was badly in need of a new coat of paint; the owner, leading us into a damp hall, admitted that he always had trouble getting the fires to draw. But the rooms were light and friendly and there was a kitchen big enough to hold a convention, if that had been our wish. A year earlier, I would have noticed nothing but a wooden beam of a suitable height from which to hang myself; now, I noticed the row of iron hooks from which I could suspend burnished copper pans. I saw myself, warm and at ease in a smell of new-baked bread; mentally, I decorated the bare windows with curtains of a cheerful checked material.

'It's not altogether up to the minute,' said the owner, a dry, long-faced man with a curious way of rubbing his hands along the length of his thighs, as though he was washing stains out of his palms. ('Walnuts,' he told me later: 'I tried my hand at a walnut plantation. You don't lose the habit of washing the juice off you. The job's better left to dusky folk. They've the skin for it.') He showed us where he had installed a generator before adding that it didn't work and that oil lamps seemed a whole lot less trouble. 'There's plenty of wood on the place, though, and

139

you'll have no problems with the stove,' he said as Chance raised his eyebrows at me.

It wasn't for the house that I wanted Appledown but the land. The lower part of the hillside was tilled as an apple orchard and a row of peach trees grew in the garden to the back of the house. I knew nothing about peaches, except for a memory of the sweet white variety cultivated by Aunt Louise in her hothouse, but my summers at Point House had given me a sound knowledge of apples, enough to make me confident. (Now, I know it only as an indication of my aunt's hidden wilfulness and pride that she chose to grow apples on a cliff top, when every gardener she encountered must have warned her of the folly of exposing their delicate buds to salt sea-winds. I still ask myself why I have chosen to follow her in this futile challenge to nature.)

We were viewing the house on a bright February afternoon. The wind was hard as a leather whip, but the sky was of the bright enamelled blue that lifts your spirits just to look at it. Frost whitened the grass below the tips of the blades. Hands deep in my pockets, feeling more at home than I had done for years, I crunched up and down the hillside with Mr van Riper, the owner, nodding wisely as he explained the reasons for preferring a Ben Davis to a Thompkins King, the advantages of a standard over an espaliered tree.

'There've always been fruit trees here,' he said. 'Not much short of two hundred years old, some of the russets.' I nodded, not listening. I was back in memories of October mornings, scrambling through the high branches above Aunt Louise's head with a wicker basket on my wrist, exulting in the childish pleasure of being freed from the ground.

I realised that Mr van Riper was watching me closely. 'Know much about apples?'

I didn't want to sound boastful. 'I'm ready to learn.'

'Well.' He rubbed his hands along his legs again. 'You'll need a couple of hired men to help with the harvest and the crating. I can give you some names. You don't want to be taking strange folk off the roads in these times. The cellar holds round about two thousand boxes and, in a good year, you should be looking at a healthy turnover. Mind you,' and he absentmindedly reached out to fondle the knotted trunk of a Rhode Island Greening, 'a good year is something of a figure of speech. You wouldn't be well advised to overprice yourselves.'

We came back to the house to find Chance stretched out on the kitchen floor and bouncing Eleanor on his knees before she slid down his long thighs like a ski-slope to sprawl, screaming with laughter, on his stomach. Spreading her plump legs to straddle his, she looked indecent, inviting.

'She'll get sick if you carry on doing that,' I said.

Chance didn't answer, just picked her up and rocked her in his arms as he sat on the floor. Over his shoulder, Eleanor's eyes gleamed at me like bright chips of flint.

'Well, I think we're settled,' I said with a smile. 'I've seen all I need to make up my mind. Would you like something in writing, Mr van Riper, or shall we leave it to the lawyers?'

Mr van Riper looked at me thoughtfully before turning his pale eyes to Chance. 'Women have a way of changing their minds,' he said.

Chance laughed and shook his head. 'Not this one,' he said.

We moved in a fortnight later.

The Taylors told us we must be mad.

'Who's going to buy apples? Have you seen how many apple-sellers there are on the streets?'

'People have to eat,' I said. 'And there's nourishment in apples and nothing to the trouble of growing them. I know what I'm doing.'

Chance nodded at them. 'She knows what she's doing. And I've started a new project.' He put his arm round Bill's shoulder. 'Come and see the study I'm making.'

From France, Isabel sent a message of goodwill, a postcard showing a jolly red-cheeked girl with a basket of apples on her hip. Mortified, I sent her back a photograph of myself on my wedding day, to show how little I resembled a beaming market-woman. I still had no physical image of her.

The summer of '34 was hot as lust. Pregnant again, too exhausted to budge, I lay out on a long chair in the porch, while Eleanor sat hunched below me, scratching designs in her little sandpit. An old umbrella, its lopped handle thrust into the ground, acted as her sunshade. A white bonnet still hid her hair, straw blonde then, with a bit of a natural wave to it; her dress, as always, had been disdainfully pulled off the minute she was out of my reach. I lacked the energy to reproach her. I remember the telegraph-wire whirr of cricket wings and the tuneless ditty with which Eleanor accompanied her slow circlings in the sand.

In the room behind the kitchen, Chance sat with his feet in a bowl of cold water and with a wet towel draped over his shoulders, dictionaries tumbled around him like the broken columns of civilisation. I am aware that this sounds snide; could I be blamed for scepticism after being told by Bill that my husband's latest enterprise was a linguistic history about the common origin of all divine words?

'And how long's that going to take?' I asked. 'And who's going to buy it? Why can't he write something popular?'

'Popular?' Bill said. 'Chance?'

'You sound just like your friend Edmund Wilson,' I said. 'It's not a crime to be popular. Being a great intellectual isn't much use if nobody reads you.'

'Isabel's writing a book about queens,' Bill said after a slight pause. 'Queen Christina, Marie Antoinette, Elizabeth I.'

'Queen Isabel of Lavalle,' I said. He twisted a rose off its stalk and started fretting the petals away from the disc.

'You don't ever think of going out there? We both think Chance would enjoy it.' He paused again. 'He does love stimulation, talk, ideas.'

I turned to face him. 'Chance isn't interested in Isabel. He likes her poetry, that's all. And he doesn't need anything he can't find here.' I looked down at the orchard. 'Besides, we can't leave all this now. Let Isabel come here, if she likes.' I touched his ruddy cheek with my hand. 'I know you love him, but you aren't in charge of his life.'

'Neither should his wife be,' he said. 'In my opinion.' He started to walk away before I could think up an answer.

The heat never let up until the last week of September. We did as Mr van Riper suggested and took a couple of hired men from his list to help with the harvest. Too heavy to clamber after apples, I took on the job of laying the fruit in paper. Chance was busy with his research, but he left his desk to watch me as I did it the way I had learned, keeping a steady flowing movement going all the time, right hand to left.

'Waltz time!' he said suddenly. 'Listen!' And he started singing one of the new tunes – 'Smoke Gets in Your Eyes', I think – beating time along with the rhythm of my hands. 'Shall we dance, my dear?' We circled, laughing, in the dark, musty-smelling cellar until I grew breathless and had to rest against the apple-crates.

'Do you want me to take over for a while?' he asked, but I shook my head. 'Make sure Eleanor isn't getting into mischief. I like doing this. It's restful. I like not having to think.'

It was true. I have often been praised for the quickness with which I can set a table. In one of the hospital therapy groups, they told me they had never seen tissue papers folded into flowers with such precision. I still love the peace I get from routine, the neat, repetitive creation of order and lines. Apples lying tidily shrouded, six by twelve, gave me the same satisfaction I take in drilling a straight row of seed, or folding the corners under on a clean linen sheet. I like visible results.

*

143

My little Tom was born in November, in Trenton Hospital. He slipped out painlessly as a fish into water. Taking the breast, he gave me no trouble, caused me no disgust. Even his crying was always to the point, for a soiled diaper or from a need for milk. People in the hospital told me I had been sent a little angel for a son.

So I was.

Six weeks later, I was strong and well enough to agree to a Christmas outing with our friends. Annie's parents were prepared to care for all the children together at the Taylors' house while we took a fifty-mile drive north up to Paterson, to look at the Passaic Falls and the hundred stone steps which go by the name of Jacob's Ladder. Going in winter, we could count on enjoying the scenery in solitude.

I was glad of an excuse to get away. We had no neighbours at Appledown and, now that the first harvest was safe and dry in the cellar, I had little to occupy me beyond the needs of the children. Chance was shut up in his study all day and the view, pretty enough in summer, was austere, gloomy even, when the leaves had been stripped from the trees. Sitting in the front of the car, I jiggled my hands in my pockets, feeling the shapes of a little blunt-nosed train, the stuffed felt hands of a minstrel doll, complete with wire-strung banjo, the smooth glass lid of a compass.

The gifts, purchased for the Taylor boys in a Trenton toyshop, were not entirely altruistic. Jay and Louis were a few years older than Tom, but they were the only boys I knew. Four years was not such a gap; Louis could be a good friend to Tom when he went to school, shield him from bullies, help him if he fell behind. All my spare time now was devoted to plans for my baby son's future and to plotting his happiness. Towards Eleanor, however, I felt no such tenderness. She had her father's adoration. She had no need of mine.

'You go in without me,' I said when we arrived. 'Take Eleanor and Tom with you. I'm making a surprise.'

Sitting in the car's cold front seat, I pulled on fur-topped boots and a bright red cape with a hood, stuffed the toys into a cloth bag and padded over the frosty flower-bed to the nearest window. Peering in, I saw a scene of fairytale domesticity. Annie, Bill and the boys were all at the door, gathered together in a laughing, clamouring group above which, like a startled eagle, my husband reared his handsome head. Eleanor was astride his shoulders, her hands twisting in his hair as she looked around for admiration. Old Mrs Goodhart was cradling Tom and smiling at me through the window. Then, after Chance had said something, the adults all went out of the room, leaving the Taylor boys to play on the floor with a brightly coloured aeroplane kit.

I watched for a while as they went about the task of construction. It struck me that they had already decided not to look at the window. I tapped. They moved round, turning their backs towards me. Wincing as I scraped my knees against the stone, I hauled myself up and banged at the glass panes, flapping my cape and nodding my head. They turned then, and I saw the panic in their eyes before they started to roar. Scrambling off the ledge, I fell heavily in the flower bed, scraping my knees and covering my hands in scratches.

Annie rushed to bandage my cuts and to excuse her children's behaviour. They were over-excited. They had such vivid imaginations! She darted apologetic glances at me under her long lashes, like a frightened deer. The room thickened with a sense of apprehension and I realised that it was I who was being watched, not the children. They were waiting to see what I would do.

'She looked like a witch,' Louis, the younger boy, mumbled, his face down. 'She kept scratching at the window and making faces.'

For Tom's sake, not the Taylors', I would be graceful, generous. I bent to their level, smiling, holding out the presents. 'Don't you want to see what I've got for you?'

Ungraciously, they took the sack of gifts and slunk towards the back of the house.

'That's two members of the party who won't be coming to the Falls,' said Bill as he looked out of the window. 'We really ought to start. The weather isn't getting any better.'

The clouds were stacked in low pearly ridges above a thin crimson line on the horizon. Wind bent the black branches of the willows at the foot of the Taylors' garden to the hissing grass.

'Do you really need to go all that way for a walk in the rain?' Mrs Goodhart asked. 'I'm sure Nancy wants to see that the farm's safe.'

'The apples are all in and packed,' I said, but she was right. The little incident had upset me. I had lost my taste for the expedition.

'I've been looking forward to this for days,' Annie said plaintively. 'All the years I've lived in New Jersey and I've never seen the Falls!'

I have no recollection of an occasion when Annie did not have her own way. Mantled and booted, we made our way out of the door.

All that long afternoon, while the others were exclaiming at the noise and force of the white hurtling water, the way it swirled and boiled up between the rocks as it plunged past us, I kept lifting my finger to the air and feeling the viciousness of the wind's bite, fresh down from Canada, cold as a steel trap.

'Smile at the camera!' cried Annie, waving to get my attention from a higher view of the Falls. 'I can't put you in my book with a face like that. You'd hate me for it.' A thin ray of sun briefly illuminated the water, spattering it with yellow as I climbed towards the bridge, my shadow limping like a bad omen over the road ahead of me.

'Careful!' said Bill as I leaned over to stare down. 'You wouldn't want to be told how many people have gone over.'

I felt the power of the water exert its seductive pull and leaned out further.

'Nancy!' he said. 'For God's sake!'

I pulled back to let him see how tightly my hands had gripped the rail. His face was white as chalk.

The wind nearly took us off the empty road two or three times on the way back. Shivering in the dark sweaty cave of the car, Annie and I sang nursery rhymes and marching songs to keep up our spirits. Chance was threatened with ejection from the car when he started declaiming Lear's blasted heath speech and followed it with Coleridge's Ode on Dejection. A wizard's finger of lightning, slicing through the blackness to strike a tree not more than a few yards from the roadside, quietened us all. A sense of dread descended. When Annie's small hand crept over the leather of the back seat to fasten its fingers around mine, I gave a scream of fright. Bill, who never swore, told me not to be so bloody hysterical. Seeing, at last, the yellow windows of residential Princeton glowing wetly at us beyond the brisk metronome stroke of the wiper, I felt weak with relief.

'But you can't be planning to drive off in this weather, dears,' Mrs Goodhart said as Chance buttoned Eleanor into her green wool coat and velvet bonnet. 'Annie, make them stop for the night. Or come over to us. The beds are made up.'

I thought of the journey and the cold, unlit farm, five miles from the nearest house. Eleanor was pale and whimpering, not having slept all day. Bill, grinning, held up a bottle of claret behind his mother-in-law's head and winked at us. 'Best I've got,' he mouthed.

'The soup's on the table and Tom's sound asleep in a cot we set up in the boys' room,' Annie threw in for good measure. And so we stayed.

I had thought that I knew about apples. All I learned from my aunt was that they get stored in paper while they ripen in darkness through the winter, ready for a spring sale. Now, too late, I discovered that apples have to be kept at a regular temperature.

147

Let it go too high, and they rot; let it chill, and they wither. We didn't need the crackling radio voice to tell us that it had been one of the coldest nights on record in the Trenton area. The hired men had been dismissed after the harvest; Chance and I carried out the desperate, futile rescue operation on our own. We covered the apple boxes with every cover and quilt we could find in the house, short of the children's cot blankets – the covers from the sofas and chairs, the curtains from the bedroom rails, bath towels, winter coats. But the damage was done and, when we crawled downstairs from a sleepless night in a bedroom brutally lit by a full hunting moon, the apples were already beginning to blacken and shrink.

On top of that, in our frantic efforts to save the gathered fruit, we had forgotten that the trees themselves needed protection. Walking among their frost-bitten trunks for the first time on a damp and drizzling January morning, I trod through a funeral pyre of broken branches brought down by wind and the weight of snow.

Spring came and we had nothing to sell. It was one of the local farmers, in the end, who said he was prepared to take some of the crop for cider and some for adding to pigswill, at ten cents a crate.

I was just about ready to quit and move back to the city after the disaster, but nobody was willing to take a shabby house and ruined orchard off our hands. There was nothing to be done but to stay where we were and hope for a change in our luck.

Isabel, receiving news of our misfortune from Bill and Annie, sent a sympathetic note in which she begged us to reconsider the idea of going out to Provence where life was far – she underlined the word in red – from expensive.

'If that's what you want,' Chance said tentatively. 'If that's what would make you happy –' I saw from the look in his eyes that he was worrying about me, fearing a return of the depression which had followed Eleanor's birth. But I had no wish to go. Remote as was the life we led at Appledown, there was a radio to tell us of the savage, ugly things that were happening in Europe. Watching a newsreel in the little Trenton cinema, I had stared with horrified fascination at the flickering images of people being hustled together and marched away from their homes, at the patient, unsurprised faces of old Jewish men, and then a smiling group of Austrian schoolchildren, holding prized photographs of Adolf Hitler up to the camera's eye.

In bed that night, I dreamed I was back at Louisburg Square. Hands stacked earth around the bed, making a mountain of soil and ash that blocked me from the light. My father's eyes glittered at me from the mountain's stony sides; the roots were his hands, clawing at me, pulling me forward until ash filled my throat and earth caked my hair. I looked all the way down through the mountain to a river of flame and my brother was there, screaming and thrashing with his face turned up towards me for mercy. I couldn't move a hand to help. I couldn't free myself. Mountain roots held me fast and the body far below kept burning and shrinking until all I could see was a skinny black tree in a seething, scarlet river. I woke sobbing and twisting in the sheets I had torn from the bed, to find myself huddled on the floor, biting my knuckles and kicking out at Chance whenever he tried to get near me.

It ended with his having to drive me into Trenton and wake the doctor at his home.

I was soon myself again. The doctor said that what I needed wasn't foreign holidays but plenty of sleep and a sensible routine. After what we had been through, he explained, anybody might be expected to become a little overwrought.

But Chance flatly refused to let me watch any more newsreels. He said I wasn't going to put him through a night like that again.

PART THREE

12

New Jersey, 1935

IT SOMETIMES SEEMED as though we'd never get back on our feet again after we lost the apple crop. But I'd already known what it was to have a miracle happen. In 1925, I met and married Chance. And, ten years later, my uncle Caleb died and left Point House with all its contents, the woods, the garden, the lovely curving stretch of shore, to his beloved niece, Nancy.

'You don't have to take on the responsibility, you know,' Chance said as we sat under the old willows on the Taylors' Princeton lawn. 'There's a lot to be said for staying at Appledown.'

Annie, handing me a bowl of peas to shell, burst out laughing. 'Oh, lots! Muddy roads, an orchard full of dead trees, dreary rooms –'

'It's not so bad,' I said. 'We've had some happy times there. And we'd miss you terribly.'

Annie lowered her eyelashes at me. 'Don't be so sure. Time to tell them about the Boston office, Bill.'

'Boston!' Chance's face brightened. 'No! Seriously?'

'Annie, you are such a blabbermouth,' Bill said calmly as he reached into the bowl of peas and took a scoopful. 'Fresh from the hand of Nancy definitely tastes best.'

'You just ate your way into a new job,' I said, pushing the bowl at him. 'Come on now, drop the suspense. What's going on here?'

It seemed that *World News* had offered Bill the job of heading their new office in Boston. A friend had already told them about a handsome old house on Fayerweather Street in Cambridge, ideal for Annie and the boys.

'And it can't be more than an hour's drive from Falmouth,' Annie interrupted as Bill began to embark on a detailed account of the house's advantages. 'Talk about fate!'

We all agreed that the coincidence was remarkable, a good omen. For myself, I was delighted. I had been aware from the moment of receiving the lawyer's letter that Chance was unlikely to be overjoyed by the prospect of moving to Point House. He had no links with New England; for him, it would simply be another humiliating demonstration of the fact that he was dependent on his wife. Secretly, I had decided to sell Point House and stay on at Appledown if Chance showed signs of distress. He had given none, but I knew that the Taylors' news would make the move easier for him to accept. He would not be among strangers.

Bill rose heavily to his feet. 'You know who should be up there with us?' he demanded and looked impatient when we shook our heads. 'Isabel and Charles! Annie, how many times do you remember Isabel saying that she wanted a house by the sea? Well, what are telephones for if not moments like this?' He looked at his watch. 'Ten o'clock their time. Not too late.'

Annie shook her head. 'Bill, you can't. It's Isabel's working time. She won't be pleased.'

He wavered. 'Maybe not. But it's a special occasion, wouldn't you say? And we've never interrupted her before.' I was struck, not for the first time, by the reverent, almost scared way they talked about her, as if she were a supreme being, not of our world. She didn't seem like that to me in the letters I had received. A little obscure and stilted, maybe, but not remote. Not frightening.

A strange look passed between the Taylors as I watched them.

Bill shrugged and spread his hands in a gesture of defeat. 'Fine. We won't call.'

And then the oddest thing happened. The telephone rang. And it was Isabel.

Bill's big tanned face was pale as the bleached straw brim of his hat when he came back to join us. 'Well,' he said. 'If that isn't the most extraordinary coincidence! Isabel knew something of importance was going on. That's why she rang.'

I wasn't comfortable with these hints at the supernatural. 'But it isn't important,' I said. 'Not to her.'

'Isn't it?' Bill wagged a finger at me. 'Don't be so sure. She sent you a message, Nancy. She asks you to make room for her.'

A cold wind, or the sense of it, touched me. I found a queer picture coming into my mind of a dark and reedy lake. Across it, staring, waiting for me, was a woman dressed in black. I wanted to look away, but her eyes would not let me. I blinked away the sense of fear. How many times had I answered Isabel's letters by urging her to come back to her own country, to join us? Wasn't that what I wanted, to feel for myself, on my own territory, the sense of the protective grace which had enhanced our friends' lives? I saw that Chance was keeping his eyes away from me, looking up to the house porch where the Taylors' new nursemaid was laying out the children's lunch.

'Why, that's wonderful news!' I said. 'When?'

'Oh, not yet awhile, I shouldn't think,' Bill said, and I saw Chance's shoulders relax. 'Isabel doesn't have the same sense of time as the rest of us. It's just a feeling she has.'

'Just a feeling,' I echoed and wondered whether the involuntary shiver that made me reach for my jacket was of disappointment or relief.

I don't know why I picked out that image of the lake. Now, I'm trying to keep my eyes away from the mirror which hangs above the desk. If I look at its mottled surface for more than a few

155

moments, I begin to see, not the specks of age where the silvered surface has worn away, but the algae on a pond's still surface, a smooth stretch of poisonous green beckoning unwary feet forward from the level banks. I can feel those secret shapes that inhabit me crawling out of their hiding places. Drawn blinds don't explain the impression of sudden darkness in the quiet room. Out into the garden, then – dazzle your eyes with the spin and glitter of light in the leaves, or let them track the slow voyage of a plump cloud across the bay, casting a safer kind of shadow that carries no threat, wakes no memories.

I wish sometimes now that I had never begun this task. I am starting to feel the return of old fears. I am afraid of what still has to be written. There are ghosts in this house, and I am the one who has called them back.

'Writing is the work of a crook,' Orage once told me. 'Rehearse the story over and over again in your head until you have every detail clear. Then, and only then, should you begin to set it down.'

But what when the details keep changing? What when, having so long known yourself to be the victim, you begin to see, in the act of writing, another side to the story?

What answer would you give me now?

13

April, 1981

A MOST UNLIKELY day! But I have enjoyed it.

I was sitting at my desk, back in our first years as the owners of Point House, when I heard the heavy pad of feet on the floorboards behind me. Startled, I felt for my stick and raised it as I turned, ready to lash out in self-defence.

'Joe!' Heart thudding, I dropped the stick on my knees. 'You should have knocked. You gave me such a scare.'

He smiled. 'Ever used it?'

'Not yet. I could. My arms aren't so weak.' I took in his appearance. 'You're very smart. Going into Boston?'

'I've come to invite you to lunch in Marblehead,' he said. 'Time you came out of the house.'

I laughed and shook my head. 'Lunch! Joe, you know I don't go to restaurants. Don't be so foolish.' I felt bad when I saw the disappointed look on his face. 'Take that fancy coat off and we'll have some soup in the kitchen. Will that do?'

'Well,' he said slowly, 'it seems a shame to waste the car, now I've hired it for the day. There's a little place that opened by the harbour. Shouldn't be much of a crowd at this time of year.' He looked down at his hands. 'I thought it might do you good – you haven't been in the garden for a fortnight.'

A suspicion shadowed my mind. I wouldn't have put it past my daughter to be gathering the evidence to put me in The

Towers. 'Eleanor fixed this, didn't she? She's asked for a report.'

His puzzlement was so transparent and his hurt so obvious that I wished the words back in my mouth. 'Well,' I said, 'I'd better smarten myself up. You look quite a film star.' I wasn't flattering him; Joe in his Sunday best was a handsome man. When he smiled, as he did now, I wondered how many of the local girls had tried their luck with him. If there was, or ever had been a woman in his life, I knew nothing of it. Extracting information from Joe was harder than winkling a hermit crab out of its home.

Upstairs, I rifled my drawers for a stick of lip salve and dabbed my nose with powder. Anxious to make up for my rudeness, I knotted a blue silk scarf round my neck and pinned it to one side with a silver brooch.

'You look smart as paint, Mrs Brewster,' he said as I hobbled down the stairs, and I gave a silly little toss of my head, the kind of gesture Annie might have made. Don't be a fool, I thought. You're old enough to be the boy's mother.

The restaurant, a long light room with big windows overlooking the water, was almost empty and the girl who brought our food was quick and attentive. Joe wanted us to have some wine; I liked the way she nudged him away from an expensive choice.

'I owe you an apology, Mrs Brewster,' he said as we sat out on the veranda after our meal, drinking coffee and enjoying the play of gulls about the boat masts below us. 'I did work at the hospital. And it was your daughter who suggested that I might like to look after the garden at Point House.'

'And me,' I said, setting down my cup. 'She asked you to keep an eye on her crazy old mother, didn't she?'

'I knew you'd upset yourself,' he said. 'No, Mrs Brewster, you never needed looking after, not in the way you think. There's nothing wrong with your mind. But you'd been living in institutions for fifteen years. It's not easy adapting to normal life after that. She was worried about you.'

I gave him a long hard look. 'And what did you think when you saw me at the hospital? Did you think I was mad?'

He shook his head. 'You kept yourself to yourself. You never said much. I thought you looked pretty sane. But I wasn't on the medical staff. I wouldn't be the one to judge.'

Relief swept over me; I had been tormented by the idea that Joe might once have been my nurse, his been the hands that held me down.

'You know what happened, don't you?'

He hesitated. 'Sometimes,' he said, 'you get too many queens in an ant colony. When that happens, the workers gather round and spreadeagle them, sting them to death. All except the chosen queen. There can only be one. It's the way of things in nature.'

'Ants don't have feelings,' I said. 'Ants don't have hearts.'

We sat in silence for a bit, listening to the chink of cutlery behind us as the girl set the tables for dinner, the ringing of boat chains as a gust of wind blew a flood of bright ripples across the harbour. Joe leaned back in his chair, looking out to sea with his hand up to shade his eyes from the probing spokes of sunlight. His nails, like mine, were cracked and rimmed with dirt. I found it difficult to imagine why he would choose to work in the grey edifice where I had spent the last five years of my imprisonment.

'What took you there? I can't see you setting out to be a doctor.'

He kept looking across the water, his handsome profile towards me. 'My father died in there when I was six. My mother wouldn't go near the place. She never took me to see him. I couldn't spend the rest of my life looking at the walls, wondering what it was like to be locked up on the other side for three years. I went there the day I left school and asked for a job. They started me off in the kitchen as a plate-washer. I spent a summer mopping corridors and dormitories. Then they said I could help out in the gardens. I liked that. I liked the peace of it.'

'If you stood on the roof of the hospital, you could see the hill where they hanged the witches.'

Joe gave a faint smile. 'If you climbed out on the roof, they put you in isolation.'

'I know.' My hands took hold of a corner of the fluttering tablecloth and held it down. In the early days at that last hospital, I joined a class for making dolls, no needles, of course, just little shapes to stuff. Sometimes I hid one up my sleeve. They never let you have anything that could be turned into a rope, but a doll could be hanged with a piece of cotton thread. I painted their faces with lipstick and knotted the thread round the bars. And then I pushed them out. Twisting the tablecloth into a plait, I remembered the brief spurt of joy I felt as I watched them fall and jerk. Joe was looking at me. I let go of the cloth, watched it slowly unfold.

'Wind's getting up,' he said. 'I'll pay.'

I leaned forward on the table. 'You say you know what happened. Have you heard what they said about me, what I did?'

He nodded. 'I have.'

'And what do you think?'

'I don't,' he said. 'No point in dwelling on the past, in my view. I admire you, the way you've carried on, made a life for yourself. Will that do for an answer?'

It was absurd, I know, but I felt quite flattered. Then I remembered why he had come to work for me.

'I suppose you admire Eleanor, too. Your employer. I should have been told about that before now, Joe. You should have said something.'

'Why – so you could have the pleasure of telling me to leave? I wouldn't have wanted that.' Unexpectedly, he reached across the table, laying his hand on mine for a moment. 'She does care about you. She has a hard time showing her feelings.' There was another hesitation. 'It's not her fault, what happened.'

I pushed back my chair and stood up. 'I'll be the judge of that. Don't you start lecturing me on what to think of my daughter.'

He held out my coat. 'Whatever you say, Mrs Brewster.'

Our drive home was silent. I was thinking about Eleanor. Before she left, she had offered to buy me a plane ticket to New York.

'I'll meet you,' she said. 'You won't have to lift a finger. You could see the girls.'

'The girls can always come and see me,' I said. The truth is that I have no wish to visit Eleanor's home. I don't need to travel two hundred miles to guess what it is like. Polished within an inch of its life. Soulless. Even on her visit here, she had the nerve to start mopping the floors when she thought I was in bed. I came down at two in the morning and found her on her knees, scrubbing like a dervish.

'You're wasting your time,' I told her. 'It was clean before you started. And you've left a trail of water all through to the stairs.'

Eleanor's self-control always impresses me. She took off the apron, put the mop back in the bucket and hung the cloth on the edge of the sink.

'Have you ever thought about visiting an optician, Mother?' she asked as she turned out the light.

I felt that I had been a bit graceless towards Joe. Still, he should have known better than to start asking questions. 'We'll do that again sometime,' I said as he left me at the door. 'But I'll pay for the meal next time.' And I held out my hand. He pretended not to notice.

'I'll be digging over the beds tomorrow,' he said. 'I finished pruning last week.'

Judging me again. I could feel it.

The trouble with me is that when I start brooding I never know how to stop. One of the penalties of living alone. Joe had started me thinking about Eleanor and it angered me to reflect on how little he really knew. Several times that week, I pushed my chair away from the desk and went to the garden door, intending to

161

find him out and tell him a few home truths about my precious daughter. In the end, I sat down again, ashamed of myself.

Point House, 1936–1939

It was late in January when we arrived at Point House. I leant forward for a first glimpse of the tall chimneystacks, standing guard on the skyline above the threadbare, shivering woods. The car wheels spun on an icy corner and the house was there, enclosed behind a wall of icicles as if waiting to be roused from sleep. I covered my mouth with my hand, not knowing whether I wanted to laugh or cry.

'There's the sea!' screamed Eleanor, hammering on the rear window. 'Sea, sea,' chanted Tom, snug and rosy on my lap. 'Sea, sea.'

Chance switched off the engine and got out. Slipping on the icy ground, he walked across the drive. Let him love it, I prayed. Let him see how beautiful it is. I watched him light a cigarette, stoop to pick a brown stem of wild parsley, its skeleton head powdered with snow. He blew off the flakes like a child puffing at thistledown before he turned to face the car. He was smiling as he came back. I wound down the window, lifting my face to the sea wind.

'What do you think?'

He stroked my cheek with the tips of his gloved fingers.

'You look just like you did ten years ago,' he said. 'The madonna of the balcony.'

I looked up, trying to read his eyes. 'And this?'

He smiled. 'Just now, I can't think of anywhere I'd rather be.'

Practically speaking, there was no great cause for ecstasy. My uncle had made little effort to keep the place in repair during the last years of his life when he was frail and sick. We spent the first few weeks carrying an army of buckets and pails from room to room to catch the swift erratic streams of melting ice that gushed

162

down through the leaking roof. Aunt Louise's garden, emerging from the quiet depths of snow, showed itself as a wild Eden. Roses and day lilies had spread beyond the neat lozenge-shaped beds; my uncle's little statue of the Madison Square Diana had been tumbled from her niche and throttled by a rapacious clematis. Panels of an avenue of wooden lattice work which had, when I last saw it, been assisting a young wisteria to climb and spread, were now held aloft in broken fragments by its gnarled branches. Nothing was quite as my memory had made it.

The air of neglect did nothing to hinder the pleasure I took in repossessing the place, making it our own. Chance was as much a victim as I of its charm and its demands. His work on the history of divine words was done in the early mornings before we shared out the job of educating Eleanor; the rest of his day was spent outside. By the end of a year, his New York friends would not have recognised the strong, brown-faced man who scythed a new path through the woods as readily as he stacked boulders at the foot of the cliffs against the wintry onslaught of the sea. Neither, I think, would they have known me in the happy, dishevelled woman with her hair tied up in a kerchief who crouched, tortoise-like, among the garden brambles, digging and weeding and planting from the moment when the sun was still only a glint of gold on the rim of the bay.

'I wonder what Isabel will think when she comes,' I said one day when we were carrying sacks of wood-ash out of the house to spread on the beds against the annual summer threat of slugs.

Chance shook out the contents of one of the sacks. 'What makes you think she will?'

'She said so to Bill Taylor – don't you remember? "Tell Nancy to keep a room for me."'

He glanced at me. 'No,' he said, 'I don't remember her saying that. Anyway, we're doing fine without her. No need to go looking for trouble.'

I didn't argue, but sometimes, walking alone and catching

sight of a yellow poplar in flower or a red-winged cardinal flashing through the beech leaves, I thought about the friendship we would have, the world I could show her. I was fond of Annie, but we would never have the deep untroubled affection for each other that existed between our husbands, for all their banter. I had always wanted a sister, or even a close woman friend. Dinah had answered that need for a time; now I had chosen Isabel for the role. I wrote to tell her that I had decided which part of the garden she would like best, and to describe the room in which I guessed she would most like to do her work. I never mentioned Mr Neville. I did not imagine that he would care to visit America. He sounded so very English.

Bill and Annie visited us most weekends. Annie and I took the children on expeditions and for picnics on the shore. Secretly, I rather enjoyed the superiority my knowledge of the area gave me, after spending so long on Annie's territory and living, to a degree of which I was always awkwardly conscious, on the charity of Annie and her parents. It gave me a surprising amount of pleasure to see her respectful stare when I showed her sons how a gull will break open a baby crab by dropping it on a low ridge of rock, or how the hermit can be coaxed out of his home by holding a lighted match under the shell. I don't think Annie had ever really looked at a sea-swallow until I showed her how to pick them out as easily as a crew of pirates in morning coats, skimming the waves. When I showed little Tom a four-armed starfish we had caught in a net and told him how its new arm would grow into place in a week or so with no pain or trouble, I felt that Annie was looking at me with real esteem for the first time.

'All this while, and I never knew you had so much information tucked away,' she said.

'Just things my uncle told me when I was a child,' I said. But I was pleased. Nobody had ever treated me as an authority before, and now I was the resident expert, the scholar of the sea shore. Nothing much to be proud of, I dare say, but I had not been overburdened with admiration in my life.

They were happy, those first two years. And then the accident happened and nothing again was quite as it had been.

It happened on a beautiful December morning, a week before Christmas. The Taylors had brought their sons over for the day and Annie and I were hanging decorations in the hall, while Bill and Chance went collecting driftwood along the shore. I remember that we had stoked up the fire with broken branches from a red cedar; the rooms smelt warm and spiced, incense laden. Eleanor had taken the boys to see a puppy she had pestered her father into buying for his darling girl. Tom, as always, trotted after them, hitting a ball along with a piece of wood I had given him from the log-basket. He was three years old by then and sport mad.

Round about midday, I looked out of the window and saw the Taylor boys playing with the little spaniel in the garden, encouraging it to run along a bank of snow with which they had enclosed the frozen fountain. I saw no sign of my own two.

'Ellie said she wanted to give Tom a special treat on her own,' said Jay. 'You know what she's like when she wants to do something. We couldn't stop her.'

Listening, I heard nothing, not a bird, not a footfall. Fear held me still. 'You should have tried, Jay. Which way did she go?'

'Why, is something wrong?' Annie, her dark curls crowned with tinsel and holly-berries, came across the room to join me. 'Did you look in Chance's study? You know how she loves playing with his typewriter.'

'She took the red sledge,' Louis said. 'I think she was going to pull Tom along the paths.'

'Then we'd have seen them through the windows.' I turned to Annie. 'Did you –?'

I hadn't finished the sentence when we heard it, a soft, distant sound, like a muffled explosion. I had just started my period; I felt a sudden flow of warm fluid leak down my thighs as I started running along the drive; behind me, I heard Annie's little leather-shod feet slipping and sliding on the icy stones.

'What is it, Nancy?' she called. 'Can't we slow down?'

Still running, I turned and shook my head at her. I could see from the shocked look on her face how frightening my own expression must have been.

'What is it? What's happened?'

I just kept on down the drive, scared of putting words to my thoughts.

Away at the far end of the woods, beyond Astarte's Grove, a small steep hill slopes down to the shore road. Eleanor had spotted it as a challenge to her sledge the first time she ran off into the woods without telling us. I slapped her and sent her to bed on that occasion. I told her she could sledge on the garden paths, nowhere else.

I knew she was a stubborn child; being forbidden can only have added to the thrill of disobedience. But I never thought she would take Tom with her.

I didn't need Eleanor's howls to tell me what had happened. The sledge had bounded straight over the ditch at the foot of the hill and out onto the road, just as a car turned the corner above it. Eleanor had rolled off as they skidded across the ditch, but Tom had been tangled in the sledge rope. The road was too narrow for the car to swerve. It had run straight over his legs.

It did not help that the driver, a young woman racing down from Maine to meet her boyfriend for a Christmas break in Boston, was hysterical. At least, Tom couldn't hear her. He looked so small. He was wearing his new red coat, a present from Annie's parents; he still had a tennis ball clutched in his hand. The blood was seeping through the red coat into the white crystals. There was no colour in his face; it was as if the

166

snow was quietly stealing his life away before our horrified eyes.

Eleanor was shrieking like a banshee, although there wasn't a scratch on her. I told Annie to take her back to the house.

'No!' Eleanor screamed. 'No!'

'Just get her out of my sight,' I said.

Annie didn't look at me. She scooped Eleanor up in her arms and carried her, noisily weeping, away up the drive. The woman and I lifted Tom into the back of her car and drove him to the hospital.

They kept him in for a month. His left leg – we were told to think of it as a miracle – was saved. The right one was amputated, just above the knee. The efficient young surgeon said this was no reason for the boy to say goodbye to a sporting career and patted me on the shoulder. A well-meaning shopkeeper from Falmouth visited the hospital with a ticket for the next Red Sox match and a baseball bat, 'to give the little boy something to get well for'. And how, I wondered, did he imagine a child on crutches was going to wield a baseball bat? But Tom seemed pleased; he kept the bat beside his bed for months after his return home.

I only saw him cry once, when I had to explain that his leg was never going to grow back. He could not understand the difference between himself and the starfish on the shore, or that the starfish, in this respect at least, was at a more advanced creative level. When he was six or so, the surgeon said, it would be time to think about fitting an artificial limb. For the moment, in his view, it would cause additional and unnecessary trauma.

Only I, it seemed, felt that Eleanor had behaved in a way which was not simply irresponsible, but wicked. She had wrecked her brother's life and she was to be allowed to go scot free.

'It wasn't her fault,' Chance said. 'She didn't understand the danger. She's only a child.'

167

'All the more reason not to spoil her,' I said. 'When I think how I was brought up!'

His light, clever eyes rested on me, thoughtful. 'Is that what you want for her?'

'Of course not.'

'Well then.'

'You're too soft. Can't you see she's got you just where she wants you?'

He smiled. 'Or where I want to be.'

She could do no wrong. It was all I could do to stop Chance bringing her into our bed every time she had a bad dream. I was never allowed to interrupt his work; time and again, I stood in the hall listening as Eleanor thumped her fists on his door, or kicked, and was received. I was an intruder; she was his cherished darling. When she and the Taylor boys started to write a children's newspaper, Chance had to be the editor and give Eleanor a typewriter of her own. He set it up for her beside his, at the same table. She would spend half a day in there and come out, swinging her skirts, pink and boastful, saying she had been helping him to write. I didn't say anything. I just looked at her until she dropped her eyes.

Tom was no better than Chance. You would have thought that the loss of a leg might have lessened his affection, but he hopped about after her like a pet sparrow. She only had to bang out a few notes on the piano or tell him she was Rapunzel come to let down her hair over the banisters, and there he was, listening and adoring.

So then he had to have a little desk set up in Chance's room and I had to listen to the three of them laughing and talking.

'I don't know how you put up with it,' I said.

'Nothing to put up with. They're no trouble, until you start shouting at poor Ellie.'

That's how it had become. I was always in the wrong.

'You have to think of the effect it must have had on Ellie when the accident happened,' Annie said with the slightly sad expression which was the nearest she ever came to a reproach.

'I think it had more effect on Tom, don't you?' No answer to that.

I remember reading *The Turn of the Screw* and thinking that our Eleanor was just like Henry James's Flora, a pretty-faced child inhabited by a demon. There were times when she looked at me across the table and said, whining: 'Mama's frightening me, Daddy. She keeps staring at me. Why does she stare like that?' Those were the times when Chance lifted her onto his knee and told her not to be a little piglet and tickled her behind the ears. Nestled against him, skirt all rucked up, legs hanging down, she would turn and give me a look of such – triumph.

The summer after Tom's accident, a German woman, a painter, rented the house nearest to ours along the shore for a few months. She invited me to visit her one day, hoping, I suppose, to sell me some of her work.

A tall, rosy-cheeked woman with her dark hair scooped up in a loose bundle behind her ears, she was dressed in a long blue overall that made me think, somehow, of a butcher. The smell of turpentine on her skin was so powerful that I winced when she shook my hand. She laughed, showing strong white teeth.

'You don't know how much a painter can miss this smell,' she said. 'In Munich, they won't let me work any more. I am what they call a degenerate.'

'A degenerate?' I sipped the mug of tea she handed me and tasted linseed.

'You don't know the term?' She sighed. 'How lucky you Americans are. I do not paint what the Führer's followers want. I do not present the image they like to see of themselves. So, I must not paint.'

She was still smiling when she told me how she had converted a cupboard in her bedroom into a studio so that nobody would discover what she was doing. A friend smuggled her art supplies into the house in a shopping basket.

'Nobody could know, not even my little nephew. But they always find out. The police came one night. They searched the house and they found the cupboard. They took everything.' She smiled again, as though she was telling me a children's story. 'But I am lucky. The penalty was not very big and here, away from Germany, I can paint as I like. I can go into a shop and order turpentine for myself.' She rose. 'So, will you come and see the degenerate art?'

My own taste is for landscapes and seascapes, quiet reflective scenes that calm my eyes. I didn't know what to say when I found myself in a room full of ugly naked bodies, yellow breasts and heavy muscular thighs sprawled out in gross indecency. I wanted to escape, but she was relentless, leading me from canvas to canvas, telling me how exciting it was to be working from the imagination. I could see that for myself; no respectable person would allow themselves to be represented looking as if they were ready for the slaughterhouse. I felt my head starting to ache.

'You don't like my work.' She stopped suddenly, her smile gone, looking at me with a piercing stare.

'It's not – not my style.'

'It's how we are.' She picked up a brush, twisted it in her fingers, set it down again. 'Perhaps the Führer should come to Boston. He would find himself in such excellent company. Oh, you need not worry,' she said. 'You are not the only one. Please go home now. I am not interested in polite apologies.'

I did not visit her again, but I was troubled by what she had said. I had put away the memory of what was happening in Germany; I had thought that Bill was being a little silly and melodramatic when he talked of terrible repercussions from the war in Spain. What repercussions could there be? What could harm us, in our safe circle of friendship? Now this woman had brought fear to our doorstep and horror into my mind with her frightening, disgusting pictures. I had hated them, but I could not put the images out of my mind.

The news came that Hitler had annexed Austria; when I asked Bill Taylor to explain what was going on, he drew me a map on the tablecloth, showing how Germany would continue to expand.

'Only over land, though,' I said. 'He won't go further.'

'Here, you mean?' Bill looked at me with friendly concern. 'Nancy, you do get the strangest ideas. Of course he won't come here. How could he? What place could there be for Hitler in America?'

'Evil spreads everywhere,' I said. 'And we don't do anything! Look at the English. They aren't doing anything. They won't stop him.' I stared at him across the table, looking for a response to my own feeling of hopelessness. But all I could see in Bill's eyes was puzzlement.

'You need to get your mind off poor little Tom's accident,' he said gently. 'We all know how badly it upset you. But he's doing fine, Nancy. He's a brave boy.' He put his hand out towards mine. 'I think you need something to occupy you.'

'I already have something,' I said. 'I just don't see why you aren't worried.'

'We're all worried.' His voice was soothing, cajoling. 'But there's nothing we can do.'

'Isabel could. She promised she'd come. Isabel would know what to do.'

But Bill was pursuing his own line of thought. 'Now why don't you think about trying to write a book?' he said. 'Get your teeth into some research. You're a bright woman. Annie's different. She's happy to look after the boys, have lunch with friends. But I've always felt you could do something more with your life. And you've a wonderful subject, sitting right on your doorstep. Why not write about the witch trials?'

I shrugged. 'I'm not a writer. We don't need more than one in the family.'

'Have a go,' he said. 'Just to please me. I think it'll do you a power of good to get your mind off the news and onto something a bit more remote.'

Just to please him, I tried. I spent a month researching the background before I abandoned the project. It didn't take my mind off anything. Everything I read about seventeenth-century Salem seemed like a sinister echo of what was in my mind now, in 1938. I could identify too easily with the terror that had driven men and women out of their wits in the summer of 1692. They were scared, like me, not by the visible world, but by the unseen. The dark ghost-haunted woods surrounded them, mirroring their own troubled minds. Walking the shadowy sunlit streets of the old town one day with my thoughts on the hanging bodies, the black choked faces, I felt a piece of cloth brush against my face and jumped, quivering with shock and disgust. It was only a cotton scarf, caught on the lowest branch of a tree, but the past had come as close to me as the dusty flutter of a dead woman's skirt, suspended from a height.

Bill was wrong. Writing was no distraction.

Listening to the radio in the kitchen, I heard the German writer, Thomas Mann, speaking at Madison Square Garden, warning us all to be alert, to guard against the presence of evil. I looked round for Chance and saw that he was swinging Eleanor through his hands, turning her until she had her nose pressed to his knees, her naked legs against his chest. Sickness rose into my throat again, although I couldn't find a reason.

'Listen, won't you?' I said and turned the volume up as loud as it would go, filling the kitchen with a storm of crackling words. I stood beside the set like a sentry on duty, forcing them to attend. At least, I succeeded in putting a stop to Eleanor's relentless attention-seeking; she marched out of the room after throwing a black glance at me for spoiling her fun.

When we had finished supper and Chance had gone into his study, I went out for what had become a habitual patrolling of the cliff top. Somebody had to be there, to search the long lines of the windblown sea for a sign of a submarine snout, an invader's presence.

Why could nobody but me feel the slippery approach of evil, sidling up on us, wrapping us round like a grey marsh fog?

Sometimes, when the days ran pointlessly along, like beads on a string, it occurred to me that the quickest way to reach an answer was to cut our throats.

We all found different explanations for Isabel's decision to return to her own country in the spring of 1939, but it was to me that she first announced it. Chance remembered the enthusiastic review he had written of her poems for *World News*.

'They don't rate her in Europe,' he said. 'And she doesn't sound to me like the kind of flower who's happy to flourish in shady corners. I don't blame her. She's a fine poet.'

I looked at him doubtfully. 'I wouldn't have thought one review was enough to guarantee much of a following here.'

'Isabel wouldn't let herself be directed by thoughts of personal fame,' Bill said indignantly. 'It's obvious why she's coming – didn't she send you a copy of her statement last year? Didn't you read it?'

Chance shrugged; I muttered something to fill the silence. The statement had been one of Isabel's most impenetrable utterances, a long rambling summons to all her friends to form a group and unite their energies in fighting what she described as a condition of world despair. The only part of it I had been able to follow was the sentence in which she defined this despair. Reading that, I knew her for my friend. She knew me. She understood.

Secretly, I wanted to take the credit, both for the statement and for her decision to join us, for myself. It was I, after all, who had written to Isabel almost every month for the past three years, reminding her of the promise she had made and begging her to fulfil it. 'We need you so much,' I wrote just after listening to Thomas Mann's warnings on the radio. 'I think of you every day. Everything in the world seems so hopeless and dreadful now, and I can't think of anybody I could trust to save us, only you. I'm signing this, but it's what we all feel.' (I was not, in fact, confident that Chance did share my feelings, however much he admired her poetry, but it was important to sound as warm and welcoming as possible.)

Isabel's reply, the letter I had just received, was not a direct response. She made no reference to mine, or to my invitation. Instead, she told me that her father had died: he was, she said, the only truly good man she had ever known. She had not seen him for thirteen years. 'My father wanted me to be a political figure, a crusader against injustice and poverty,' she wrote. 'My aims are not so different from his own, but poetry is my medium. I hate the vulgarity of oration, the treachery of rhetoric! At sixteen, I ran away from home. I knew what needed to be done. I knew that I had to free myself from his will and from the sense of obligation with which he was trying to shackle me.'

It took Isabel's letter to teach me about right times and wrong times. I don't think I would have been able to take up Uncle Caleb's generous legacy, to make a life for myself in the country of my youth, until the death of my parents. I don't think Isabel felt able to come back to America until her connection to her father was severed and she was able to return on her own terms, to live without guilt. Again, I felt the strengthening of a silent bond between us.

Later, when my thoughts were less forgiving, I wondered if she had come to America because she was scared. In the spring of 1939, I still had no idea that March was not her real name. I had no reason to make a connection between her own background and the fate of Jewish families in Europe. I don't quarrel with the fact that she wanted to speak out, to take action. I just note that she chose to do so from a prudent distance.

My only disappointment was that she said she would be

coming with Charles Neville. I had so wanted to have her all to myself.

They planned to arrive in May. The four of us convened at Point House on a bright Saturday afternoon in mid-April to discuss where they should stay.

'I think you've put on a little weight,' Annie said as she kissed my cheek. 'Doesn't Nancy look well, honey?'

'I wasn't ill before,' I said. Annie's smile was intrusively knowing.

'Not ill, exactly,' she said. 'But not yourself. We were worried about you.' She dropped her voice. 'So was Chance.'

'Nonsense,' I said. And I turned away to catch the attention of the others before she could say any more. 'Now, if nobody else has a plan to put forward, I'd like to suggest that we have them to stay here. We've plenty of spare rooms and we all know Isabel wanted to live near the sea.'

Bill shook his head. 'That's handsome of you, Nancy, and I'm sure Isabel would be the first to acknowledge your generosity. But you haven't met them. I don't think you quite appreciate the need they feel for privacy. Besides which', and he glanced at my husband, 'I'm not sure Chance would welcome the idea of sharing his workspace with two writers. And two writers with, wouldn't you say, Annie, quite difficult personalities?'

'I wouldn't share a house with them both,' Annie said. 'Not for anything. You'd have to give up two bedrooms, for a start.'

I looked at her in surprise. 'They're not a couple? Then why's he coming with her?' Evidently, I had failed to keep the resentment out of my voice; the Taylors looked at each other with broad smiles.

'Let's call it a spiritual affinity,' Bill said. 'My crude guess is that Charles would prefer something a little more down to earth, but Isabel is not in favour of –'

'Not at all in favour of,' Annie said with a giggle.

175

I felt ready to knock their heads together. There's nothing more objectionable to my mind than couples who talk in coded conversations. 'Of what, for goodness' sakes?'

'Why, sex, you sweet innocent thing,' Bill shouted with a roar of laughter. 'Isabel doesn't approve of it.'

I stared. 'Not for anybody?'

Trying to look solemn, he failed. 'I'm afraid not. Not much of a lookout for the future of the human race, not if we stick to Isabel's creed. Still, she's splendid in every other respect. Sound as a bell.' He shook his head. 'Poor old Charles. He's a handsome man, too.'

'I don't think he minds,' Annie said. 'After all, it gives him something to be wretched about. I can't imagine what Charles would do if he was allowed to be happy.'

'Well,' Chance said drily, 'it certainly sounds as though we're in for an interesting visit. Am I allowed to put in a suggestion?'

Knowing that he was far less enthusiastic than I about the prospect of our new, shared life, I was afraid he would suggest that a house near the Taylors in Cambridge might be the solution. Instead, to my surprised delight, he reminded us that the gardener's cottage at the end of our drive was empty, and that it had two bedrooms.

'I know it's a bit of a wreck,' he said, 'but you say they aren't due to arrive for a month. I don't mind knocking it into shape. Something to do.'

I wasn't alone in being struck by the flatness of his voice. Bill looked at him sharply. I hoped he wasn't going to ask in his usual slightly condescending way about the progress of Chance's book. His own success had given Bill quite a taste for running the lives of his friends.

'You may not mind,' he said, 'but I'm darned if you're going to do it. I'll take care of the repairs. Just hire the men and tell me what the cost is. Damn it, Chance,' he said as my husband shook his head, 'you don't even know Isabel and Charles. Tell him not to be such an idiot, Nancy.'

Through the window, I watched a small army dirigible moving steadily along the rim of the horizon. If I looked hard, I could see the tiny black figures on its deck.

'Doesn't look much like a German invasion to me,' Bill said and I blushed and laughed.

'I don't see how we can turn down such a generous offer.'

'Neither do I,' said Bill and there was a sudden sense of lightness and relief in the room. It was done. And, in a few weeks, Isabel would be among us, guiding us forward, away from the sense of deadly inertia and hopelessness which had dragged my spirit so low. Together, we would be strong and certain again, locked into a sense of purpose.

I turned as I felt a soft hand touch my shoulder. Annie was there, smiling at me, her eyes swimming with tears.

'I know,' she said. 'I know exactly how you feel.'

14

May, 1939

WE WERE AT the docks to meet them, struggling to keep together in a group as the crowd surged towards the narrow line of passengers emerging from the liner's grey flank.

'There they are!' Bill, the tallest of our party, raised his hand to point. 'Coming out now.'

Charles Neville looked older than the photographs I had seen on the jackets of his books. His face was pale and puffy under a mop of dark curls, streaked with grey. The woman walking ahead of him was small and slight as a girl although Bill had told me that she was thirty-eight, the same age as Chance and himself. She wore a spotted shirtwaister dress in buttercup yellow and a cream fedora was pulled forward to shadow her face. She could have been a society lady or a gangster's moll; I couldn't, from her clothes, have been sure which.

'Oh, look!' I said, 'they're taking photographs of her.'

'Nancy.' Annie shook her head at me. 'You're such a fan. Nobody knows who she is. It's Charles they're photographing.'

'Hush up,' said Bill, 'she's coming – why, Isabel!'

I hung back, feeling suddenly shy as Bill and Annie smothered her in embraces and compliments. I was, just for a moment, disappointed; she was so very unlike the handsome, queenly woman I had imagined. I watched her fiddle with her hat brim and push it back. Her forehead was broad and mild; above it, a neat schoolgirl ribbon kept back a soft cloud of wavy brown hair. Her mouth was small and firm above a strong, slightly rounded chin. Just like a governess, I thought, and then, as she began pulling her gloves off, she turned to look at me and I saw her eyes.

'No need to tell me who you are,' she said. 'I still have the photograph you sent me.' Her voice was flat, hard and void of any hint of an American accent; later, I realised that she had taken some trouble to achieve the clipped English which came naturally to Charles Neville. She took my hands in hers, stroking them as she looked into my face. 'You are kind to take us into your lives in this way,' she said. 'Very kind.'

I was still transfixed, like a rabbit in the sudden glare of a torch, by the snapping, almost electric intelligence of her eyes. Her hands kept stroking mine, soothing me. I heard myself stammer out something about everything being pretty well fixed and ready. 'Only we haven't quite finished work on the cottage yet –'

'Cottage?' She frowned as she released my hands from her own light clasp. 'But you wrote that we were going to share a house. You mentioned a particular room.'

Chance came to my rescue. 'Bill and Annie thought you might prefer a little privacy. But we're close by, only a few minutes' walk.'

She looked up at him, tipping her hat brim to protect her eyes from the stabbing brightness of the morning sun. 'So you must be Mr Chance Brewster.' And then she held one of her hands out to him with a funny little almost regal gesture. 'I was gratified by that review of yours, Mr Brewster. The meaning of my poems has not always been clear to the literary critics. Your interpretation was almost faultless.'

I didn't expect Chance to let that 'almost' pass without comment, but he didn't say a word. Instead, to my surprise, for he did not often make courtly gestures, he lifted her small hand to his mouth and kissed the tips of her fingers. I wondered what

179

they smelt of – lilies? frankincense? Something truly exotic, I felt sure.

'Bloody newshounds.' Charles Neville, after a brief nod of greeting to us, had turned back to Bill. 'I know it's your profession, but I wish you fellows could think what it's like to come straight off a boat into a pack of photographers.'

'Two,' said Isabel. 'I counted two. Not a pack.' She reached up to straighten his tie with a surprisingly wifely gesture. 'Last exit,' she murmured, bafflingly.

Charles Neville's full mouth suddenly twisted, as though he was holding back a smile. 'Games again? All right. Mortal portal.'

'Not bad,' she said. 'Terminal cigarette?'

'Choke smoke,' he said and gave her a familiar slap on the behind. 'But you're not having one. She's given up,' he added with a glance at us. 'For the twentieth time.'

'Not any more,' Isabel said. 'And not when you say "she" like that.' She turned a dazzling smile on Chance. 'You'll indulge a depraved woman in her hour of need, won't you?'

'I'd rather you didn't, old chap,' Charles Neville said in his comically polite English voice. 'She gets the most frightful cough. Anyway, it doesn't look nice for a woman, not in the street.'

'Isabel was born to break the rules,' Bill said gallantly and he drew a thin silver case out of his breast-pocket and offered it with a flourish. 'Egyptian – will that do?'

'Nectar,' she said, stooping over the cupped flame of his lighter. Inhaling, she blew out a perfect ring of smoke, something I had never been able to do without coughing. 'I can't tell you how sick I am of the smell of his Woodbines,' she said and I saw her dart a quick, malicious glance at Charles. Theirs, I began to think, was not a relationship in which to become too closely involved.

We had planned to take them back late in the evening after a visit to the newly opened World Fair; I had been rather looking forward to riding on the much-publicised rollercoaster which travelled at over eighty miles an hour, and to whirling around the giant Perisphere on a 'magic carpet' platform. But it was not to be. Charles said at once that he loathed being in crowds and Isabel had, it seemed, arranged to spend her first week apart from us.

'I shall stay with friends in Brooklyn for the first five days,' she said. 'We have important matters to discuss. They don't know Charles. You can take him with you. You'll be doing him a favour.' Lightly, she brushed his cheek with her hand. 'He can't bear travelling on trains. Or boats. He's been sick as seventy cats on the crossing, poor, sensitive thing.'

'Stop it,' he said, but not so softly that, even in the roar of the crowds swirling around us, we didn't all hear him.

There was an embarrassed silence. Bill broke it with his big, easy laugh. No problem there, he said. Charles would just have to stay with them for a few days until Isabel was free to join him and travel up to the Cape. Annie, I thought, looked relieved; she would be able to show off her illustrious guest at a few dinner parties without the anxiety of seeming to neglect or diminish Isabel.

'It's not that Isabel's jealous of Charles,' she had said to me earlier that morning while we were waiting. 'But it is difficult. Everybody's heard of him, you see, since the novels. They don't understand why we feel as we do about her. She isn't – she's not a name.'

'So that's settled,' Isabel said, although I was not aware of Charles having spoken a word. 'Time for me to go and find my cases. Oh, but wait! I almost forgot.' Delving in a soft velvet bag which was draped over her arm like a scarf, she drew out a little parcel, something wrapped in a square of black silk. 'A present for Nancy,' she said and she put it into my hands with another of her charming, confiding little pats. 'Don't open it now. Wait until you're home.'

*

'I haven't seen enough of her to judge,' Chance said when I tried to extract an opinion of Isabel from him in the car. 'I thought she was quite pretty.'

'Pretty! She's extraordinary. Didn't you look at her eyes?'

'Striking, then.' He smiled at me as he pulled up the car outside the house in Cambridge where we had left the children with the Taylor boys. 'Don't work yourself up so, Nancy. You know how I admire her poems.'

I did, but I wanted more. I wanted him to share my sense of passionate fascination. I had never known him to be so annoyingly calm and reticent. Still, he had kissed her hand.

Eleanor was furious to have been left behind: the Aquacade, glowingly described to her by young Jay Taylor, featured two hundred girls, a water-curtain and a swimming ballet. Tom had heard Louis' account of a circus and railway trip which went to every country in the world, with real wild animals at every stop. There were snivels in the back of the car, despite my explaining that none of us had gone to the Fair.

'How big was the liner?' Tom asked, rubbing his eyes. 'Bigger than a house?'

'Much bigger,' I said, unwisely. Tears broke out again.

'Why don't you open the present?' Chance suggested, a little desperately.

'For us?' Eleanor bounced on the back seat until the leather squeaked.

'For me. From Miss March.' Reaching into my bag, I took out the black silk parcel and unwrapped it. Two layers of soft crepe tissue, blood red, lily white, and then a box.

'A dagger!' Eleanor shrieked in my ear.

'A paper-knife,' I said, holding the amber handle up to catch the light. 'And a very pretty one.'

'Watch that point,' Chance said as I showed the children how well it could stab. 'It's not a toy. Pretty strange choice, I'd say.'

'She didn't give anybody else presents,' I said, rolling the tissue carefully around the blade. 'Just me.'

'*Timeo Danaos et dona ferentis*,' Chance said. 'And do you know who the Danaans were, Ellie?'

I slept for most of the drive home.

Charles asked us to meet them at Salem station, although there are any number of daily trains to Falmouth. The heat of the afternoon defeated their wish to be given a conducted tour of the town; there would, as I pointed out, be plenty of time for that.

'No time like the present,' said Charles, but he climbed obediently into the front of the car when Isabel said that Nancy must be worried about leaving the children.

'We aren't here to disrupt your lives,' she said.

She sat close to me in the back of the car. The weather was humid, more like late summer than spring, but she wore a dress of bottle-green velvet with a white satin collar. Several times, she took a lace handkerchief out of her bag and dabbed at the base of her throat, where the skin was pale and creamy. She looked older and more tired than when I had first seen her, an impression which was accentuated by the heaviness of her make-up. I wondered, anxiously, if she was expecting a lot of social goings-on.

'Just peace and friendship,' she said. 'But I do want you to take me round Salem yourself. Bill says you're writing a book about the witch trials.'

I shook my head. 'I gave it up. Chance is the writer, not me.'

'Everybody should write,' she said. 'It's only by writing words down that we can be sure they make complete sense. And that's what we're all about, isn't it, making a solid basis for human communication.' She patted my hand. 'Charles will help you. He's fascinated by witchcraft.'

'Not witchcraft,' he said, staring out of the window. 'Magic. All poets are magicians. It's part of our trade. Orpheus was the first poet-magician. You need magic to outlast a pack of maenads.'

'Speaking from experience?' Chance asked, a little drily.

'Certainly,' he said. 'Orpheus's head continued to sing and I see no reason to regard his resurrection as mythical. I did not become a true poet until I was reborn.'

I thought for an uneasy moment that he must be talking about reincarnation, but Isabel explained that Charles had been hit by a fragment of shell when he was at the front and left for dead.

'He survived, as you can see,' she said, lighting a cigarette. 'Charles is uncommonly resilient.'

'It was a resurrection,' Charles said solemnly.

'And that', Isabel said, 'was when he became a poet in the full sense. He was saved, you see. From all the poets who died, God had picked him out. The chosen one.'

'It's not a subject for jokes,' Charles said in a low furious voice. Isabel smiled at me.

'Nancy doesn't think I'm joking, do you, Nancy?'

'I'm not sure I know what to think,' I said, conscious of Charles's rigid back. 'It sounds very romantic.'

'Charles is nothing if not romantic,' Isabel said. 'The heir to Shelley. But I don't think that Shelley filled in his spare hours by writing potboilers.'

'There's quite a good view from this corner if we slow down,' I said nervously.

'Still, Orpheus,' Isabel said. 'That's quite a claim. I'm not sure that being torn to pieces by maenads is quite the same as being shipped out of the front line into a comfortable bed in a London hospital. Not really.'

Charles didn't say a word for the rest of the journey.

The cottage still smelt of paint and turpentine and I had not finished making curtains to hang at the bedroom windows, but Charles, who seemed to have recovered his temper, expressed total satisfaction.

'It's quite like that first place we lived in at Lavalle,' he said to Isabel. 'On the hillside – do you remember?' His smile was tender and I saw him try to take her hand in his, to make up, I supposed, for his surliness in the car. But Isabel was looking with horror at something in the corner of the kitchen where we stood.

'What's that?' She shrank towards me and I heard the soft rustle of petticoats under her velvet skirt. 'Why, it's a bat!'

'It won't harm you,' Chance said and he picked it up by the tips of the wings and carried it to the door to be released, squeaking with agitation, into jagged flight.

'It's a lovely cottage,' Isabel said slowly. 'You've all made so much effort to welcome us. But I did want to be with you.' She smiled at me. 'And you did promise me a place in your home.'

'Well, there's no shortage of rooms,' I said hesitantly, not knowing what Chance would think. 'But we thought you'd want to be together and it seems a shame not to make use of this.'

Charles lifted a heavy book from one of his cases and stood it on a windowsill. 'I'm staying,' he said. 'Isabel's free to do as she wishes. As always.'

Her smile at me was bright as a child's. 'I won't be any trouble. I'm a very good guest.'

It took less than a week for Isabel to transform our lives. Chance was happy and at ease. Charles seemed content to work in the cottage for most of the day and to join us in the evening for meals at which I tried to follow their conversations. It wasn't easy. Somebody only had to express a literary opinion for Isabel to fly off to some rarefied plane of knowledge, quoting Dante and Shelley and Voltaire by the yard and explaining how poets had a duty to change the way people think. Chance loved all that; I could see it gave him real pleasure to get into a dispute with Isabel, with Charles throwing his cent's worth in whenever they left him space to speak. I generally went off and cleared up the kitchen, waiting for the moment when I would have Isabel to myself again. Alone with me, she was a different woman, light and playful. She was the sister I had hoped to find. Sometimes, still, I pictured the darkness over Europe sliding towards us in a poisonous, enveloping cloud and wondered when Isabel would tell us what we were to do. She only had to take my hand and speak to me for the fears to ebb away. I felt – I can think of no better word – blessed.

It seemed a shame that the Taylors should be excluded from this sense of serenity. I could do nothing to help them. Every day, they rang with a new excuse and a request to speak to Isabel; every day, Isabel gave the same smiling response.

'Not yet. Tell them that and nothing more. Not yet.'

'What on earth does she mean?' poor Annie asked as I dutifully transmitted this message into the receiver. 'Have we annoyed her? Is there something we should know? She must have told you something, Nancy.'

'Nothing that I can think of,' I said with a guilty sense of triumph. 'I'm so sorry.'

The children were fascinated by Isabel in that first week of her visit, although they eyed her suspiciously when she came down on the first morning, dressed in a scarlet kimono and asking if she could grind some coffee. Eleanor stared at her with narrow, suspicious eyes while I explained that we did not keep a supply of coffee beans.

'Why do you put paint on your eyelids?' she asked.

'To look pretty,' Isabel said calmly.

'But it doesn't,' said Eleanor. I sent her out of the room, apologising for her rudeness. That afternoon, Isabel invited Eleanor into her bedroom and allowed her to make use of the tiny sable brushes, the small pots of creams and powders which she kept in a painted wooden tray on her dressing-table. Eleanor came out beaming an hour later, announcing that she was Princess

Cinderella and requesting us all to admire her rouged lips and blackened lashes. Tom, presented with a set of magic dice, a pack of trick cards and a conjuror's wand, glowed at the news that he was now enrolled in the worshipful company of sorcerers. Isabel's capriciousness was less easy for them to accept. Eleanor was sent away, weeping noisily, when Isabel found that she had, without permission, visited the magic tray of cosmetics a second time; Tom's pleading requests to be taught a trick to perform were met with a small, regretful shrug.

'I have none to teach,' she said, lying back on a sofa in the drawing-room and holding up a book to shut him out.

He stood his ground. 'Then why did you give me the wand?'

'To please you,' she said, reading. 'All the best sorcerers are self-taught.'

My heart bled for him as he hopped forlornly away, but I knew that there was no point in remonstration. Nobody, not even Charles, told Isabel what to do or how to behave. It was unthinkable.

She insisted on joining in our system of home education, a method for which she expressed strong approval. Charles was drafted in by her to give Eleanor lessons in French, which she did not enjoy, and English, which she accepted with resignation, while complaining that Mr Neville only talked about old foreign poets who had been dead for years and years. The classes ended after Eleanor informed me, weeping, that she had been smacked on the hand and called a little idiot for spelling 'ghost' as 'gost'. Mr Neville had then instructed her to write the word correctly a hundred times. When I explained, rather coldly, that we were trying to liberate the children from just this sort of schooling, Charles shrugged and marched off to the cottage for the rest of the day. I cannot say that I felt his absence to be a great loss.

Isabel taught the children history, in the form of elaborate and mysterious stories which had them both begging for their lessons with her to be extended. Listening through the window one bright morning as I weeded the gravel paths in the garden, I heard her telling them about Anne Hutchinson, a woman who braved the fury of her prim, puritan society to hold meetings for her fellow religious malcontents and who was massacred in an Indian attack after she and her family had been driven into exile.

'Massacred?' I heard my daughter say with relish. 'Was she cut into tiny little pieces?'

'As tiny as your smallest fingernail,' Isabel said. 'But they couldn't massacre what she had done. She was a brave, strong woman.'

'Was her husband mastikered?' I heard Tom ask. 'Why don't you say he was strong and brave?'

'Massacred,' Isabel said. 'We don't know about him. He just followed his wife.'

'Like Mr Neville and you,' said Eleanor, who had already drawn my attention to the way Charles waited on Isabel at meals.

'Mr Neville and I are not a married couple.' There was a small pause, a creaking of chairs.

'Why not?' I heard Tom ask. I listened intently.

'I do not believe in marriage,' Isabel said. 'But that is a grown-up subject and the lesson is over. Your mother has come to teach you some more geography.'

'Now, how did you guess that?' Laughing, a little shaken by the ease with which I had been discovered, I leaned in over the windowsill. 'Do you have eyes in the back of your head?'

'Magic!' Eleanor shrieked. 'Miss March is magic!'

'Like a witch,' said Tom, round eyed.

'Not in the least like a witch,' Isabel said. 'And I do not expect you ever to use that word in relation to me again.'

Tom, subdued, ducked his head, but Eleanor was not so easily crushed. 'How did you do it, then?' she demanded, although I frowned at her. 'You have to tell us.'

'I do not,' Isabel said. And then, unexpectedly, she smiled.

'But I will. Turn your head and look at the wall behind you. Mirrors give reflections, Eleanor. Without the help of witchcraft.'

To tell the truth, I was as disappointed as my daughter. Isabel, in my dazzled eyes, seemed entirely capable of sorcery. But the subject of witchcraft distressed her. When I took her on the promised tour of Salem, she was far more curious to see the settings of Hawthorne's stories than the weatherbeaten Danvers house in which Rebecca Nurse had planned to enjoy her old age or the hill on which, so I was always told, the accused men and women had been hanged.

'I'm glad now that you decided against that book,' she said, squeezing my hand. 'Not that I don't want you to write – everybody should, if only as an exercise in discipline – but I was troubled by your choice of subject. It would have done you no good.'

'Oh, I don't believe they were real witches,' I said. 'Poor things. And the power of those awful, crazy girls –' I shivered. I hated to think of what it must have been like to sit waiting for an accusation to be lodged and to know you had no way of fighting it.

'What if the girls were right?' Isabel said as we strolled along the harbour road. 'Did you ever wonder about that? Don't you believe in evil, Nancy?'

I slowed my steps to hers, conscious that she was having a struggle to keep up and knowing she would be too proud to say so. 'Evil in a general sense? I think what's happening in Europe is evil. It scares me.' I smiled at her. 'Not so much since you came.'

'That's good,' she said. 'But it's not what I meant. How about the evil which can settle, make its nest where there's a waiting mind?'

I imagined she was thinking of the covenant by which the early church bound its members to watch over each other, to become spies in the cause of general salvation.

'I think,' I said, trying to concentrate in the way which always made my head start to ache, 'when people are scared, when they're living in strange times, they get some comfort out of looking for a scapegoat to pin their fears on. I think that's what happened here with the witches.'

My eyes followed hers from the calm stretch of houses up to a cloudless sky, spattered white by the wings of circling gulls. 'So you don't believe in witchcraft,' she said.

I shook my head. 'If I don't believe in God, I can't see much reason to put my faith in devils.'

Isabel's hands came together, palm to palm, as if she was about to preach, then slid away to smooth her skirt over her hips. 'You have to believe in something, Nancy.'

'Well, you,' I said. 'I believed you could make our lives happier and you do. There's a belief worth having.'

She didn't smile, as I had expected. 'It's not enough,' she said.

'Not enough for what?'

'To protect you.' And, to my considerable astonishment, she raised her hand and pointed it at me. 'Neglect not walls, and bulwarks, and fortifications for your own defence.'

Two people had stopped to stare at us. I saw them whispering together and laughing as they walked on. 'You do say the oddest things!' I said, embarrassed. 'And I don't know what you're talking about. Defence against what?'

'I thought it would be familiar,' she said, lowering her hand. 'One of John Cotton's sermons at the time of the witch trials. He knew.'

Knew what? I wondered, but Isabel reminded me that we still had the museum to visit. Showing her my favourite prints and the battered smiling faces of the old ships' prows, I forgot my moment of unease.

A lack of servants and my alleged indifference to domestic hygiene were the only subjects on which our guest and I came near to quarrelling. Isabel was as feverish in the pursuit of dust and cobwebs as a princess searching for the pea hidden under her mattress. Once, teasingly, I told her that I suspected her of hanging cobwebs up at night in order to enjoy making a public discovery of them in the morning. She gave me a reproachful look. Her index finger glided along the projecting wooden frame of one of my uncle's whaling prints and was extended to me, slightly grimed. 'Did I steal down in the night to do this?'

'But nobody notices,' I said.

'I notice,' she said. 'You're just like Charles. He could live in a stable and never notice the dung in the straw.' And she sighed.

I let her have her way. Who would want to contradict a woman so remarkable, so superior as Isabel about a matter so trivial as the rearrangement of china ornaments or the number of times a passage should be swept?

They had been living with us for about ten days before Isabel chose to tell us what it was that she worked on in her bedroom every afternoon and – I had seen the light shining under her door – late into the night. She had, for the first time, consented to spend a weekday afternoon away from her desk. The room, she said mildly, was a little hot and the air in the garden was so delicious. We lay, all four of us, on the grass under the apple trees that fringed the lower lawn. Distantly, the sea swished and lapped; above us, the blossoming branches made Japanese patterns against a deep blue sky. I felt half asleep with pleasure.

'So are you going to tell us what the book's about?' Chance asked Isabel.

'A dictionary,' Charles said. 'Not any dictionary. The dictionary. The book of final, ultimate definition.'

'Don't try to be facetious, Charles,' she said.

'Me?' He pulled a blue cotton handkerchief out of his pocket and spread it over his forehead. 'The stage', he said from underneath it, 'is yours. Go on. Tell him about the book. But don't think I don't know what you're up to.'

'We all know that without a true understanding of language, an exact use of every word,' Isabel said in her clear lecturer's voice, 'there can be no moral development. The only way forward is through the use of a language in which there is no obscurity, no possibility of misunderstanding.' She looked at Charles. 'There was a time when I thought that Charles and I could achieve this together. But Charles has other interests.'

'I'm a poet, Isabel,' he said, very mildly. 'It's what I do.'

'It's what he does,' she said, still looking at his pink, half-covered face with amused, almost tender eyes. 'And he does it very well. But poetry doesn't offer us an honest language. It's a panacea, not a solution.'

'Allow me to interpret the goddess's wishes,' Charles said. 'I can't provide the level of dedication she needs. She's asking you to help.'

'I'd be honoured,' Chance said. 'If that's what you want.' He hesitated. 'And if you really don't object, Charles. I don't want to step into your shoes.'

Charles laughed. 'Chance, my dear chap,' he said, 'haven't you realised yet that you and I don't have the luxury of minding or choosing, where Isabel is concerned? It's all ordained. Just give yourself up to fate and be glad you had a part to play.'

Isabel threw a sprig of blossom at him. 'The rubbish you talk! I'm only asking for a little help on reference work.'

'What about your book, Chance?' I looked at him, puzzled. 'Do you have the time to spare? I mean, if it's only reference work, I'm sure I could –'

'Nancy, I knew you'd say that. You are so sweet,' Isabel said. 'But Chance isn't working on his book any more. I wouldn't have dreamed of suggesting this if I thought he was otherwise engaged.'

I kept on looking at him, trying to hide the sudden feeling of hurt and bewilderment that she should know more of his writing life than I did. He pushed his hair away from his face and leaned forward, his arms folded around locked knees. He didn't seem eager to meet my eyes and I couldn't wonder.

'It wasn't going anywhere, Nancy,' he said. 'I should have seen that for myself. It wasn't bringing anything new to the world.' His voice hardened. 'It was self-indulgent.'

A blackbird, perched in the branches above me, widened its beak in gurgling appeal for company or, perhaps, to proclaim its territorial rights. For once, I listened without pleasure. Six years, I thought. Six years, and you're ready to give up everything you've cared for and struggled over to help work on someone else's stupid dictionary. I didn't know what to say.

'There's some pruning I want to get done,' I said. 'I'll go and get my clippers.'

Chance came up to me when I was bent over a bush and laced his hands gently around me. 'You're not too cross, are you? You went off so suddenly.'

I leaned back against him, comforted by the warmth of his body and the easy way his arms enclosed me.

'Just a bit startled. You hadn't said a word.'

'Well,' he said, 'I wasn't sure you'd be interested. Don't worry. It's the right decision.' He kissed the back of my neck. 'You did want me to get on with her.'

'Of course I did. I do.' I tilted my head back, looking up into his eyes. 'Stay and talk to me. It's nice having you to myself for a while.'

I felt him loosen his hold. 'I'd like to, but I promised Isabel I'd sit with her for a while, go through some preliminary ideas.'

'It's only words,' I said. 'Don't you just look them up?'

'Nancy!' He pressed his mouth to the crown of my head. 'Sweet Nancy. If life was so easy. No, there's a bit more to it than that. Sure you don't mind?'

I smiled. 'Now, how could I, if it makes you happy?'

'Charles minds,' he said. 'He's putting a good face on it, but he minds like hell.'

'Let him,' I said. It felt rather agreeable, to be so superior in my attitude, so gracious in my understanding.

At dinner that night, Isabel wore a dress which was new to me, a dark blue velvet robe with an elaborate bodice of gold brocade. The velvet brought out the colour of her eyes. Her pale skin had caught the sun a little; she glowed almost like the harvest queen I had pictured from the Taylors' first descriptions. As soon as we had all taken our places, she announced that Chance and she would spend every afternoon in his study, working on the dictionary.

'Did Chance tell you he was once going to write a dictionary himself?' I asked, looking towards where he sat at the other end of the table. 'Do you remember, Chance? We all went to that speakeasy near the Brevoort to celebrate it.'

'The Brevoort. I used to go there,' Isabel said. 'Which year was that?'

'The year I stopped reading Yeats,' said Chance, at just the same time as I said, 'The year after we got married, 1926.'

'Well, isn't that a strange thought,' Isabel said. 'We could have met each other all that time ago. It's enough, almost, to make me wish I'd never gone to Europe. Perhaps I would have stayed, if I'd met you.'

'But then, my sweet, you'd never have met me,' said Charles. 'And we all know that goddesses need a willing human sacrifice.'

'All I know is that you've drunk too much,' Isabel said.

Charles shrugged and poured himself another glass. 'Well, Nancy, ready to toast the joint project?' He held the glass up, squinting at its colour against the light. 'Or shall we drink to our own exclusion from the glorious, unassailable and wholly unpublishable gospel of Isabel?'

'I don't think you know what you're talking about,' I said, but my voice came from far away. I felt dizzy and light headed; for a moment, as I looked down the table, I saw only darkness. I heard the soft low slop of water on mudbanks. I saw, as I had seen once before, a woman dressed in black watching me from where she stood across a stretch of reedy lightless water.

'All right, Nancy?' I heard Chance ask, a little anxiously. I smiled, shook my head and opened my eyes wide. 'Here's to friendship,' I said and drained my glass.

15

May–June, 1939

THE DICTIONARY MARKED the beginning of the end, but I didn't see it that way. It seemed to me that Isabel had chosen, in her usual graceful way, to divide herself between us. The children and I had her to ourselves in the morning, while Chance was given the opportunity to think and argue as he hadn't, I think, since his college days, in the sleepy afternoons they spent together in his study. He never criticised her now; I teased him for prefacing every second remark with the words, 'Isabel thinks –'

'Don't you think for yourself any more?' I asked. He laughed.

'It's like starting all over again,' he said. 'What a mind! Like a sword!'

Once or twice, I felt curious enough to linger in the passage and listen. Their voices were muffled; all I could hear was a rustle of paper and the occasional stutter of typewriter keys. My main feeling was astonishment that anyone could choose, when the sea glittered with light and the woods were cool and green, to stay cooped up in a dusty room. Even Charles went out every day now to pace through the marram grass on the shore where I saw him, a little forlornly, skittering pebbles across the backs of the waves or watching razor clams bury their length in the sand.

Eleanor was the one who felt threatened. She came into the

kitchen where I was presiding over the funeral of a small party of crabs. Standing on a chair, she stared morosely into the pot of seething water.

'Don't,' I said. 'It'll only make you feel sick.'

'I don't care,' she muttered, and she kicked the side of the stove.

'Go and play in the garden. See how Horace is doing.' (Horace was a tortoise Charles had found in the road and brought up to the house as a peace-offering to Eleanor, who received it in cold silence. She seemed, nevertheless, to have become attached to the idea of keeping the poor creature in a little enclosure of rocks.)

'I don't want to,' she whimpered. 'I want to go in the study.'

I scooped the pink crabs out of the pot and dumped them on the table. 'Well, you can't. Miss March is busy with your father.'

'I hate Miss March,' she said. 'When will she go away?'

I looked down at her scowling face. 'Not for a while, so you'd better stop hating her.'

'Tom hates her too. She's ugly. And she smells.'

'It's a nice smell,' I said. 'Lilies of the valley. And Tom only hates her because you told him you did.'

Eleanor, taking this as a compliment, allowed herself a small smile and gave herself up to admiration of her new red sandals.

'Daddy spends hours and hours with her,' she said. 'He likes her better than us.'

'That's not true.' I bent to her level. 'You stop this, Eleanor. Stop it right now.'

She moved away from me, twirling her skirts. 'I'm going to make her go away from here.' Her eyes narrowed. 'I'm going to make a spell.'

'Really?' I put my hands on my hips. 'And just what are you going to do? Stick pins in a doll? Say abracadabra? She *will* be scared. You've been spoiled for too long, Ellie, that's your trouble. You can't have everything your own way in this world.'

Eleanor's rages were violent and sudden as summer storms. Scarlet faced, fists doubled up, she ran at me, battering my knees. 'Can so, can so,' she screamed through her sobs. I gripped her by the arm and marched her to the garden door.

'Out you go and don't come back until you're fit for human company,' I said. 'And not one more word against Miss March, do you hear?'

Howling, she stamped away down the path.

After supper, pink and subdued, she allowed Isabel to kiss her goodnight.

I felt pretty pleased with the way I had dealt with the situation. No harm had been done.

The heat kept building. I had never known a May like it. Up in the study, Chance and Isabel worked with their feet in saucepans of cold water; in the kitchen, I wrapped a tea towel soaked in vinegar round my forehead as I rolled out pastry and chopped potatoes into the thin sticks which reminded Isabel of France.

The kitchen was my fortress, the safe refuge in which, with nobody to make fun of me, I could hitch up my skirts and dance to the piano of Eddy Duchin, Mr Magic Fingers, crackling out of the radio into the steamy air. I was quite annoyed when I spun round the table one day to find Charles Neville staring at me from the doorway. I straightened my skirt and picked up a rolling pin to flatten the pastry.

'You're like Isabel,' he said. 'A solitary performer. She used to go off to all-night dance halls when she lived in New York. On her own.'

I pressed down on the thin sheet of dough. 'A bit risky, I would have thought.'

He smiled. 'She likes risks.'

'Well,' I said, when he showed no sign of moving, 'and what can I do for you?'

'I thought you might know something about catching butterflies,' he said. 'A *nymphalis antiopa*, to be precise. A Camberwell Beauty. I've never seen one in England. You Yanks call them Mourning Cloaks. I saw three outside the cottage this morning.'

I turned off the radio. 'Well. Let's see. You'll find my aunt's old net in the cellar, bottom of the stairs. Then you need a pin, a box and a pinch of chopped laurel leaves. Prussic acid. But you'd better hurry. They don't spend all day in one place. Mostly, you'll find them round the pond in the woods.'

'I know,' he said. 'You told Isabel.'

'Off you go then,' I said. 'Happy hunting.'

He looked past me. 'The thing is, I'm not awfully keen on woods,' he said. 'When I was shot. It happened in a wood. Bad memories.'

A thought came to me. 'Did she ask you to do this? A sort of test?'

He gave a sheepish smile. 'Something like that. So, will you help me out?'

I didn't feel able to refuse. Sighing, I picked a jar of honey off one of the shelves. 'Just in case you don't have any luck with the net. Something sweet and sticky usually brings a butterfly in. Unless you're after Purple Emperors. They like a nice bit of rotten meat.'

I should have known better than to gamble my small hoard of knowledge against Charles Neville's erudition.

'Serbians think butterflies have the souls of witches,' he said as we walked along the drive. 'And the Maoris believe that we descend from giant butterflies. I wonder how that relates to the Greek sense of the butterfly as the soul? There are people in the Solomon Islands who choose to become butterflies after their death, of course.'

'I used to call them flutterbys,' I said.

'Pretty,' he said, 'but unsound. It seems to be connected to the German *Schmetterling*, *smetana* being the cream on top of the milk. The earliest form of butterflies were probably Brimstone yellows.'

I looked at him curiously. 'Is this the kind of conversation you and Isabel have when you're on your own?'

'How we used to talk, you mean,' he said, and his mouth twisted.

Passing the cottage, I was startled – and none too pleased – to see my uncle's little cast of the Madison Square Diana standing on the porch with her arm drawn back to spring an arrow at the woods. 'Pretty, isn't she,' Charles said affably, quite as if he owned her. 'Isabel brought her down yesterday morning.' He glanced at me. 'Quite rightly, in my opinion. She looks splendid here.'

I shook my head. 'It's not Isabel's to bring. I do still own the place, you know.'

'Dangerous thing, a possessive nature,' Charles said. 'You want to watch out for that. So, is this the path?'

Condescending pig, I thought. 'Looks like it,' I said.

Even on a summer's afternoon, I felt jumpy and nervous by the pond. Close on a month of unnatural heat had brought the mud near to the surface where algae floated, laying bright serpent trails of green over the stagnant darkness. The smell of decay was bad enough to make me cover my mouth with my hand for a moment.

'Not a place I'd care to visit alone after sunset,' Charles said with a glance at me. 'What do you call it – Hades' Mouth?'

'Astarte's Grove,' I said. 'It's just a joke. Local people like to say this was where the witches held their rites. But there never were any witches in Falmouth.'

'Wherever there's fear –' he said, peering across the water. 'Yes, there they are. And I count eight. We should be able to get one of them, don't you think?'

I handed him the net with the pot and brush. 'You ought. I don't care for the sport, myself.'

I had never understood why my gentle, kindly aunt should

enjoy trapping such pretty, harmless insects; it pleased me to see how easily they swooped out of Charles's reach. Eyes half shut, I watched their strong brown wings carry them across the black water and up to the height of the silver-trunked birches as he stumbled in the ferns and brambles, stabbing futilely at empty air. Looking down, I saw the alert red eye of a little whippoor-will watching me from under a dead branch. I felt a kind of friendly kinship with it.

'No use,' Charles shouted. 'I can't get near them.'

'Try the honey. Spread it on one of the birch trunks.'

Walking towards me round the pond, he stooped and picked something up from the grass. I saw him stare at it.

'What have you got there?'

'I thought', he said, standing over me, 'that it was all nonsense about the witches. So how do you explain this?' His voice was triumphant, excited. In the palm of his hand was a small figure of baked dough. Chips of stone had been wedged into the flat circle of its face for eyes; a few stems of dried grass lent the appearance of an Indian headdress. There was a pin stuck through the centre of the body. I knew as soon as I saw it whom the doll was intended for.

'Throw it away, Charles. Go on. It's no use to you.'

'I don't know about that.'

'Do as you like, then.' I turned my head away as he pocketed it and dropped heavily onto the ground beside me.

'So,' he said, oblivious, intrusive, 'how are you enjoying the new arrangement? Don't you feel anxious about leaving the two of them alone every afternoon?'

I stared across the water. 'Should I?'

His sour breath told me that he was leaning closer. 'You don't wonder what they – do?'

'Since Isabel hates sex and Chance is my husband, no, I do not.'

'I've slept alone for six years,' he said. 'It hasn't been easy.' He sighed. I felt pleased by this confirmation of the Taylors' account of their odd relationship. I did not like to think of his large hands on Isabel's delicate, graceful body.

The group of birches under which the butterflies were gathered was still dappled with light, but the soft plumage of an old cottonwood blocked the sun from the pond. The water was dark, unfriendly. I looked at my wristwatch. 'I ought to think of going back. The children have their supper at six.'

'Don't leave me,' he said, and he gripped my arm. 'Please.'

'Ten minutes,' I said. An hour later, we were still waiting for the butterflies to leave the last patch of pale green glimmering under the trees.

'Actually,' Charles said suddenly, 'I have met a woman. She was with us in London before we came over. I'm hoping to bring her here.'

I turned to stare at him. 'Have you told Isabel?'

He shook his head. 'Not yet. But she'll understand.'

'What complicated lives you lead!' I pointed across the water. 'There's your butterfly. Let's take the box and put it out of its misery.'

'Well, they only have a day and it has had most of it,' Charles said as we walked briskly round the water's edge.

'So well informed and you believe that old wives' tale?' I put my hand over the soft, furry wings and felt for the underside to press until it subsided, limp in my cupped hand. 'Open the box, Charles, don't just stand there staring. Now shut it.' He looked green, but he did as he was told.

'I can hear it moving.'

'It takes five minutes. You needn't worry. Laurel always works.'

'How long do they live, then?'

'Weeks. Months, in some cases. Not a day.' I stared him out. 'Well, that should make your gift all the more valuable.' I tried to keep my voice light, but I felt wretched, I wished I had stayed in the kitchen. Safe. Untroubled.

'I've put the children to bed,' Chance said when we came into the dining-room. 'Where on earth were you? I searched the shore.'

'Helping Charles.' My eyes were on Isabel, sitting quietly in my chair at the head of the table.

'I didn't intend to take your place,' she said, but she didn't move. 'Chance suggested it. I'm always more comfortable in a chair which has arms. I told him you wouldn't like it.'

'Don't be silly,' I said. 'Of course you shall sit there. You should have told us before. Sorry we're so late, but Charles was determined to bring you back –'

'Don't, Nancy,' he said. 'It's a surprise.'

'A surprise!' We all watched her as she smiled and turned the box over, shaking it, patting it, relishing the sense of mystery. Opening it, she pulled sharply away, her breath hissing through her teeth. 'But it's horrible,' she said. 'Please Charles, take it away. How could you?'

He snatched it up. 'Bring me one, you said. Bring me one. I spent all afternoon in that bloody wood on your behalf. You know I hate woods.'

'You killed it,' she said in a small, stony voice. 'I never asked you to kill it.'

Charles walked out of the room with the box in his hand. We heard the front door slam and the tension went out of the air.

'What a fool that man is,' Chance said when we lay in bed later that night. 'I wonder why Isabel ever took up with him. He's not fit to kiss her shoes.'

I stroked his back. 'At least we don't have to share the house with him.'

'You didn't mind about the chair?' he said a little later. 'It seemed awful, if she was in pain. You know.'

I kissed the curve of his shoulder, pressing my mouth to the warm familiar scent and taste of his skin.

'I know. I'm just so glad you love her too.'

*

203

Isabel was sitting up in bed and staring at herself in a little hand-mirror when I brought up her breakfast the morning after the butterfly episode.

'My first grey hair,' she said, and held it out.

'I can show you a handful if you want,' I said, amused by her anxious vanity. 'One hair!'

'The first.' She sipped at her coffee. 'My mother's hair went white when she was forty. And I'm thirty-eight.'

I pulled back the curtains. 'Look at the light on the water! You'd almost think you could walk on it.'

But Isabel's mind was elsewhere. 'What is it you're so afraid of?' she asked suddenly. 'What is it you want from me?'

I sat down on the bed, watching her as she absently started stripping the petals from a rose I had laid on the tray. 'Well, friendship. Comfort. A purpose. I don't know – you're the one with the answers. I only know that I'm scared of what's happening to the world.' I looked at her. 'Do you think there will be a war? Do you think we'll be safe here?'

'Listen to me, Nancy.' Her hands arranged the petals in a near star pattern. 'Once there was a man who had a vision. He had a vision and he started running away, calling to all his friends to escape while they could. He ran to his sister's house, he rushed in, and he jumped down the well.' She lifted her head. 'Let those persist who can bear the truth.'

I could see that she was waiting. 'I don't understand what you mean,' I said and I saw a weary impatience in the way her hands gathered up the petals. 'I'm sorry,' I said. 'I know I'm stupid.'

'You can't run away from endings,' she said. 'And things are ending. Things are running down.'

'No,' I said. 'No, that's not true.'

'True is what's inside us,' Isabel said softly. 'And I can't help you until you let me in. So I'll ask you again – what frightens you?'

'Things that happened long ago,' I said after a long silence. 'Things you wouldn't want to hear about.'

'Don't expect to frighten me!' she said and she reached for my hands. 'Tell me.'

But I thought of the way she had written about her father and of the love and reverence she had felt for him. How could I tell her and not cause disgust? 'I don't know you well enough,' I said. 'Not yet.'

'Not well enough!' She stretched her white arms up above her head so that I could see the delicate blue veins pulsing on her wrists. 'There you are – what you see is absolutely all there is. Clear as a goldfish bowl.'

'If you filled it with ink,' I said, laughing and somehow relieved that the moment had passed.

'Did Charles kiss you when you went butterfly hunting?' she asked as I carried the tray to the door. 'You needn't be embarrassed. It wouldn't be the first time. He's very susceptible.'

I shook my head. 'And I'm very married. It may sound dull, but I don't believe in behaving badly.'

'It's only behaving badly if you don't want to do it,' Isabel said. 'So nothing happened?'

I put away the memory of the little doll which Charles had thrust into his pocket. 'He did mention a woman,' I said. 'He spoke of bringing her here. So you can see he wasn't very interested in seducing me!'

She didn't smile. 'She's married,' she said. 'And don't worry about being invaded. She won't come. Charles is far too afraid of displeasing me.'

'Aren't we all, your highness!' I dropped her a mock curtsey from the door. She didn't respond, just left me to wipe the silly grin off my face and get out of the room.

I didn't give much thought to the fact that Charles might be jealous of my husband's friendship with Isabel until he challenged Chance to, of all ridiculous things, a wood-chopping contest. Isabel, the children and I were asked to judge the competition. Shortly after breakfast, we went to the edge of the woods where Charles, stripped to the waist, was waiting beside a young pine that had come down in the winter storms four months earlier.

'You can't win, you know,' I told him. 'Chance has been chopping wood almost every day for three years.'

He flexed his arm, showing off the swell of the biceps. 'And what do you think I did in France?'

'I thought you wrote books.'

'In the war,' Isabel murmured as we retreated to a safe distance. 'Charles's activities in the war grow more surprising with every year that passes. I've never seen him chop wood. I don't believe he even knows how.'

We watched as he stepped forward and took a wild angry swing at the trunk. Eleanor giggled.

'The blade's stuck, from the look of it,' Chance said kindly as Charles, purple with annoyance, tugged and swore. 'Shall I take a turn?'

'Trial run,' said Charles. 'I've got my eye in now. One – and – two! Damn!'

'You're coming down on it too heavily,' Chance said. 'Try and put more of a rhythm into the swing. Look.' And he drew the axe up above his shoulder until the light through the leaves flashed along the blade.

'It's like Arthur and Excalibur,' Eleanor said in a clear tactless voice as the trunk splintered and severed. She clapped her hands. 'Daddy's won.'

'Daddy's won, Daddy's won,' Tom chorused happily.

'I think Charles is going to kill him,' Isabel said, and her eyes sparkled. Instead, Charles picked up his shirt and draped it over my husband's shoulders. 'Victor's mantle,' he said. 'I don't know about anyone else, but I'm ready for a swim.' He looked at Isabel, but she shook her head.

'Chance and I have work to do. And you know swimming makes my back hurt.'

'We could paddle. You used to have time for work and play.'

'Times change,' she said and she slipped her hands into Chance's and mine.

'When are you going home, Miss March?' Eleanor asked as we strolled towards the house.

Chance shook his head at her. 'You don't ask things like that, Ellie. It's not polite.'

Eleanor gave us the length of a flower bed before returning to the attack.

'Have you finished the book yet?'

'No,' Isabel said calmly. 'No, we have not.'

'Will it soon be finished?'

'Stop it, Eleanor.' I smiled apologetically at Isabel. 'They're so used to having their father all to themselves.'

Isabel stooped to Eleanor's level. 'I thought we were friends,' she said. 'You don't really want me to go away, do you?'

It seemed to me that she spoke in the kindest of voices, but Eleanor stared at the ground with mutinous eyes. Not even when Chance gripped her by the shoulders and shook her could she be persuaded to speak. And then, to my dismay, Isabel drew out of her pocket the little dough doll with the pin still sticking out of its stomach.

'And what the heck is that?' Chance stared at it.

'I think your daughter knows,' Isabel said and she held it in front of Eleanor's crimson face. 'Did you do this?'

'No!' She started to scream and Tom, taking his cue from her, burst into a fit of noisy tears. 'You're frightening me! I'm scared!' She rammed her face into my skirt as if she was trying to burrow into a nest. I felt quite dizzy with the noise and the heat and the sense of this small butting body. For a moment, I almost wished Isabel would go away and then I saw the sadness in her eyes, the look of puzzlement and hurt.

'It's just a doll,' I said. 'Charles found it by the pond. It could have been there for years.'

Chance took it from Isabel's hand, turning it over. 'It doesn't look so old,' he said. 'But I can't believe Ellie would do something like that.'

'Of course she wouldn't.' I smoothed Eleanor's hair although, knowing perfectly well what she had done, I felt more inclined to pull it out. 'Nobody wants you to leave, Isabel. You know how we all love having you here. Say you're sorry, Ellie, and then we'll have some lemonade in the kitchen.'

'Sorry, then,' Eleanor muttered. But a halfwit could have told that she didn't mean it, and Isabel's face did not lose its wistful expression.

Was that the night on which, as we tossed beside each other in the humid darkness, Chance mentioned that he was going to move a spare bed into the study in order not to disturb me when he was working late?

'I know you've been having a hard time sleeping.'

'It's just the heat. Nothing to do with you. There's no need for a spare bed.'

'It's just a case of convenience,' he said. 'Come on now, Nancy. Nothing to make a fuss about.'

I propped myself on my elbow, staring down at him with sudden pain. 'What about Isabel? Will she be working half the night with you now, as well as every afternoon?'

'Isabel is a law to herself,' he said softly. 'As you well know.'

'But what's it all for? A dictionary: why should a dictionary be so important? Aren't there enough of them already?'

'Too many,' he said. 'Breeding confusion. Breeding lies. If only you cared about words, Nancy, you'd understand the danger better. Isabel is our hope. And she came to us. To you as well as me. Surely you're not going to squabble about a few extra hours of work?'

I shook my head. 'Do as you want.'

The next step towards a new ordering of our life. And I had done nothing to prevent it.

They had been with us for three weeks when Isabel came out into the garden and told me that it was time to call Annie. Only my sense of relief brought home to me the fact that I ached for a return to normal life. Aloud, I started to plan picnics, expeditions with the children, pleasant unadventurous schemes which would usurp the place of the dictionary in our lives.

'I'm so sorry,' Isabel said, a little stiffly. 'I'm not sure we quite understand each other. It wasn't picnics that I had in mind.'

The smile I produced did not come easily. 'You surely don't expect them to work on the dictionary?'

She stroked my arm in that charming and affectionate way she had. 'Don't look so cross, Nancy. I'll try to explain. What we are going to do is something quite difficult and serious. It isn't a game for children. Eleanor and Tom must learn to amuse themselves for the next few days. I'm sure they won't object to missing their lessons or to seeing a little less of me. But we – we have to concentrate ourselves, every bit of us, all of the time.'

'On what?' Bewildered, I looked at her.

'Thinking,' she said. 'Thinking and watching.'

'Watching what?'

'Each other.'

'And what good is that going to do?'

'That's for us all to find out.' She stroked my arm again. 'It's all we can do. It may be enough.'

Only then did I realise that this was the solution she was proposing, the answer which I had waited for so eagerly. I couldn't help myself; I burst out laughing. I laughed until the tears came into my eyes.

'Look,' she said. 'You've frightened the birds.'

'I'm sorry.' I shook my head. 'I couldn't help it. The idea of our thinking being the solution!'

Isabel's face was as composed as if she was reading a lesson in church. 'Please call our friends now,' she said. 'Ask them to come tonight. And don't underestimate the power of thought. You should know better than that. And you will, Nancy. You will learn.'

I don't know what came over me for I was so fond of her still, and so admiring, but the way she spoke was so condescending that it made me tremble. My arm flew up and the palm of my hand caught her across the cheek with a crack as smart as a whip. The force showed in a flat red stain on her pale skin. Slowly, while I stammered a horrified apology, she raised her own hand to touch it.

'Your husband said you had a temper,' she said. 'He warned me of this.'

'You spoke as if I was a child,' I said. 'I won't have that, I won't. I may not be a literary genius, but I'm not a fool. I haven't objected to your taking over Chance for the book. I'm willing to go along with these, these thinking sessions if you really feel they're going to solve the world's problems, but I won't stand for being patronised. This is my home, Isabel, I'd like you to remember that.'

She pressed her fingers to her temples, as if she was driving out a pain. 'I'm more than a guest,' she said, 'and you know it. Now go and call Annie. Tell her that we are ready.'

'I'll call her,' I said. 'But because I want to, not because I'm ordered. And don't think you can scare me by looking at me like that.'

'I'm looking at you', she said, 'as I look at everybody. It's not me you should fear, Nancy, it's yourself.'

'And tell me something,' she called as I went away from her up the path. 'If your daughter didn't make that unpleasant little figure and stick a pin through its heart, then who did?'

I turned, hands on my hips. 'Are you saying I did it?'

'Not saying,' she said. 'Asking.'

My indignation was so great that I couldn't trust myself to utter a word. Bending over the rosebush from which I had been taking a few sprays of buds to grace her dressing-table, I began to snip with short, savage cuts, letting the roses drop where they, severed, fell. Her long skirts brushed against my bare legs as she made her way past me.

16

June, 1939

'THIS WEATHER!' ANNIE fanned her face with her hand as she came through the door that evening. 'At least you've got the sea wind. It's worse than a steam bath in Cambridge. You look awfully pale and thin, Nancy. Haven't you been sleeping?'

'Not much.' It was true that I had lost my appetite for food, but I hadn't troubled to look in a mirror of late. From Annie's expression, I judged that it was just as well.

'We thought you'd never call,' she said, following me into the drawing-room. 'My, but you've been busy! I've never seen the place so shiny. But that's not it. I know! You've changed the furniture round.'

'Not me,' I said drily. 'Your friend.'

Annie opened her eyes at that. 'Seriously? Without asking you? Poor Nancy. Still, she has made it look bigger, more airy, somehow. So where is she? Bill went upstairs to look for her.'

'She's there,' I said. 'In the study. With Chance and Charles. They're talking.' My voice seemed to come from a long way off. I had been feeling dizzy and strange since my conversation with Isabel in the garden. I couldn't get over the way she had spoken to me, as if I was her enemy. 'Oh Annie,' I said, 'I'm more glad to see you than you can begin to guess.'

'Snap,' she said, hugging me. 'Three weeks! We've been

chewing our fingers off, wondering what was going on. Well, what's the news?'

'They're working on a new kind of dictionary,' I said. 'She and Chance. She keeps him at it.'

Annie laughed. 'That's how she is. The energy she has!' As if exhausted by the thought, she flopped into a chair, swinging her legs over the arm. 'So Isabel's living here and Charles is on his own in the cottage. I don't suppose Charles is too pleased about that.'

'I'm not sure.' I sank into a chair opposite her, feeling ease return at the calming spectacle of Annie's pink soft untroubled face.

'That's it,' she said companionably. 'You rest yourself. You really don't look well, Nancy. You've been working too hard. I can tell.'

'Just cooking and stuff.' I closed my eyes.

'So what do you think of them?' she asked after we had lain in silence for a few minutes. 'Aren't they astonishing?'

'I found him trying to iron her dress yesterday,' I said sleepily. 'He'd burnt a hole in the sleeve and he looked terrified. Absolutely terrified. She treats him like a worm.'

'Only because that's what he wants.' Annie looked wise. 'I made quite a study of them when we were in France. I know it looks strange, but they suit each other.'

'I could do with them being a bit more normal myself.'

'But it's so exciting!' She leaned towards me. 'I always thought the air felt as if it was vibrating whenever I was near Isabel. As if something was just on the verge of happening.'

'And it is.' Startled, we turned our heads at the same time. Isabel stood in the doorway with the three men grouped behind her. She was wearing her blue velvet robe and her hair was bound back from her face by a thin gold fillet. She looked magnificent. You could imagine men following such a woman into battle and dying for her. That, at any rate, was the impression she made on me.

'Why, Isabel dear!' Annie said, half rising from her seat. Bill shook his head at her.

'We are together for a reason,' Isabel said in her high, slightly flat voice. 'We are going to concentrate all our thoughts on the evil which is here, waiting to be uncovered. It will be done now and it will be done here, in this room.'

Turning in my chair as I sit here in the dusk, scribbling with an aching hand, I can call her out of the shadows, pale and radiant, her hands as white and pretty as two nestling doves as she held them towards us in a kind of benediction.

'Come,' she said, and Annie, with a little cry, ran towards her. I sat where I was, almost exactly where I am sitting now, gripping the arms of the chair.

'Come,' she said again, looking at me. I shook my head.

'What evil?'

'I had to wait until I was certain,' she said. 'Until I knew. There could be no mistake. The evil is here, Nancy. It is with us, in this house. We will wait and watch each other until it shows itself, as it must.'

I stood up, confronting her. 'You're wrong. We came together because we were worried about what's going on in Europe, not because of anything here. That's what I thought we were going to concentrate on. Well, weren't we? Wasn't that what all this was to be about? Chance? Bill? Annie? Aren't any of you going to speak to me?'

'Come to us, Nancy,' Isabel said again. But they stared at me coldly, as if I were an object of hate.

'Five against one,' I said. 'How can I possibly win?' And I went away into the kitchen and sat down with my head against the cool wooden boards of the table, keeping very still.

Annie came in after a while. I kept my eyes shut but I could tell it was her from the quiet metallic clink of pans being put on the stove, food being chopped. Isabel was no more capable of helping me prepare a meal than of ironing her own clothes. Goddesses don't trouble themselves with menial tasks.

'It isn't how you think,' Annie said softly. 'Isabel's been explaining everything to us. Nobody's against you. It's just a process to clear the air before we decide what to do next.'

'Clearing the house,' I said. 'Taking it over.' I lifted my head from the table. 'You know that story I told the children about the starfish growing an extra arm? Well, I'll tell you another clever little trick the starfish does.' And I told her how, when the starfish wants a clam supper, it hugs the clam and slips its stomach through the smallest gap in the closed shells and eats the clam up inside the clam's own cosy little home. 'And that's what's happening to me, if any of you had the brains to see it.'

'Nancy.' She put her arm round me. 'You shouldn't be talking like this. You'll make us worried. You do seem so nervy and odd.'

'No,' I said. 'I'm the normal one. He doesn't even share a room with me any more.' And I started to cry.

In the days of the witch trials, women were bound to a chair and ducked in a pond to bring the spirits out of them. I don't think they were doing anything so different in the 1940s when, to punish me for violent behaviour, they padlocked me into a covered bath of cold water for twelve hours a day, six days on end. The witches usually calmed down after a few duckings. I learned to be meek.

I could tell you stories to make your hair stand on end about the things I saw in hospital, the humiliations I endured. I could tell you about being beaten for telling a nurse that she had a kind face, about having clothes, even underwear, taken away, about trying to sleep on nothing but a brown rubber sheet that smelt of burning hair, about begging, crying for the privilege to go once, just once, into the garden of bright flowers where the nurses and doctors stirred their tea and strolled at leisure, within our view. I could tell you of the days and weeks of watching by a window for the visitors who did not come. I could tell you of the terror of the treatments that rob you of your past, stealing it away in a bolt of fire, a light that seems to crack your brain in half. And locked wards. And fear. And the hopelessness that follows broken promises.

I do not think I could tell you of anything that was more terrible than the days at Point House when I waited for the disclosure, for my fate to be sealed.

Perhaps, when Isabel first decided that we should join together as a group, she believed that she was doing something of importance in the world. Perhaps in a world filled with terror, she thought that a sacrifice, a scapegoat, would appease whatever powers it was she worshipped. And then again, perhaps she just fell head over heels in love with Chance and decided to strike me out of her path. The most generous interpreter would have to agree that her motives were, at the least, mixed.

It was never a battle between equals. Isabel believed in herself, more strongly than anybody I have ever known. All I knew about myself was that I would be at her mercy the minute I showed a chink in my armour.

I drove away from the house one afternoon, out to Danvers. I went to the meadow where old Rebecca Nurse, hanged in the summer of 1692, lies quiet in an unmarked grave. I looked at the wild flowers, pink, yellow, blue. I laid my face down to the earth and watched the busy ants running to and fro over channels of baked soil, so diligent, so purposeful. I listened to a couple of women talking about a painting holiday they were planning to take in Nantucket. I couldn't believe that life had once been as normal, as gentle as this.

'You shouldn't have gone without telling us,' Isabel said when I came back and walked into the drawing-room, singing at the top of my voice. 'How many times must I tell you, Nancy? We all have to take part. We all have to be here. Do you understand that?'

'I understand what you're trying to do,' I said. 'I do understand that.'

An hour later, I was sitting at the table, all joy gone, listening while Isabel, in language that seemed to become more elaborate and obscure with every day that passed, enjoined the evil to show itself, to make itself plain.

'We can only be worthy of the world when we are worthy of our own minds. Order must be discovered before peace can be discovered. Thought taking is the preface to order bringing. Through thought taking, we will expose the thing that takes order from us. The inside minds that work together bring outside happiness. Let the evil show itself and order will return.'

Sometimes, sitting there, with her eyes flaming at me like twin torches, I thought of the whales I had seen in old prints, of the harpooner, his weapon held high. He looked so proud, the harpooner, as if he was doing something glorious.

It can take hours for a whale to die, suffocating as the blood floods its lungs.

The days grew hotter. The nights were a blaze of stars. Four light years to the nearest star. Twenty-five billion miles of silent distance. No help for me in the heavens.

Sometimes, in the early hours before dawn when I could not sleep, I crept into Tom's room and sat by his bed, staring down at his face, soft lashes lying on soft cheeks, at peace, beyond her reach.

Eleanor spent all day in the garden, playing with her tortoise, keeping out of our sight. Wise Eleanor. She knew how to protect herself.

'Do you remember Stalin's moustache?' I asked Chance one day. (One day. Which day? They had all become one by then.) He looked at me with the eyes of a stranger.

'His moustache?' His voice was so polite and careful. 'No, Nancy, I can't say I do. Should I?'

'You said it was like Gurdjieff's. You always were capricious.' It seemed an important thing to say, but I couldn't remember why. Chance looked at me with cool and thoughtful eyes.

'That was you, Nancy, not me. You forget things.'

217

Perhaps I did. Everything seemed unsure. Stepping across a floor, I saw cracks in the boards and took care to avoid them. A white dinner plate glistened queerly up at me like the jellied white of an eye. Holding a kitchen knife in my hand, I carved my name into the table where I still chop vegetables. It took me a whole hour to do it.

Out of a pattern in the bedroom curtains, my mother's face stared down with a hard smile.

'I'm disappointed in you, Nancy,' she said. 'Fantasising. Making trouble. You should have died back then, not your brother. And now you're paying for it. That's as it should be.'

I saw him, too, although he hadn't been in my dreams for years. I heard the screams. I saw the burning van, bodies piled by a dusty road like lumps of charred wood.

I couldn't sleep. I prowled the house at night, touching the furniture, pulling the curtains open and shut, making a blanket lair for myself under the kitchen table. I felt safe there.

My senses quickened. I could smell the want they had for each other. I saw how she quivered when his body brushed past hers in a passage. I saw the tenderness with which he watched, even, the way she lifted a glass of water to her lips. Once, coming from the kitchen, I saw her body in his arms, her face turned up, her eyes fastened on his as if she was sucking his soul out. I walked back into the shadows, shivering as I hid myself away.

Bill and Annie knew what was going on. Five days after the vigil began, they left us to it. I watched them drive away and knew they would not come back until it was all over. Isabel didn't try to stop them and I couldn't blame them; there was no help that they could offer. But their absence increased the pressure on me to submit. Night after night, Isabel's eyes stared into mine across the table, willing me to break.

Even the care of the children offered no escape. Now, it was always Chance who, hearing a cry or a call, went up the stairs. She let him go without protest. He was not needed. His only function at the table was, like Charles, to act as witness, to record the moment at which the evil would unveil itself.

Once, passing her on the stairs, I took hold of her wrists and pushed her back against the wall. 'If you had the integrity you talk so much about,' I said, 'you would go to my children and tell them that you are planning to take my place. You would tell them that you will never leave this house until you have forced me out of it, you and your acolyte. The only evil here is the harm you mean to do me.' I put my hands around her throat, using no force. 'My home,' I said. 'My family.'

That was my first mistake and I knew it when I saw the faintest of smiles lift the corners of her mouth. She told Chance that I had threatened her life. Later that day, standing in the kitchen where I was kneading dough, my husband told me that the three of them had decided I needed treatment.

'We want you to see a doctor.' He spoke quietly, as if I needed to be soothed. 'You aren't well, Nancy. You haven't been well for a long time.'

I didn't answer him.

'She showed me the marks on her wrists,' he said.

'There were no marks. I hardly touched her.' I looked at him across the table. 'You don't need to threaten me with treatment, Chance. I know what's going on.'

'So you won't let a doctor see you?'

'I'll have lunch ready in half an hour,' I said with a bright smile. 'Mustn't delay the afternoon thinking session.'

The following morning, I woke to the sound of a car being driven away.

'Chance didn't want to wake you,' Isabel said. 'He's taken Eleanor to a summer camp. It will be good for her to be with some children of her own age.' She sipped at her coffee. 'Poor little things, they've had no attention from any of us for far too long.'

'That was not my doing,' I said. 'Or my wish. You should at least have allowed me to say goodbye to her.'

Isabel lifted her eyes to my face. 'It didn't seem a good idea to distress her unnecessarily.'

'And me,' I said. 'What about me? She's my daughter. Do I have no rights at all?'

'Of course you do, Nancy,' she said. 'You have exactly the same rights that we all have.'

'You won't take Tom from me,' I said.

She gave me a sweet, wondering look. 'But we all know how close he is to Eleanor. Don't you think it would be rather selfish to keep him here on his own?'

I stared at the floor. 'It's all settled,' she said. 'Chance is going to see if the camp can take him. I'm sure there'll be no difficulty.' She smiled. 'And then we'll have nothing to distract us, will we?'

I wouldn't go when they called me into the afternoon session after Chance's return. I sat alone in the humid kitchen, pressing my hands against the sides of my forehead as if I could keep my brain steady just by holding it in.

The heat was past bearing, like a weight of iron lying over the house. On the radio, they said we were to expect local storms. I went round the rooms, closing up the shutters. Tom was sitting on Ellie's bed, his arms around her pillow, his head nuzzled into it.

'We're going away,' I told him. 'We're going to leave this place, yes we are.'

'Will you read me a story?' he asked.

I tried. The letters jumped off the page at me; I couldn't put them back into words.

In Chance's study, I saw two heads lying on the pillow of the bed he had set up in the corner. It wasn't two heads, just the way the pillows had been pushed under the sheet, but the sight of them made my eyes swim. I picked up a pen and went to the pages scattered on top of the desk. I wrote EVIL EVIL EVIL all over the typed lines before I pushed them out of sight behind the bed. Then I went outside.

The sky was growing dark, turning from far-off lilac to midnight blue. The waves lashed the shore like little whips. I could hear them talking in the dining-room. I peeked through the window and there they all were, hand in hand, bent over the table. Praying for me to come dancing into the room, stark naked, with a carving knife, so they could ship me off to the snake pit. I smiled.

I went back into the drawing-room. I decided to call the Taylors and tell them what was happening, so they could come and rescue me. I went towards the telephone, my heart thumping. The heat was making me dizzy. I felt weak. I put my fingers in the holes around the dial. I couldn't think of their number. I dialled the first number I thought of. I heard the tone and tried to remember whom I was going to call. A voice spoke, a voice I knew. It said: 'Hello. Hello? Who is this, please? Hello?'

I stood there, dumb, shaking. I put the receiver down. Then I went up to my bedroom and locked the door.

I heard heavy steps and a voice outside the door, calling me out, ordering me. I shut my eyes. The steps went along the passage and down the stairs.

Far away, I heard the throaty wail of a ship's horn. There was a growl of thunder, a flash, bright enough to light up the room like a funfair. Then the rain started coming down in long, hard rows, drilling the windowpanes like gun pellets.

Time to go.

I went into the room where Tom was still lying on Eleanor's bed. Nobody had fed him. Nobody cared for him but me. I took a handkerchief and tied it round his mouth. His eyes were round and afraid. His foot kicked out at me. But I was strong. I held him fast.

The wind was howling round the outside of the house like a banshee, blowing the rain in my face. The tall trees bent and

moaned, sharing my pain. I ran across the grass, my feet slipping and sliding on the slippery green. A low sad sound came
from the woods, like the droning of bagpipes. I followed it in,
pushing my way through the undergrowth. I heard the crack of
a falling tree. All around me, the great trunks were groaning and
vibrating as the wind tore the leaves apart, opening up a waste
of black sky. I wanted to jump up through the trees and be there,
flying through the night with the wind and the clouds.

I felt my mouth twisting and turning as I walked on, kicking
the broken branches out of my way. Frogs can copulate for a
whole month in spring, I thought. Imagine that! And isn't it odd
that cats, which love to eat fish, hate to go in water? I wonder
what will happen to Eleanor's tortoise? Isn't there an island
somewhere, where people manage to live on seabirds? Seabirds
to eat, seabirds' feathers to keep them warm, seabird fat to give
them lamp oil. I could do that. I could.

I was in the grove and the pond was in front of me, all thick
with green velvet, like a carpet. Would it hold me if I walked? It
looked so soft and comfortable. Wouldn't it be good just to lie
down on it, to sink under the velvet, down into the black water,
soft lapping water, away from all the noise of the sky, the beating
of the blood in my head?

I took Tom a little more tightly in my arms and closed my
eyes.

Then I walked carefully forward on to the green carpet.

Charles must have felt himself the hero of the hour. He was the
one who, walking home to the cottage down the drive, saw me
running across the grass with Tom in my arms. Charles was the
one who woke the others and brought them out to hunt me
down. And Charles, so they told me afterwards – I remember
none of it – was the one who waded out into the water and
dragged us back to the bank. I hope it wasn't Charles who took
my sodden clothes off. I was wearing a nightdress when I woke

to find myself on the sofa in Chance's – Chance and Isabel's – study, with the three of them staring at me from the door.

'Let me be,' I said. 'I need to sleep.'

Isabel sat down at Chance's desk and the two men drew up chairs on either side. The Grand Inquisitor and her jury. I sat up on the sofa and folded my hands in my lap, keeping my eyes trained on her.

She was dressed like an Austrian governess that morning, clean and neat in a white tucked blouse and a sandy-coloured skirt. All in control. Chance and Charles looked shot to bits, by comparison.

'I blame myself,' she said. 'I want you to understand that, Nancy. You gave us your warning long ago. It was wrong of me not to take it. Reckless.'

I saw Chance put out a hand to cover hers, quite lightly, just for a moment. I just kept staring at her.

'The doll,' she said. 'I knew then. I knew you were using evil forces.'

I moistened my lips. 'Eleanor made the doll, not me. She wanted you to go away. She wanted her father back.'

The three of them exchanged glances. Chance seemed anxious to speak to me, but Isabel shook her head. 'Don't reproach her,' she said, as if I was deaf. 'We have to make her understand why we are doing this. It's important that she understands.' She leant forward. 'We know everything now, you see. It's all in the open at last, as it should be. The evil has shown itself.'

I turned my head away from her and stared at the wall while Isabel explained that they had evidence to show that I was not only mad, but a practiser of witchcraft.

'Witchcraft!' I swung back to confront my husband. 'And she says I'm mad? Oh Chance, don't tell me you believe her.'

'Quiet now, Nancy,' he said. 'It's for your own good.' His face was as solemn as if he'd been asked to take the Fifth Amendment. Charles was looking down at his hands.

I sat and listened while Isabel presented her evidence. I had shown an unhealthy interest in the events at Salem. I had, from the first days of marriage, revealed a strange side to my character. 'You have been violent, Nancy,' Isabel said. 'I myself have been the witness to that.' Watching her fingers touch her neck, I clamped my hands between trembling knees.

'Can't you just tell me what you want?'

'Not what we want, Nancy,' she said. 'What we have to do. For your own sake as well as ours.'

And then she explained that a decision, by common agreement, she said, had been taken to have me committed. Chance was prepared to request it. I was to be taken to a doctor, not our own family doctor, but a man I had never met, recommended over the telephone by Bill Taylor. Insulin courses were said to be effective. 'Whatever is done', she said, 'will be in your own best interests.'

I didn't speak.

Isabel rose to her feet. I heard the chink of car keys in Chance's jacket as he pushed back his chair. They looked at each other.

'Well,' she said. 'I don't think I have anything more to say.' She came towards me and, brave woman, laid her hands on the madwoman's shoulders. 'I'm only the agent,' she said, 'not the cause. You must remember that.'

I lifted my head and spat at her, full in the face. 'To peace and friendship,' I said.

It must have disappointed them greatly to find that the doctor was unwilling to accept that I was insane. Instead, he prescribed a period of rest in a nursing home. I behaved carefully. I ate what I was given. I went to bed when I was told. I didn't make a fuss when one of the other patients stole my coat, or complain when one of the nurses said that women who tried to drown their children ought to be given the death penalty. At the end of ten days, I persuaded the administrator that I was well enough to be released. I got on the bus to Falmouth and walked up the hill to Point House. Charles opened the door.

'Let me in,' I said. 'Don't argue. I want to see my son.'

'Shut the door,' I heard Chance say. 'She mustn't be allowed in. Close it please, Charles.'

'No.' Isabel came to the door. She was wearing her blue velvet robe and her feet were bare. 'We have nothing to fear from her,' she said, and she kissed me on the cheek. 'The house is pure now. You can do no harm.'

Entering, I saw that everything was different. It could have been another house. Puzzled, I walked ahead of her, looking for all my favourite little possessions, keepsakes I had kept since childhood, gifts from Chance, a set of Cantonese plates from the house in Louisburg Square. The tables and shelves were bare as church pews. Upstairs, I opened my cupboards. My clothes had gone: Isabel's robes and brocade skirts hung stiffly on the wooden hangers.

'We destroyed them all,' she said. 'It had to be done. But I kept this for you.' And she held out the little amber-handled paper-knife. 'Would you like to take it with you?'

'Take it with me?' I sat down on the rumpled bed. 'I'm not going anywhere. Where's Tom?'

'He's gone away,' she said. 'And so, I am sorry to say, must you.'

'Gone where?' I fastened my hand around a bit of the sheet, as if I could keep myself safe just by holding onto a piece of cotton. 'I'm quite well. They said so. They told me I could go home.'

She sat down beside me and put her arm around my waist. 'But we know better, don't we, Nancy? Look at you now, winding that sheet round and round your hand. That's not normal. And look at your stockings! One blue, one brown. That's not normal, is it?'

'It's not normal here,' I said dully. 'It's not normal to destroy people's things and take away their husband. Where's Tom?'

'You asked me already,' she said. 'He's with the Taylors. Tom's fine. And so will you be. But it takes a while. You didn't think you were really going to be better in ten days, did you?' She brushed the hair away from my face with her hand. 'You *are* in a mess. But don't worry. The administrator is sending a car to collect you. He understands things better now.'

I lifted my head to stare at her. 'You asked them to take me back?'

'Not precisely,' she said, smiling. 'You're going to a place where you will be safer, better treated. We all think that's the best thing. The administrator will bring the papers for Chance to sign.'

The last time I saw Isabel, she was standing on the porch with Chance, waving at the car as I was driven away. She could have been any courteous hostess, graciously attentive to the departure of a last, unwelcome guest.

Charles went back to England a month after they put me in the asylum. Annie wrote me that he had a nervous breakdown. I'm not surprised, but I don't excuse him on those grounds. He, as much as Isabel, was responsible for what took place in my home that summer before the war. He knew her. He understood what she was doing.

Chance and Isabel married as soon as he had his divorce papers. Isabel arranged for Eleanor and Tom to be taken in by the Taylors.

Tom was twelve years old when he hanged himself in the pleasant, airy room overlooking the garden which Annie had chosen for him. I didn't know; I continued to get cheerful news bulletins from Annie. She was probably afraid of upsetting me. I didn't learn the truth until one of the doctors broke it to me, very kindly and gently, in the summer of 1950. He'd been dead for three years. I don't suppose he had ever escaped the memory of that night at the pond. The news set me back, quite badly. I spent the next year in the ward for hopeless cases.

Bill and Annie are both dead now. So is Chance. Isabel lives alone in the house they built together, where she is occasionally reported to be completing their life's work. There is no communication between us. How could there be?

I still think of Chance. I never seem quite free of the thought that I'll look up and find him back here. I can see him in my mind as clearly as if he was, and he doesn't have the grim disapproving look she brought to his face. He's the Chance I knew, the man the Taylors loved and with whom I wanted to spend the rest of my life.

He could have been so happy with me. It took Isabel to make a failure of him.

So there we are. And perhaps Dr Storrow was right. I don't feel better for having written all this down, but I do feel as though the past has been dealt with. I've lost the taste of ashes from my mouth.

I had a friendly little letter from Eleanor today, saying that Judith is planning to do volunteer work with poor families in the Lower East Side. I'm pleased about that. And Cathy's done well in her exams. They're hoping she'll go to Eleanor's old college, Bryn Mawr.

They! I'm going soft in my old age. It's the first time I've written of Eleanor and her fancy man as a couple. Well, she seems happy enough, and not a word in her letter about shipping me off to a retirement home. I take that as a good sign.

Eight o'clock and the sun's almost down to the horizon. A sea as level and placid as a tray of milk. Shadows coming up over the grass and a little cool wind tossing the tops of the trees. Time to go for a walk in the garden and see if Joe's still out there working.

Author's Note

ALTHOUGH THIS IS a work of fiction, readers may be interested to learn more about the actual events on which it is partly based. These can be found in the biographies of Robert Graves, written by the author, by Martin Seymour Smith (no relation!) and by Richard Perceval Graves. Deborah Baker published the most recent biography of Laura Riding, *In Extremis*, in 1993.

The early life of Nancy Parker, specifically her relationship with her father, is pure invention, and was chosen by me as a way of giving a context to her later emotional turmoil. In reality, there was no such previous history. The friendship of Nancy and Chance with the Taylors loosely reflects the actual relationship between Katharine and Schuyler Jackson and Tom Matthews and his first wife, Julie. I have made use of their short involvement with Gurdjieff and his followers and of Matthews's account of his friendship with Edmund Wilson. The location of Riding and Graves's home in Mallorca has been shifted to Provence, and I have omitted their subsequent experiences in England, Switzerland and Brittany between 1936 and 1938. The scene of the coming together of the three couples has been shifted from Pennsylvania to New England. No resemblance is intended to the children either of the Matthewses or of the Jacksons.

Katharine Jackson was committed for a period during which her husband and Laura Riding lived together. Their marriage followed Mrs. Jackson's divorce from her husband in 1940–1. Katharine Jackson was awarded custody of their four children.

Graves returned to England in the summer of 1939 and, after a nervous breakdown, began a new life with Beryl Hodge, who subsequently became his second wife.

The disabling accident and death of Nancy Parker's son are fictitious events. Mrs. Jackson's 'crime' was to have been found attempting to strangle one of her daughters.

Schuyler and Laura Jackson became fruit farmers in Florida, where they continued to work on their dictionary, which evolved into *Rational Meaning: A New Foundation for the Definition of Words*, published in 1997.

Katharine Jackson converted to Catholicism and remained friendly with Tom Matthews, who retired as editor of *Time* magazine to live in England.

Robert and Beryl Graves returned to Mallorca, where he died in 1985. Laura (Riding) Jackson remained in Florida after her husband's death in 1968. She published a personal statement of faith, *The Telling*, in 1972 and continued to seek a new and truthful definition of words until her death in 1991.

Katharine Jackson survived her and shows a kind and unembittered interest in the work of biographers seeking her version of the extraordinary events by which her life was so disquietingly shaken and almost destroyed in the summer of 1939.